THE HUNT

A MAX AUSTIN THRILLER - BOOK FOUR OF
THE RUSSIAN ASSASSIN SERIES

BY JACK ARBOR

D1167051

THE HUNT
(A MAX AUSTIN THRILLER - BOOK FOUR)
This book is a work of fiction. The characters, incidents, and dialogue are drawn from the author's imagination and are not to be construed as real. Any resemblance to actual events or persons, living or dead, is fictionalized or coincidental.

ISBN: 978-1-947696-07-5

Requests to publish work from this book should be sent to:
jack@jackarbor.com

Edition 1.0

Published by High Caliber Books

Cover art by: www.damonza.com
Bio photo credit: www.johnlilleyphotography.com

For the firefighters that fought the Lake Christine fire in Basalt, Colorado in the summer of 2018, especially those who saved the El Jebel trailer park and nearby neighborhoods on the night of July 4, 2018.

We are eternally grateful.

"History is a set of lies agreed upon."
~Napoléon Bonaparte

"Maybe you are searching among the branches for what
only appears in the roots."
~Rumi

ONE

Aras Valley in Turkey Near the Armenian Border

A peregrine falcon soared in lazy circles, her outstretched wings and tail forming a triangular silhouette against a pink morning sky. The bird of prey flapped her wings once and arced against an air current before pointing south and floating with the slip stream. A moment later she pumped her muscular wings again and soared in a broad figure eight while sinking closer to the arid ground.

A breeze ruffled the pale green buds of a goosefoot plant as silence blanketed the dusty steppes of the barren desert.

The falcon arched her back and glided lower, her razor-sharp eyes looking for movement on the ground below. Without warning, she dove with knife-like talons outstretched. A cloud of dirt exploded from the ground, and the bird flapped her massive wings once to propel herself back into the air while clutching a struggling long-eared hedgehog in her claws.

Five klicks to the south, Max Austin pulled his eye from

the scope in time to see the culmination of the falcon's hunt. As the powerful bird rose into the eastern sky, he grinned in admiration of the near-perfect display of Darwinian evolution. Since the dawn of time, stronger hunters prevailed over weaker prey. A comforting thought.

A disturbance on the horizon caught his eye and he scanned the valley. A plume of dust rose in the air against a tan and green background. The dust cloud's grainy tail dissipated in the light breeze as it moved along a barely visible double-track road. Max tapped the arm of the man lying next to him, who gave him a thumb's up.

The source of the dust plume appeared in his scope. A caravan of three tan-colored vehicles sped along the trail as their headlights cut a swath through the early morning gloom and swirling dirt. He tracked the approaching convoy with the muzzle of a Knight's Armament SR-25 Mk 11 sniper rifle. The flat desert-tan hoods and reinforced cattle guards of three Humvees bounced along the rutted track three klicks from their position. No markings were visible along the vehicle's flanks, but machine gun turrets jutted from behind armored plating on the lead and trailing Humvees. Helmeted heads swayed to the rhythm of the vehicles. Max's intel indicated the vehicles were operated by a team of Russian soldiers.

Ex-Russian soldiers, actually. The worst kind. With nothing to lose and heads filled with visions of plunder. Everyone in Russia was getting rich, why not them? Max checked his watch. Right on time. Just like his intel indicated. The intel that was just too convenient, too easy.

A gravelly voice with a thick accent sounded through his comm device. "Three bogeys at one klick."

Max grimaced. His old Iraqi friend had a penchant for mixing his military slang. Toggling his mic, he whispered,

"Sammi, bogeys are unidentified aircraft. Are you saying we have aircraft to deal with?"

Sammir Hassim, camouflaged in desert fatigues and armed with an M16 rifle he picked up somewhere during Desert Storm, was positioned along a scrabble-covered ridge on the far side of the valley to Max's left. Sammi also had a set of Steiner M2080 binoculars attached to a short tripod. The Iraqi clicked his comm device to indicate the negative.

Max panned his rifle left, following the road ahead of the speeding convoy. According to his intel, their destination was a gathering of four massive tents erected along a steppe at his eleven o'clock position. The green canvas-sided buildings had aluminum frames, galvanized supports, and were the size of half a football field. They resembled the mess hall tents used by the Russian military.

As the edge of the tent colony appeared in his scope, a door flung open and two soldiers in black ducked into the sunlight. Each man wore a standard-issue flak vest and a ball cap devoid of insignia. Their uniforms were common to military contractors, and their actions indicated they were well trained. Their skin was light, but otherwise their nationality was indecipherable over the long distance.

His spotter lay prone next to him on the dusty ground among a stand of goosefoot and bramble. A thatch of indigenous flora was affixed to their helmets, and they wore desert camouflage and tan flak vests. His rifle barrel stuck out from the stand of goosefoot, but otherwise they were invisible.

Thanks for the training, Dad. It keeps coming in handy.

The man next to him, the indomitable ex-CIA black-ops operative named Spencer White, watched the scene through a Leica rangefinder balanced on a small tripod. A filter was affixed to the Leica's lens to eliminate reflections from the harsh desert sun.

The three men had been in position for hours, the only action interrupting the monotony was the occasional bird soaring overhead and the banging of a tent door loose in the early morning wind.

"Eight six two meters to the middle Humvee," Spencer whispered.

Max slipped his finger into the trigger guard. A little over half a mile. "Wind?"

A hesitation from his spotter. "Quarter to from the east at three miles per hour."

Quarter to meant the wind was coming toward him at a forty-five degree angle to his rifle. Max studied the ballistics chart before putting his eye back to the scope.

Fish in a barrel.

Two more soldiers in black uniforms emerged from the tent and hastened to positions twenty meters on either side of the structure. Max followed the approaching vehicles with his rifle until they ground to a halt a dozen meters from the encampment in a flurry of dust.

A calm settled over the camp. The pale morning light grew stronger as the dust and dirt settled. Out of sight, a falcon chattered. Bramble waved in the breeze.

At last the canvas door to the tent swung open with a bang that echoed across the dusty landscape. No one appeared.

Despite the activity at the tent, Max kept the crosshatch of his scope's reticle centered on the middle vehicle's rear door. *Come on. One shot and we can get outta here.*

Max spoke in a low murmur. "Tell me if anyone emerges from the tent."

His spotter made a minute adjustment to his scope. "Nothing moving yet. So far, the intel is holding."

"It's too easy," Max whispered. *This is a trap. But I can't*

*ignore it, can I? Alex and Arina's lives are at stake. No other
option.*

A month prior, an electronic dossier had come to them
through Max's sometime lover and trusted hacker,
Goshawk. She had received it from an intermediary who
gave no indication of the origin of the file. Although the
dossier was detailed, professional, and organized in a way
that reminded Max of his old days at the KGB, the true
source of the information proved untraceable, even for the
resourceful Goshawk.

A gritty creak rang out over the desert as the middle
Humvee's door opened on metal hinges caked with dust.
Before anyone emerged from the vehicle, a flurry of activity
stirred clouds of dirt as men exited the vehicles in unison
and fanned out in a defensive position. Max counted eight
gray-clad men, each with rifles, sidearms, and ball caps.

Everyone has their own private army these days.

A glossy black boot appeared from the middle Humvee,
followed by a compact man with a head in the shape of an
anvil. He wore Russian military fatigues in desert camouflage and a black-and-white checkered keffiyeh around his
neck. A pair of wraparound sunglasses adorned an otherwise bare head. His hand drifted to the leather flap of a hip
holster as he surveyed the valley around him.

Max placed the crosshairs directly on the man's forehead before shifting a fraction to the left to compensate for
the wind.

Sammi's voice hissed in his ear. "Action at the tent."

Max kept the rifle frozen on the Russian's oversized
head.

Sammi continued. "Two more. Makes six soldiers
outside, plus one guy in a funny suit with one of those hats
like Indiana Jones wore in that movie. Take a look."

His curiosity piqued, Max let his finger off the trigger and shifted the rifle to his left. The mystery dossier indicated the meeting was a weapons transaction. The seller was a former Russian major named Spartak Polzin, who was peddling five crates of new AN-94 Nikonov assault rifles and assorted spare magazines and ammunition. Spartak was Max's target, but the file was silent on the buyer's identity or the intended use of the weapons.

His scope found a man wearing a tailored linen suit and a fedora standing just outside the tent doors, feet planted, arms crossed.

Max did a double take. *It's not possible.*

This was the last person he expected to see in the Eastern Turkish desert buying weapons from a man he intended to kill. The buyer, the man in the panama hat, was Victor Dedov, former head of the Belarusian KGB and his father's old boss.

Victor Dedov. His pulse quickened.

Diminutive in stature but commanding in presence, Victor only cared about what's best for Victor. Since the devastating bomb that killed Max's parents and his sister's husband, Max and Victor had developed a stormy relationship. Max believed Victor had concealed the real culprits of the bombing, had tried to swindle Max out of ten million dollars, and revealed a love affair with Max's sister, Arina. Now Arina and her son, Alex, lived under Victor's roof in a heavily guarded castle in Switzerland. But what was Victor doing here, in the Turkish desert, meeting a member of the consortium to buy weapons?

Dedov stood with feet planted, the pleats on his linen suit rustling in the wind. Sun glinted off a metal case sitting on the ground near his leg. No one moved.

Max swung the scope to find the broad head of the

Russian, who started toward the tent flanked by two body-guards. Max's finger curled around the trigger as he waited for his target to halt. The two short men cut a stark contrast against the military contractors guarding them. Dedov, trim and neat. Spartak, broad and muscular. The scope's detail was fine enough for Max to see the pores on his target's nose.

Sammi's voice hissed in his ear. "Four men at the back of the lead vehicle. Unloading crates."

A Russian military officer selling surplus weapons on the black market was nothing new. Vast inventories of weapons had gone unaccounted for in the aftermath of the breakup of the Soviet Union. Russian-made rifles, hand-guns, grenades, and other small arms had made their way into conflict zones across the globe while their purveyors—current and former Russian military leaders—spent the profits on exotic sports cars and chalets in the south of France.

What made this transaction different was that Spartak Polzin, a former major in the Russian army and special operations commander in the Russian Spetsnaz, was also known as number five in the consortium, the shadowy group that had placed a bounty on Max's head.

"Can you confirm the target's identity?" Max whispered.

A lizard darted along the hard dirt while Spencer accessed a file photo on his phone. "Spartak Polzin. Confirmed."

Max's plan to save the lives of his sister and nephew was simple: He would get to the consortium members before they got to them. The more consortium members he killed, the more turmoil and fear festered in the group. To date, he had killed one of the twelve. Spartak was about to be the second.

His finger tensed on the trigger as the Russian extended a meaty hand to his customer. Max centered the crosshairs on Spartak's head just behind his ear and moved the muzzle a fraction to the left. As he applied pressure to the trigger, wind kicked up a cloud of sand that dispersed into the air. Max eased up on the trigger.

Victor Dedov grasped Spartak's hand, and both men laughed as the major said something and gestured at the four men unloading the crates. The buyer nudged the metal case with his foot, and Spartak pointed at one of his men. As the dust settled from the men's activities, Max waited a beat for his heart to slow.

A shout sounded from somewhere among the tents. Soldiers scattered, raising another plume of dust and obscuring Max's vision. His finger froze with pressure on the trigger. Dedov dove into the tent while Spartak vanished around the fender of Humvee.

Damn it. What just happened?

A tiny crack, like a twig snapping underfoot, sounded from behind their position. Max shifted his hand from the rifle's stock to the pistol at his waist.

He eased the pistol from its holster while straining to hear any more sounds. *Was it just an animal? Risk a turn of the head and violate his cover? Nope. Trust the camouflage.*

Through the lens, Spartak's gray-clad men formed a defensive position behind the vehicles while Dedov and his black-uniformed crew disappeared. The long morning shadows faded as a hot sun rose in the east. A crushing silence descended.

A pop, like a pebble dropping on a larger rock, jolted

him. Max instinctively rolled to his right, away from Spencer's position, while bringing the pistol around.

He froze as two rifle muzzles stared him in the face and the hulking figures of four gray-uniformed soldiers blocked the sunlight.

TWO

The fist slammed into his cheek with the force of a cast-iron pan. A sharp crack filled the tent and Max fell sideways, only to be jerked back to his knees by two Russians. Sparks sprang across his vision and blood spattered as another blow hammered his nose. A punch landed on his temple and he sagged against the grip of his captors, unable to keep himself up.

A slap to his cheek cleared his senses as a voice rang in his ears. "Come on. Stay with me."

Blood and mucus dripped from his face onto his bare stomach, and his muscles bulged and strained as he struggled against the strong hands holding him. Despite the cold air in the tent, his skin was covered by a sheen of sweat.

Come on, is this the best you've got?

The bull-chested figure of Spartak Polzin stood in front of him, stripped to a white tank top and fatigue pants. Sweat flew from his brow and dripped onto his polished combat boots as he put all his effort into rearranging Max's face.

Max shook his head sending beads of sweat flying. "You look angry."

Spartak wiped his knuckles on a towel and put his face close enough so his spittle pelted Max's face. "Do you know how much money you just—"

With a jerk of his forehead, Max connected with the bridge of the major's nose, spraying blood across the room. Spartak staggered back while flailing his arms. Max lunged, but four strong hands held him down. A sharp kick to the back of his knee made him crumple to the dirt. A gleaming boot whistled at his face. He shifted so the boot glanced off his bare shoulder and pain radiated up his arm and down his spine. He was jerked to his knees.

The Russian major planted his feet in a boxer stance and struck Max's face and torso with well-timed jabs, each one feeling like a piston. After the sixth strike caught his jaw, the daylight blinked off, and Max hit the ground hard, out cold.

———

The daylight blinked back on as a blast of cold water shocked his system. A spasm throbbed in his neck, and his chest burned near his ribcage. Swollen cheeks prevented his jaw from functioning. Something like rough sandpaper grated against his cheek. A rust-colored mixture of dirt and blood pooled near his face. He struggled to rise, but his body was rooted to the ground.

Boots crunched in the grit, and a hulking figure knelt near his face, blotting out the light. Through the smell of blood, Max caught the fetid odor of old socks. It reminded him of the locker room at the KGB academy. He forced his jaw to work. "Good morning, sunshine. Still mad?"

The major's voice was gravelly. "One of my men reminded me to be grateful. It's not every day that a man with a bounty on his head lands in your lap." When Spartak stood, Max braced for a kick. Instead, the major walked away, his hand resting on his pistol holster. "Get him up so we can have a talk."

As Max was yanked to his feet, an abrupt kick to his hamstring sent him staggering to his knees. His head swam as the sand rushed at his face. Before his chest hit the deck, he was jerked upright and shoved into a chair where he was held by the soldiers.

He studied the interior of the tent through eyes hazy from pain and blood. A weak yellow light from an electric lantern faded into shadows at the edges of the room. A long wooden table sat beside one canvas wall, and six chairs were scattered and tipped as if their occupants had made a hasty exit. The crumpled form of a lanky man lay on his stomach in the shadows opposite the table. He wore fatigues that looked like Spencer's, but Max's blurry eyes prevented him from telling whether the man was breathing.

Spartak stalked into the light, his nose covered with a butterfly bandage, the skin around his eyes turning red and puffy. He grabbed Max by the chin to yank his head around. "He's alive, if that's what you're wondering. But not for long."

Max worked his jaw to form words, but his mouth was full of marbles. "Surprised to...see us? Since you're going to kill us... Tell me...how you found us."

Someone snapped something under Max's nose and his surroundings turned to technicolor before his vision cleared.

Two soldiers stood at attention along the wall, each clutching 9mm pistols in their hands. Those two plus the two men holding him in the chair in addition to Spartak made five.

Max rolled his neck to loosen the muscles. "Your face is lookin' good."

Spartak planted his feet a meter from Max's chair. He had donned his fatigue shirt, but the Arab scarf lay on the table. "It'll heal. You, however, will not."

Max groaned. "Good one."

The major produced a gleaming chrome-plated pistol from his leather holster, racked the slide and slid out the magazine, examined the visible brass bullet, and shoved the magazine back into the handle.

Max spit a wad of phlegm and blood into the sand at Spartak's feet. "Whatever you're going to do, you better hurry. There's a German BND tactical squad about a klick away. You don't want to be here when they get here."

The Russian major stole a look at the door of the tent. Max strained against the men holding his arms. "Aren't you wondering how we knew you'd be here?"

Spartak stepped in front of Max and swung his arm. The butt of his gun crashed into Max's cheekbone and sent stars cascading through his vision.

How am I still awake? Must be the ammonia still in my nervous system.

The major took a step back. "That's exactly what I want to know. You're dead either way, Asimov. You can suffer for weeks as we dismantle you piece by piece or you can tell me what I want to know and end it. You know how—"

Max spit another wad of blood and snot, hitting the major's boot. "Yeah, yeah. I don't know where—"

Spartak thrust his fist into Max's abdomen, using his weight to maximize the power of the blow.

Max doubled over and retched, tasting bile as he gulped for oxygen. When he looked up, gasping, a pistol muzzle was jammed in his face, Spartak's finger firm on the trigger.

A deep breath. "Okay...okay. You win." Max sucked in more air. "It was one...of your consortium partners." *Was that flicker of panic in Spartak's eyes?* "Come on, everyone knows you guys...are fighting among yourselves. Who's against you?"

Spartak's brow furrowed.

"Think...hard," Max said. *The silence confirmed it. But who on the consortium sent the dossier? Who wanted to interrupt Spartak's gun deal?* He forced his swollen face into a weak smile.

The major waved his gun at the tent's entrance and yelled at his men. "Get out. All of you." When the soldiers hesitated, Spartak bellowed at them, spittle flying from his mouth. "Get out!" Two men glanced back as the group filed out of the tent.

When they were alone, Spartak held the gun in a meaty hand and pointed the muzzle at Max's face. "Talk."

Fueled by the ammonia, Max ran through the list of consortium members he had long ago memorized. The leader was Nikita Ivanov, a name so common Max assumed it was a pseudonym. The second, third, fifth, sixth, and seventh names on the list were Russian—heads of petroleum conglomerates and senior intelligence officials in the Russian government. The fourth and tenth names were Chinese, while the rest were from former Soviet states like Ukraine and Latvia. Max gambled. "It was the Chinese."

This time, the strike was lightning fast but lacked

power. Spartak's left fist bounced off Max's chin, causing pain but no real damage.

Spartak laughed, and the gun wavered. "Bullshit. Now I know you're lying. What I don't know is—"

As the major regained his balance from the punch, Max coiled all his energy into his legs and launched himself. His shoulder plowed into Spartak's ironlike abdomen while his right arm grabbed for the gun hand. When the two men plowed into the sand, Max dug for purchase, trying to gain leverage and control of the gun.

"*V rot mne nogi!*" Spartak bellowed.

As the major brought the gun around, Max found purchase on his wrist and clamped on. With the smaller man gasping for breath underneath him, Max banged the gun hand on the sand repeatedly to dislodge the weapon.

Spartak held tight, caught his breath, and heaved upwards.

Max held on and locked his legs around the major.

"Guards!" The major screamed.

Running feet and shouts came from outside the tent. Max drove his left elbow into the major's nose, and Spartak screamed. Max banged Spartak's gun hand into the sand with a final heave, causing the weapon to come loose.

Sand flew in a panicked scramble as both men dove for the pistol. Max closed his hand around the bare steel of the grip, spun on a knee, and pulled the trigger.

The gun fired just as the butt of a rifle struck his jaw. Bright light exploded, and he crumpled to the sand.

THREE

Aras Valley in Turkey Near the Armenian Border

Am I underwater?

The voices were muddled, the words barely discernible. He strained to hear.

"Load up, we need to leave."

Blackness surrounded him. Grit ground into his cheek, and his limbs were dead weight. Max strained to move a finger, but the effort yielded nothing. A dull ache radiated through his head, and his ears rang. *Don't puke. Keep it down.* A few words came through.

"What do we do with these two?"

"Bring the Russian. Shoot the other one. He's dead weight."

Panic forced his eyes open. Pain pulsed in his head, and he bit his tongue to keep from crying out. The blurred movement of men made him dizzy.

I'm Belarusian, damn it.

Rough hands dragged him through the sand, and more

pain crushed his abdomen as his torso was wrenched around.

At any minute, he'd hear the sharp report from the pistol that meant the end of Spencer White's life. Visions from his recent operations with the former CIA man spun in his mind. Spencer limping through the dark warehouse until Max grabbed him by the shoulders and threw him into the van. Spencer, wielding an assault rifle, appearing in the basement of the safe house in Poland to free Max from the clutches of Nathan Abrams. Spencer on the porch of his Colorado ranch nursing a bourbon.

As Max was dragged through the tent door by two men, the morning air was filled with gunfire.

Crack.

Heavy caliber. Men shouting. Another shot.

Crack.

Max pitched face-first to the sand, free from the strong hands. He rolled, sending pain coursing through his rib cage.

More gunfire, lighter caliber. The distinctive sound of the M16.

About time, Sammi.

Two gray-uniformed men standing next to the lead Humvee went down. Max dug his toes into the sand and propelled himself at the vehicle, adrenaline spiking. *Remind me to give you a hug, Sammi.* He snatched a rifle from the ground left by a fallen soldier and pushed his back into the cold steel of the Humvee.

He checked the rifle's safety, found it off, and whirled to face the tent with the rifle held against his cheek. Two more soldiers lay on the ground, blood seeping into their gray uniforms. He took a step at the tent but froze as more gunfire filled the air.

Pop, pop, pop.

The tent doors flew open and a hail of gunfire poured from the interior. Bullet's sang past Max's face and plinked into the hood and radiator of the lead Humvee.

Max hit the dirt, ignoring the pain in his ribcage. He rolled to his right as the sand where he was standing was chewed by bullets. Another burst of gunfire followed him as he jumped to his feet and scrambled behind the lead Humvee. Flinging the barrel of his rifle over the vehicle's hood, Max aimed at the tent's door and waited. An eerie quiet settled over the desert as Max kept his finger firm on the trigger.

Spencer is still in the tent.

As he counted the seconds, he scanned the camp. Made from thick canvas, the tents looked permanent, each with walls, a frame, and poles resting in their own foundations. They were as large as a medium-sized house. There was no evidence of Victor Dedov or his black-uniformed men.

I need to get into that tent before they kill Spencer.

A lanky form in dusty combat boots and a full beard materialized and positioned himself next to him, bracing the barrel of a scratched and dented M16 on the Humvee's hood. Sammir Hassim, Iraqi and former leader of the resistance against Saddam's Sunni-led government, wore a knit kufi skull cap covering wild hair and a dirty red thawb over ripped fatigues, giving him the look of an extremist.

Max knew better. A devout Muslim with a large brood of children and a devoted wife, Sammi hated the taint the extremists put on his beloved faith. Since Desert Storm and Saddam Hussein's demise at the hands of the Americans, Sammi now sold his services to those fighting ISIS, al-Qaeda, and other militants, and led dozens of missions with Soviet special operations groups, lending local support, translation services, and helping with local connections. Osama bin Laden had placed a fatwā death sentence on Sammi's head in 1997 for the operative's activities in aiding and abetting foreign governments.

Max's voice was low. "Took you long enough."

A guffaw. "I headed for home. Figured you were handling it. What of *Agha* White?"

Max yanked the Humvee's door open. "Unknown. Last I saw, he was lying against the right wall of the tent, alive. Who knows now."

Sammi nodded at the military vehicle. "I read your mind, sadiqi."

While Sammi followed, Max flung his rifle into the vehicle, climbed over the passenger seat, and plopped into the cracked vinyl driver's seat. He cranked the starter and the V8 turbo-diesel rumbled to life. Sammi jumped into the gunner's cockpit, grabbed the big machine gun, and swung the barrel to the front.

Max ground the transmission into gear. "That .50 caliber is too big for where we're going. Don't kill the major. I need him alive."

Sammi slammed the lid down on the big gun's ammunition port and grabbed the two handles. "Shock and awe, sadiqi. Shock and awe. Hit it."

Max punched the accelerator while spinning the wheel to the left. The three-ton armored truck bounced over the dead Russians, and the Humvee's cattle guard plowed into the side of the massive tent. The entire structure swayed before the canvas ripped and the vehicle roared into the tent's interior. Chairs crunched under his wheels as he scanned the interior for the enemy.

There. To the left.

The tent's interior was filled with the deafening sound

of .50 caliber machine gun fire and the lighter pop from the
Russian's AK-74—a newer version of the venerable AK-47.
A stinging scent of gun powder filled Max's nostrils, and
brass casings rained down on his head. Smaller bullets
plinked off the Humvee's armored plating and he stomped
the brake.

As he wrenched open the door and dove out, pulling the
rifle with him, one of the Russian soldier's heads exploded
into a pink and gray vapor from the .50 caliber. Max
crouch-walked around the back of the Humvee, keeping the
big truck between him and the enemy, holding the AK
against his cheek while looking for a target. A lumpy form
lay in the shadows to his right. *Spencer!*

The .50 caliber went quiet, and Sammi cussed in
Arabic as rifle fire cracked. Shots plinked off metal while
the Iraqi slid into the driver's seat of the Humvee. Notorious for jamming when poorly maintained, the .50 caliber
had either run out of bullets or a casing was stuck in the
breach.

Max poked the rifle muzzle around the rear end of the
vehicle and squeezed off three rounds to cover his reconnaissance of the tight room. Smoke hung in the air. The
Russians had flipped over a heavy table in an attempt at
cover, and a large chunk of wood was chewed away by the
.50 caliber rounds.

Two left. Spartak and a guard.

He remained hidden behind the rear bumper as the
Humvee lurched forward with Sammi behind the wheel.

A soldier darted to Max's right, firing as he ran, the
bullets passing to Max's right. There was no sign of Spartak
as Max nosed his gun from behind the truck and put three
rounds into the soldier's torso. The Russian staggered,
dropped his rifle, and fell.

The Humvee plowed into the table, splintering the wood beneath its heavy tires before its momentum carried it through the canvas side of the tent. As the vehicle ground to a halt halfway through the tent wall, Max whirled, rifle up, and scanned the tent's interior.

Nothing moved. The tent was empty.

Spartak had disappeared.

FOUR

Aras Valley in Turkey Near the Armenian Border

Max banged his hand on the rear of the Humvee. "Go."

The vehicle heaved over the table's remains and caught on the canvas wall before it freed itself and lurched through a jagged hole in the tent's side.

Rifle at the ready, Max approached the debris and kicked pieces of the table away finding only sand and shards of wood. Sunlight blinded him as he stepped through the ripped canvas. When his eyes cleared, he scanned the immediate area for activity while ignoring the throbbing in his rib cage.

Sammi appeared from the driver's side of the Humvee holding the M16 and shaking his head. "Nothing. The *khanzir* disappeared."

Max marched away from the tent and gazed at the horizon. Nothing moved out in the scrub. "He must have used the running soldier as a distraction and cut his way through the canvas."

The Iraqi threw up his arms. "But where did he go?"

A diesel engine roared to life on the far side of the tent, followed by a turbo whine and the sound of wheels crunching on rock.

Max wrenched the Humvee's door open and crawled inside. "Motherfucker. Get in, Sammi."

Sammi dove in and stuck his long torso out the window as Max spun the wheel in the direction of the front of the tent.

Spartak, forced by the cumbersome vehicle to make a sweeping turn, picked up speed as Max and Sammi rounded the front of the tent on a collision course with the Russian. Gunfire erupted as Sammi squeezed off rounds from the M16, the bullets bouncing harmlessly off the Humvee's armor.

The major's sweat-covered face was visible through the window while he attempted the wide turn to escape. Max pushed the accelerator to the floor. "Sammi, jump!"

The rebel commander pushed the door open and leaped, robes flying, and rolled when he hit the sand. The front cattle guard of Max's Humvee plowed into the side of Spartak's truck with a grating of metal on metal, lifting Spartak's Humvee onto two wheels. The force of the collision hurled Max into the steering wheel, sending blinding pain through his body.

Through the burning agony, he kept the accelerator down, his truck's wheels digging into the sand and straining against Spartak's vehicle, keeping it pinned so two tires were just off the ground.

With his rifle in one hand, Sammi ran to the driver's side of Spartak's truck and wrenched the door open. He grabbed Spartak by the shirt collar and yanked him from the vehicle and jammed the M16's muzzle into his chest.

———

They left Spartak facedown on the sandy floor of the tent, his ankles and wrists secured behind him by duct tape—the only thing available—while Sammi searched the other tents and Max tended to Spencer. Using a packet of smelling salts he found among the major's possessions, Max brought Spencer around. The former CIA black-ops agent blinked his eyes open and shook his head before permitting himself to be led to a chair.

"Guess we're even now," Spencer mumbled, the characteristic brightness in his eyes slowly returning.

Max placed Spartak's pistol in Spencer's hand. "Not even close, my friend. Shoot him if he even blinks wrong."

It took a few minutes for Max to find his shirt along with his rifle, pistol, combat knife, pack, and other gear in a corner of the tent. After shrugging into the T-shirt, his ribs protesting, he stuck his phone in a pocket and shoved his knife into his waistband. He rummaged in his pack and grabbed a plastic baggie of heavy-duty painkillers, dropped two in his mouth, and swallowed them dry.

Sammi stuck his head into the tent. "Clear. No one else around. Tents are empty. Six dead guys."

Max squatted next to Spartak's prone body. "Search the vehicles and bring me a tool kit." *Where was Dedov? Waiting out in the desert somewhere or halfway to Ankara?* "Stay vigilant. Dedov might still be around."

"Aye, captain." Sammi ducked back out into the morning sunshine.

With Spencer's help, Max heaved Spartak into a chair, where he used more of the duct tape to secure his captive. The major's face was swollen and puffy, and the butterfly bandage hung loose. Sand and grit clung to blood-covered abrasions on his cheek and neck.

Max crossed his arms and studied his prisoner. Spartak was the number five man on what was known in intelligence circles as the consortium, a shadowy group of twelve men who controlled the oil and natural gas production of the Russian Federation and much of the black market in the former Eastern Bloc countries. Spartak, known as a fearsome warrior and a tough-as-nails special operations commando, glared at Max. *Can't let my guard down.*

He strolled behind his prisoner, whose arms flexed and moved to loosen the tape around his wrists. "Don't bother, Spartak. You so much as flinch and my friend there will shoot you full of holes."

The captive kept flexing his arms.

"Fine. Your funeral." Max walked around to look Spartak in the eye. "Back when I was with the KGB, one of the captains in the Second Directorate led a long and detailed study of interrogation and torture techniques. It took him four years, and when it was done they named it the Chernov report, after the guy who wrote it. Are you familiar with it?"

Spartak scowled.

Max dug in his pocket and fingered the bag of pills. "I'm not surprised. The report was buried. Probably didn't make it to the Spetsnaz. Chernov's assertions were so controversial that the KGB didn't want its conclusions made known to the KGB general population."

The tent door banged open as Sammi entered carrying a large roll of oil-stained canvas along with a leather shoulder bag. He tossed the canvas roll at Max, who caught it and dropped it onto the ground before unrolling it on the sand to display a row of tarnished and grime-caked tools.

"You know what the summary of the report was, Spartak?"

Sammi dropped the leather shoulder bag at Spencer's feet and nudged Spartak's chin with the barrel of his rifle. "The man is speaking to you, *ya kalb*."

Spartak's eyes flicked to the leather bag.

Max stooped and selected a tool from the canvas roll on the ground. "Right. How could you know? Like I said, the report was buried."

He stepped in front of Spartak, his arms crossed, the tool cupped in his hand, hidden. "The report looked at dozens of interrogation and torture techniques, including the Reid technique, water boarding, pain, solitary, and all kinds of drugs. The normal stuff. He reviewed thousands of cases across all thirteen of the Soviet states. You know what he found was the single most effective method of gaining information?"

The major drew back and spat a wad of blood-laced phlegm at Max, who shifted fast enough so the mucus struck his arm.

With a flash of a dirty red thawb, Sammi crushed the butt of his rifle into the major's jaw, pitching the former soldier onto his side, where he landed with a thud.

Max helped Sammi yank Spartak upright. "Check the tape. I think he's working the old stretch-the-duct-tape trick."

While Sammi wound a few more strands of tape around Spartak's wrists, Max showed his prisoner the screwdriver. To his credit, Spartak's expression remained steady.

By now, the hydrocodone had taken the edge off the pain in Max's rib cage. "As I was saying. Do you know what Chernov found to be the most effective technique for obtaining information from captives?"

Fresh blood flowed from the wound on Spartak's temple, but the fire in his eyes remained.

Max hurled the screwdriver into the sand, where it landed pointed end down, handle sticking up. "Rapport."

This time, Spartak's eyes flickered.

"That's right. We were all surprised too. Put the subject into a comfortable setting. Use respect and relationship-building techniques to build empathy. Pretend to be a friend. Make them think there's a chance. Allow them to regain their self-respect. The report said that physical or psychological torture is ineffective because the subject will say anything to make the pain stop. Makes the results unreliable."

Max withdrew the tactical knife from his waistband. Its silver edge caught the sun shining into the open side of the tent. The hilt was covered in well-worn leather, and a thong loop was attached to the end of the handle. Spartak's eyes tracked the knife as Max spun it in his hand. "You can imagine why the KGB leadership wanted that report buried."

"Too humane." Spartak choked on the words.

In a flash, Max used all his weight to drive the knife deep into Spartak's thigh.

The major screamed and heaved against his bindings as his wide-open eyes stared at the knife hilt sticking from his leg. A sheen of sweat appeared on his brow while his screams died away.

Max grabbed Spartak's chin and held him steady. "Wrong. Too slow." Max let go of his captive's chin and pushed gently on the knife hilt, eliciting another round of screams. "What do you think?"

Spartak growled through clenched teeth. "Go fuck yourself, Asimov."

As Max yanked the knife from Spartak's thigh, the colonel ground his teeth against the pain. Max wiped the blade on his captive's shoulder. "Let's begin with an easy one. Why are you selling weapons to Victor Dedov?"

Spartak stayed silent.

Spencer's feeble voice sounded behind him. "Take a look at this."

The leather bag was open at Spencer's feet, its contents spread on the sand. Stacks of US one hundred dollar bills lay next to a semiautomatic pistol, a tactical knife, a bottle of pills, and a sheaf of papers bound with a binder clip. The papers were dog-eared and covered with scribbles in blue and red ink.

Max picked up the bundle of papers and thumbed through a long list of weapons, colorful brochures, and schematics for various weapons systems along with bills of lading and invoices. A set of ledger pages with a list of entries written in Cyrillic followed by numbers was at the back of the stack. "What d'ya got here?"

Spartak scrunched up his face. "Fuck off."

Spencer's voice again. "Something else. Hidden in an inside pocket."

Spencer tossed him a black box-shaped device made from metal about the size of a cigarette pack, except thinner. Max flipped it over. The back was smooth with no markings. Along one narrow side was a USB port. Another side held a button set flush into the box's side. When he pushed the button, the front of the device lit to display a number pad and a field asking for a PIN. He held it up.

Spartak's face went slack. "Where'd you get that?"

"It was in the case."

Spartak's voice raised an octave. "Impossible."

Max grinned. "Not yours?"

His captive's face hardened.

Max waved it in the air. "What is it?"

Spartak shrugged. "Never seen it before."

"What's the pin?"

Scowling, the major struggled against the tape binding his wrists. "We're both being set up, Asimov. I tell you I've never seen that thing before. Someone planted it in my bag."

"Explain."

Spartak stared at a point on the far side of the tent.

Max twirled the knife until it rested in his hand in a reverse grip, with the blade close to his little finger. "We can do this a couple of ways. We can stuff you in the Humvee and take you to one of Sammi's safe houses in Mosul where we can spend a few weeks building rapport. Or we can stay here while I use the old method."

As he said the word *method*, Max drove the knife into Spartak's left thigh and braced for the howls of pain.

The major sat frozen, his head still and his jaw clenched, while his eyes roamed the ceiling of the tent before his body went slack and his head slumped, his chin falling to his chest.

Max shook Spartak's shoulder. "What the hell?"

Spencer walked over, put his fingers on the man's neck, and shook his head.

"He's dead."

FIVE

Aras Valley in Turkey Near the Armenian Border

"His heart gave out. The sudden shock was too much."

After cutting the major's hands free, Spencer grabbed a wrist and held it before letting it flop back to his lap. "Nothing. No pulse." He snatched the pill bottle and dumped the contents in his hand. "Beta blockers. Used to treat systolic heart failure. There's also a few nitroglycerins for angina. This guy was a walking time bomb."

Max yanked the knife from Spartak's thigh and wiped the blood on the dead man's shirt before stalking out of the tent into the stifling heat. Another falcon flew lazy circles against the azure-blue sky. The elegant creature floated on an air current before disappearing over the rocky ridge. Otherwise, the desert was still.

He kicked a Humvee tire, banged his hand on the hood, and squatted in the sand so the sun warmed his back. Spencer walked out of the tent followed by Sammi. The

CIA man crossed his arms and studied the ground while the Iraqi inspected the remaining Humvee.

Spencer leaned on the Humvee's grill, his arms still crossed. "At least that's two consortium members dead."

Max grabbed a handful of pebbles and tossed them into the sand one by one. "We lost an opportunity to learn some valuable intel. Like what was Victor Dedov doing here?"

"True." Spencer nodded once. "But you planned to kill him anyway."

Casting away the remaining pebbles, Max stood. "We only get so many opportunities."

"I'm sorry I didn't look at the bottle." Spencer kicked the sand. "I might have been able to warn you."

Max punched Spencer lightly in the shoulder. "My fault. I got carried away."

"Help me with these crates," Sammi called from behind the Humvee.

Spencer ambled over to help Sammi load the crates of weapons into the back of the Humvee.

Squatting, Max stared into the dim interior of the tent while going over the past month. Goshawk's discovery of the intel indicating where and when the weapons sale would take place. The time of the deal in GMT, the location in GPS coordinates, the number of vehicles, and even the count of Spartak's men. Funny, the dossier didn't mention Dedov or specifics on his soldiers. *Was this a setup by Dedov to capture Max, kill Spartak, and make off with the weapons?* That complex of an operation was not beyond Dedov's abilities. When Max failed to kill Spartak and was instead captured, the former KGB director disappeared.

He stood too fast, fought off a wave of dizziness, and removed the small metal box from his pocket. *And what about this thing? Was Spartak feigning surprise? Or is it part of the set up?*

Behind him, a diesel engine started. Sammi yelled and pounded the side of the Humvee. "We should go."

The Iraqi was right. The longer they stayed, the more they invited unwanted attention from a wandering band of ISIS fighters, a Kurdish patrol, or Dedov's men coming back to claim the weapons. As his adrenaline faded, the pain in his ribs surged. He surveyed the partially destroyed tent and the two wrecked Humvees. A gaping hole stood in the side of the tent where the Humvee drove through, and flies hovered over the soldier's bodies. His eyes roved over the encampment.

Something was off.

It didn't add up. Sure, Sammi was an effective fighter, but could he take out four highly trained soldiers with a single rifle?

A door creaked as Spencer climbed into the rear of the Humvee. Sammi had his elbow out the window and watched him with a curious grin. He should get into the vehicle and make for the Iraqi border. Instead, Max walked into the tent and let his eyes grow accustomed to the murk.

The former Russian major sat slumped in the chair where he died, a swarm of flies buzzing around the wounds in his thighs. Two dead soldiers lay where they were shot, one by the big .50 caliber gun, the other by Max's rifle. He approached one of the soldiers and rifled through his pockets but found only a plastic lighter and cigarettes. He tapped one out, lit it with the lighter, and inhaled the strong Turkish smoke.

The taste reminded him of his father, who favored the short but heavy Turkish cigarettes. He smiled at the memory of his father standing in the backyard of their gated estate west of Minsk and talking on his mobile phone in a hushed voice while cradling one of the smokes in his fingers. His father wore the cigarette in his hand like an accessory. Despite the constant smoking, his father's health never suffered. Andrei Asimov could run for miles in heavy boots through the tundra before putting a bullet through a man's forehead at eight hundred meters, earning him the nickname The Bear. Max shrugged off the melancholy, knowing that he would never see his father again, and flicked ash into the sand while looking around the tent.

Thanks for leaving me with this mess, papa.

Another glance around the tent, but the niggling sensation in the back of his neck didn't go away. *What the hell had happened here?*

He exited the tent into the sunshine and examined the bodies of the dead gray-uniformed soldiers sprawled around the vehicles. Two lay in pools of sandy blood with their chests torn apart by small caliber fire from Sammi's M16.

The other two dead soldiers lay on their backs where they crumpled halfway between the tent and the line of Humvees. Max squatted and flicked ash into the sand.

One man's head was shorn off at the neck. The second's man's face was intact, but the top of his skull was a ragged mess. The two wounds bore the signature of a large caliber sniper rifle, not the smaller M16. *What the hell?*

Rising to his feet, Max banged on the hood of the Humvee. "Sammi, how many guards did you kill outside the tent?"

The Iraqi revved the engine. "Two? Three? Four? Don't know. Bogeys for real this time. Let's beat feet."

Rotors thumped in the distance. It was a sound that brought either fear or hope to any soldier—the fear of an approaching enemy or the hope of swift rescue. These weren't rescue birds.

He took a last drag on the cigarette and dropped the butt into the sand. While he ground it out with the toe of his boot, he gazed around at the surrounding desert.

Was it possible?

A buzzard, her dull orange plumage ruffling in the breeze, circled lazily in the blue sky above a far-off ridge. Max scanned the ridge line for glints of light or telltale movements among the scrub but saw nothing.

"Damn it, Max. Time to go." Spencer's voice was urgent.

He let his eyes linger over the landscape for a few more beats before yanking open the front passenger door and jumping in. He didn't stop scanning the surrounding desert scrub until their Humvee crested a hill and the cluster of tents disappeared. As he settled in for the long ride and wondered who the sniper might be, he remembered one of his father's favorite quotes.

All things are possible, son, until they are proven impossible.

———

Max clutched Spartak's leather bag between his feet and gripped the plastic stock of an AK-74. The Humvee bounced and careened over the rutted dirt track, and they left the valley behind and sped south in the direction of a Kurdish encampment, where Sammi's friends would usher them farther south and across the border into Iraq.

As he watched the arid landscape fly by the window, he thought of Kate Shaw, the woman who rescued him from

Belarus and welcomed him into the protection of the CIA, only to herself be pushed aside by a CIA director with her own agenda. After Kate risked her career and livelihood to help Max in his fight against the consortium, she was arrested and incarcerated by that same CIA director, a woman named Piper Montgomery. Now Max was once again on his own, without help from an agency. *It's better this way.*

Max shouted at Spencer to make himself heard over the Humvee's drone. "Any word on Kate?"

Lines of pain were etched on the older man's face behind the scraggly white beard and blazing brown eyes as he gazed at the passing landscape. He shook his head.

Spencer, who spent years under Kate's command, had watched as she was taken prisoner by a band of blue-suited government-issued men after she was ambushed by her former boss, Bill Blackwood. Spencer shouted to be heard over the Humvee's rumble. "Now that another consortium target is in the ground, what's next?"

Max guessed what was really on his friend's mind. The idea of finding and rescuing Kate was troubling. He owed Kate Shaw a debt, and he had grown fond of the stoic and resolute woman in the short time they had known each other. The idea of her shackled in a stockade, eating prison food, and subjected to horrific interrogation made him nauseous. *Where are you, Kate?*

He also worried about his ten-year-old nephew, Alex, and his sister, Arina, and the home in Switzerland where they were confined, surrounded by dozens of guards, virtual prisoners themselves, their lives in constant danger. *How can I look for Kate when my own flesh and blood is in constant and mortal danger?* "Goshawk has intel on number six. Guy by the name of Leoniod Petrov. Russian oligarch involved in some shady oil deals. I'm heading to her place to start the planning."

As they bounced south, and the relentless sun beat down on them, Max ignored the slow burn of Spencer's glare on the back of his neck.

SIX

Unknown Location

The walls in the ten-foot-square room were made from water-stained cinderblock, and the air was heavy with moisture. A loamy, earthy smell of flora laced with citrus dominated. The floor was hard-scrabbled dirt, treated with a chemical to form an impenetrable surface, and was crisscrossed with furrows from dripping water or mad captives digging with their fingernails. The ceiling was far overhead, too high for any prisoner to jump or reach. A dim light flickered from a single yellow bulb set in a corroded fixture halfway up one wall. The socket buzzed faintly, which did nothing to convey confidence that the light would remain lit much longer. Set in the center of one concrete wall was a metal door. The thick floral aroma barely hid odors of mildew, feces, urine, and the stench of decaying flesh.

A rat the size of a small racoon sat on its haunches near the door holding a hard roll between its paws, working on the crunchy niblet with buck teeth. Resting in the dirt was a tin tray holding a bowl of beige-colored powder and water mixture the guards called God's Gruel, which the rat ignored.

A narrow access panel beneath the door's plexiglass window popped open, and a yellow bloodshot eyeball next to a black eyepatch appeared. The single eye shifted back and forth before the window shut with a bang.

If the naked woman curled in the fetal position heard the window shut, she gave no indication. She stared through blank eyes partially covered by dirty strands of curly brown hair and rocked, a faint moan escaping her lips, while her arms clutched her knees to her chest. She made no attempt to wipe the dried mucus from her upper lip nor did she try to clean the blood from her mouth or temple. Instead, she rocked and shivered in the damp heat, fighting the madness that had already come.

SEVEN

Somewhere in Bavaria

Wind howled through the parapets as a flash and crackle in the nighttime sky lit the castle grounds and illuminated the leafless trees surrounding the keep, their crooked branches swaying in the gusts while casting long shadows over the forlorn grounds. A crust of snow from a storm that raged through the valleys and mountain peaks covered the property, while the clouds spit frozen pellets of water and the trees groaned under a coat of ice.

The castle's main fortress was a hulking affair constructed of stone by craftsmen who were unaware that their life's work would withstand the millennia. Despite hundreds of years of harsh northern weather, occupation by tyrants, decades of misuse and vandalism, and the onset of decay, the structure remained stout enough to repel an attack from even a modern army. Narrow windows, called embrasures, looked out over the barren valley. A dozen fortified spires and towers allowed observation for miles in any direction. What was once a deep moat surrounding the castle was now full of detritus, trash, and mounds of decaying brush.

The man pacing the castle halls resembled the very structure he owned and inhabited. Massive, almost giantlike —he suffered from a pituitary gland tumor that caused his monster proportions. His features looked as though they were carved from the same granite that made up the castle walls. A jutting brow cast shadows over already dark eyes and a proportional nose and a short Caesar cut peppered with gray softened his harsh features. A pair of thick but fashionable spectacles in muted black complemented a modern-cut wool suit and silk shirt. Gnarled hands the size of baseball mitts, strong enough to rip phone books in half, hung from muscled arms. A Bluetooth communication device hung perpetually from his ear—so much so that his aides wondered if he slept with it, if he even slept at all. He went by the name Nikita Ivanov, but his actual name was lost to the annals of time.

Despite the abrupt impression, he radiated a charisma that women found hard to resist. Early in life he learned that the power of persuasion had little to do with physical appearance and everything to do with making an emotional connection, so he worked hard at combining his strength, power, and wealth with a charm and magnetism that over-compensated for his harsh exterior.

His work ethic was as legendary as his size. Known to subsist on only four hours of sleep a night, he demanded identical dedication from his staff. Those who struggled to keep up with him were summarily dismissed. To the best of anyone's knowledge, he never married, he was not known to seek sexual relations with females or males, and he discouraged social chatter in his presence. He followed a strict vegetarian diet and never smoked. He was attended in his personal quarters by a small staff sworn to secrecy. In an attempt to charm a comely chamber maid, a valet once whispered a description of his master's choice of pajama pattern. The next day the valet's body was found in a mountain ravine after the brakes on his vehicle mysteriously failed.

Now his footsteps pounded along the slate hallway as he stalked from his personal quarters to his offices where his staff and guests waited, despite the late hour. His mind churned and calculated, at once pleased with the knowledge of Spartak's death and the success of his plan's inception yet troubled by the machinations of those on the consortium who conspired against him. Despite the weight on his broad shoulders, he took smug satisfaction that the traitorous army major was dead, and he permitted himself a moment of amusement at the events he would set off with this next meeting.

His earpiece buzzed, and he tapped the button to activate the connection. "Go."

"Sir. Your second guest has arrived. Shall I show her into—"

"Put her in the sparring room with Magnus, and leave them alone together. Make sure you're recording with both audio and visual, and send a feed to my phone." His pace never faltered.

"Roger that, sir."

He severed the connection while working through the possible outcomes of the series of events he was setting into motion. The operation in Turkey went as planned, and it was only a matter of time before Asimov took the bait. The killer from Belarus was a robot, programmed to follow one set of instructions. All he had to do was issue those instructions, and the killing machine would do the rest.

His visitor was another matter entirely. The woman was as unpredictable as a toddler but as effective as a Cray computer. He had one lever with her, and the little test he was about to enjoy might prove out his hunch. If his test failed, he would switch to plan B or plan C. His mind, equal to that of a chess grand master, had plotted through endless thrusts and parries. Each move was to be savored but not celebrated. *Will final victory bring me peace?*

He stopped at the end of the corridor. Here the stone walls towered overhead while LED sconces cast a soft light and blended in with the medieval décor. Unseen to all but the sharpest eyes were video cameras sending feeds to a data center in the basement that rivaled those at most Fortune 500 companies.

A few taps on his phone revealed a video feed showing the sparring room. The space was large with shadows that hid a variety of workout equipment mixed with his private collection of ancient torture devices. Spotlights illuminated a large square mat in the center where a young woman with vague Japanese features and dressed in a black leather biker jacket stood with her arms crossed over her chest. On the far side of the room was a broad man in a form-fitted dress shirt, his cufflinks glittering in the room's pale light, a tattoo on his neck.

The giant's skin broke out into gooseflesh.

Here we go.

EIGHT

Somewhere in Bavaria

The giant strode into a small command room adjacent to the sparring room where monitors were mounted on three walls and a one-way mirror covered the fourth wall. Through the glass, the woman in the biker jacket and the muscled man circled each other. Felix, his personal bodyguard—what he called his utility man—sat watching the activity on a monitor with his lanky arms and legs crossed.

His utility man barely hid the glee on his face. "You sure this is a good idea? Remember what happened last time we used them both on an op?"

The giant parked himself in front of the glass and ignored his craggy reflection in the window. "No, I'm not sure."

"Care to make a wager, sir? I'll put two hundred on Magnus and give you two to one." Felix toyed with a ring on his index finger.

The giant grunted and kept his attention fixed on the action in the room.

The arched ceiling high overhead the sparring room was covered in aged and fading frescos of medieval violence and war. Walls made from stone dripped with moisture forming puddles on the floor. Arranged around the room's perimeter was a mixture of barbaric torture machines intermingled with modern workout equipment. A weight rack sat next to bumper plates that were stacked next to an ancient wooden rack with rollers at both ends. A speed bag hung next to a heavy bag, both of which were beside a chair made from cane and covered with spikes and straps. The center of the room contained a large blue mat, similar to those found in a mixed martial arts cage.

The woman, her arms and back rippling with muscles, dropped her leather jacket to the floor. Underneath, she wore a white halter top and black tights. The male had the broad upper body and tiny legs of a gym rat who liked to skip leg day. As the woman circled the center of the room, he sidestepped away. He deposited his suit jacket and rolled up his sleeves, revealing arms covered with tattoos in bright colors. A set of hidden microphones relayed their conversation.

The woman took a step onto the mat. "Hello, Magnus."

"Kira. What a surprise to see you here." Magnus rolled his head around causing a crackle to echo around the room.

The lithe female advanced another step. "It's just like our large friend to do this, no?"

Magnus snickered as he stepped onto the mat. "Just you and me, honey. Mano a mano. Old-fashioned fisticuffs, like it should be." The fighter bounced on the balls of his feet while shaking out his arms.

In the observation room, Ivanov cleaned his glasses with a silk handkerchief. *She doesn't stand a chance.*

The woman took two running steps and launched herself at Magnus with a flying kick and struck her target's chest with two heels. He flew back and performed a summersault while she landed and took three running steps, sprang, and delivered a butterfly kick that connected with his jaw. Blood and saliva flew from his mouth as he spun and landed on his chest with a jarring thump that rattled the glass.

She's not fucking around.

The female executed a series of quick but vicious kicks that sent more blood spattering across the mat. A Brazilian kick landed on his neck while he struggled to stand and a sweep sent him hard to the mat once again.

Kira bounded away and stopped in a Kokutsu-dachi, a karate stance with her weight on her back foot while Magnus staggered to his feet. He took a tentative step, wavered, almost fell, and caught himself. He wiped blood and sweat from his brow before settling into a front stance, hands low in leopard hand. "Come on. Fight me, you bitch."

Felix snickered. "She's toying with him." He slapped two green-hued one hundred euro notes on the table.

"I'll take those odds." Ivanov removed a single one hundred euro bill from his pocket and laid it on the table.

The two fighters traded a series of blows that tested each other but did no real damage. She feinted and slipped, letting the strikes glance off her arms and shoulders, parrying the more direct hits. Magnus moved slowly, but the giant knew better. He'd seen this tactic before after watching countless cage fights where Magnus played possum in the beginning only to emerge later with a vicious energy after his opponent tired.

As the next strike sailed past the woman's shoulder, she used Magnus's momentum to toss him to the ground. Instead of pouncing and closing like her opponent might expect, she landed a series of stomp kicks on his torso and head, sending more blood spattering to the mat. He rolled away and struggled to his feet, shaking his head, sending a spray of sweat and blood through the air in a slow arc. Again he attacked with a series of jabs and punches, which she parried with blocks and a series of kicks, before he backed away on shaky legs while she bounced on the balls of her feet. Kira wore a mask of easy concentration, and she showed no fatigue.

He's playing possum.

A light went on in Magnus's eyes, and he attacked again with a variety of his own kicks. A strike found her solar plexus, and she barely managed to parry another with her forearm. Off balance, she struck at him with a right jab, which he caught in an arm lock, pulling her close where she had no leverage against his superior strength and weight.

The glint in Magnus's eyes grew brighter.

She kicked out at his shin again and again but failed to dislodge the hold.

He tightened his grip on her elbow, threatening to break it.

Behind the glass, the giant's toe tapped a rhythm on the floor. *She's finally met her match.*

The action on the mat slowed as the utility man joined the giant at the window. The two fighters stood locked in a stalemate, and the female's face contorted in pain. Felix scooped the bills off the table.

She's done. Then Ivanov's jaw dropped.

Balancing on the ball of her left foot, Kira angled her right leg back and spun it around until her foot swung around her back, over her head, and the top of her foot hammered her opponent's forehead in a perfectly executed scorpion kick that released his hold and sent Magnus to his stomach, where he lay stunned.

Landing on Magnus's back, Kira hooked her arm around his neck, flexing her bicep so his windpipe was cut off. Veins popped from her neck and forehead, and her shoulder muscles rippled and pulsed as her arm tightened around his neck. Her eyes changed from shimmering with the fight to a clouded faraway stare.

In a split second the giant sprinted from the control room while drawing a pistol from a shoulder holster. As he threw open the double doors to the sparring room, he cursed his one miscalculation. "Kira!"

The pistol was in the giant's hand, but he wavered.

The woman's gaze was locked onto the ceiling, her mind somewhere deep in her past. She straddled Magnus's back while her arms encircled his neck, holding him in a cobra-like position, bent awkwardly at his lower spine. His face was contorted and his eyes bulged as he gasped for air, and he slapped the mat repeatedly.

The giant halted two meters from the pair. "Kira. Let him go. He's tapped out."

She tightened her grip. One of Magnus's arms flailed at her shoulder and his eyes grew wide as he ran out of air.

Goddamn it. "Let him go," Ivanov yelled. "I command you."

Her lips curled in a sneer as her right hand crept around to grasp Magnus's chin.

Hands up and palms out, Ivanov realized the significance of the shift in her grip. "Don't do it, Kira. Felix, get her off him."

The utility man strode at the pair.

There's no time. "No. Kira. Don't—"

With a sharp wrench of her hands, Magnus's neck snapped with a sickening crunch. She pushed his body into the mat and leaped to her feet to meet the oncoming attack.

Felix stopped and pushed his stringy blond hair behind an ear before checking Magnus's pulse. "Dead."

The giant clenched his free hand into a fist. "Damn it, Kira. Why'd you do that?"

She stepped back. "What did you think was going to happen?"

Felix walked to the end of the room and perched himself on the torture rack.

Ivanov spread his arms. "I thought you two would work out your differences. We needed him for this operation."

She pointed at Magnus's body. "Now they're worked out."

Bowing his head, Ivanov gathered his thoughts. He pushed away his anger and holstered his gun. "So be it."

The woman remained tense and poised as her eyes darted between Ivanov and Felix.

Reaching into his suit jacket, Ivanov pulled out a glossy four by six-inch image, which he held out to her.

After a moment's hesitation, she snatched the picture and examined it while keeping a wary eye on both men.

From memory, Ivanov visualized the picture. It depicted a surveillance shot of a fit-looking man in his mid-forties wearing a suit jacket over a casual shirt. His head was shaved, and he sported a pair of aviator-styled sunglasses and held a cigarette in a curled hand.

Kira's face remain stoic. If she recognized him, there was no indication.

"You recognize this man?" He asked with a wry grin.

Kira handed back the photo. "No. I thought so. But no."

Was that a slight shift in her eyes? He shrugged. "Felix, the dossier please."

The utility man rose, ambled to the double doors, disappeared for a moment, and returned with a file, which he handed to Ivanov.

After paging through the folio to ensure it was intact, Ivanov held it out to Kira. "Your next assignment."

With her chin up, she grabbed the file and looked inside. "My usual fees apply, you know."

Ivanov chuckled. "You're going to want more for this one. You could have used Magnus's help."

"I work better alone."

The file was thin, containing only a few photos of the male subject along with a sheaf of dog-eared papers held together with a paperclip. In the back of the folder were several photos of a curly-haired woman with tan skin. Kira examined each image, and Ivanov knew from experience that she was committing them to memory.

He shoved his hands into his pockets. "The assignment is simple but won't be easy. We don't have much to go on, but what we do have is there. This deal is different than our past engagements. You can't just kill him. Track him instead. Watch him. Keep a log. Report back. He's searching for the woman—well, he will be. Shadow him, and when he gets close to her, when he reveals her location, take him out. But not before—and this is important." Ivanov shook his finger at her. "Not before you learn this woman's whereabouts."

Kira kept her eyes on the file. "Who is she?"

"The woman's name is Kate Shaw. Ex-CIA. Went rogue. Apprehended and imprisoned by the CIA. No one knows where she's imprisoned. The details we know are in the file. It is of the utmost importance that we find this

Shaw woman before he does. Before any other intelligence agency does. Before the Russians do. Got it?"

Kira nodded, still examining the file. "Why? What does she know?"

Nikita laughed to hide his displeasure. "That's need to know. Are we clear?"

The slim assassin snapped the file closed and grabbed her jacket as she walked to the door. "Crystal. Track him. Find her. Kill him."

NINE

Corsica

The crusty tan-skinned local with the wiry hair brought the old flatbed truck to a halt in a cloud of dust outside the fence and yelled at the men in the rear bed through the cab's rear window. "As far as I go."

Spencer handed the old man a handful of euros through the rear window, who accepted the wad of bills with a sniff. Both men jumped off the tailgate as the driver spun the wheels and roared off, leaving them under a hot orange sun in a swirl of dust.

A silver fence rose over their heads and coiled razor wire along the top gleamed in the sunlight. Signs warned of the fence's high-voltage status, and there were security cameras in weatherproof housings at regular intervals along the barrier. Through the fence, rolling dunes covered with a tangle of prickly pear, eucalyptus, juniper, and the occasional wild olive tree dotted the landscape. Behind them, spanning for miles across the center of the island, grew the

Corsican thicket, also known as the *maquis*, filled with a dense thorny forest of hundreds of species of flora. Men were known to get lost for days in the maquis, sometimes emerging with tales of wild cork oaks, sightings of the elusive Corsican Finch, and even discoveries of the remains of former cultures.

Max eyed the sky and dug out his Blackphone, a device that used custom software designed by Goshawk to encrypt transmissions and prevent tracking. Overhead, a red kite hawk soared, her black-tipped wings spread wide. The elegant bird had white wing feathers, a reddish-brown underbody, and a hooked beak. In a blur, the hawk dove into the maquis thicket before rising to resume her hunt. Next to him, Spencer had his back to Max. They hadn't talked much since the operation in the Turkish desert.

Max typed a text message on his phone.

A few seconds later, the gate whirled to life and creaked sideways.

As they followed a sandy double-track approaching a squat terra-cotta house, the scurry of pawed feet was followed by a melodic command. The men rounded a corner in the path to see Goshawk's willowy form standing with her hand resting on the head of a black-and-brown Doberman Pinscher. The dog's ears were up, and her broad chest heaved, ready to leap. Goshawk bent to whisper something in the dog's ear, who immediately lost interest in the two intruders.

Max caught his breath. *Damn, she looks good.*

Goshawk offered Max a long hug and pecked Spencer on the cheek before leading them along the path through dense foliage. A moment later the trees parted to reveal waves crashing beyond a set of short dunes, while the azure expanse of the Mediterranean filled the horizon. The salty air was tinged with rosemary and honeysuckle. The Doberman didn't stray more than a meter from Goshawk's side as they stepped onto a narrow wooden deck. "Meet Cerberus. She was a gift from Don Paoli."

Max grunted. "Cerberus, as in the hound of Hades?"

"The one and the same." Goshawk smiled. "She guards the gates of the underworld and prevents the dead from leaving."

"Prophetic, I guess."

As she led the way through doors hewn from eucalyptus into the cottage, Max followed and Spencer remained outside.

The interior was cool, dimly lit, and appointed with a colorful mixture of wooden furniture in the Corsican tradition. Max picked out several miniature video cameras, and he knew there were more that evaded the naked eye. "Nice place."

Max leaned against the kitchen doorjamb while Goshawk put a kettle on the gas burner. Her previously long coal-black hair was now cut into a tight crew cut and dyed blond. Her long fingers, usually adorned with silver jewelry, were tan and bare, and her nails were unpolished. She wore a pair of short cutoff jean shorts and a gauzy blouse that hid little. Her skin, adorned with an array of tattoos depicting bloody scenes of Japanese samurai battles, was tanned and leathered from the Corsican sun. The quiet Corsican life treated her well.

Their eyes met as she handed Max a steaming mug of green tea. *Were those newly formed wrinkles around her eyes?* Wordless comfort passed between them, and he followed her out to the porch where Spencer sat staring at the placid ocean.

A cane chair crackled when Goshawk settled into it and

crossed her legs. Her gaze settled on Spencer as she handed him a mug. "I have news."

The old operative's eyes darted to Goshawk. "About Kate?"

Goshawk blew into her tea. "They found Bill's body."

Spencer shot to the edge of the seat. "And Kate?"

She placed a hand on his forearm. "She's alive. But that's about all I know."

Max squatted next to her chair. "Tell us all you can."

She grimaced as she sipped her hot tea. "Bill's body washed up on the Eastern Shore of the Chesapeake Bay, near a place called Deal Island. His death was ruled an accidental drowning."

Spencer made a guttural sound. "Bullshit."

Goshawk set her tea on a rickety table. "Agreed, but it's hard to get more information. The official coroner's report ruled the death was a drowning. The public files were conspicuously light on details."

"And Kate?" Spencer fidgeted.

"I've been digging. I've followed trails down rabbit holes that led me through government servers to private servers to anonymous servers and back to government servers. They went to great lengths to hide her location."

She lifted her tea cup and blew into it again. "I found her at some kind of CIA black-ops prison. It's an off-the-books kind of place, buried deep within US military land, disguised by a fake company name and protected with top-level clearances. I doubt the executive branch of the US government even knows the prison exists. With all the drama surrounding Guantanamo, these are where they keep their high-value targets away from the US justice system. And the media."

Spencer teetered on the edge of his chair, his eyes focused on Goshawk. "Where is it?"

Goshawk shook her head. "I don't know."

His face fell. "What else can you tell me?"

"They're interrogating her regularly, although from the reports I was able to dig up, they're not using physical torture. Instead, they're using isolation, sleep deprivation, noise therapy, and other methods to break her down. I haven't found any files or records on what they're learning or her physical condition—"

"Can I see what you have?" Spencer stood.

Goshawk glanced at Max, who gave an imperceptible nod. "Sure, hon. Follow me."

————

While Spencer paged through files on her computer, Goshawk sauntered back outside to sit with Max. "Is that your next move? Find Kate?"

During the multiday overland trip from Iraq to Corsica, designed to throw off any pursuit or surveillance, Max concluded that his next step might be determined by what was contained on the tiny device they found in Spartak's briefcase. Spencer lobbied hard to attempt Kate's rescue, but Max had difficulty justifying the distraction against determining the true goals of the consortium and ensuring his family's safety. Max shook his head. "It won't help keep my family alive."

Goshawk ran the tip of her tongue over her bottom lip. "But you love that woman."

Max scoffed. "What are you talking about? I barely know her."

Goshawk tilted her head. "That didn't stop us."

"Is that what you call it? Love?" Max winked.

The computer hacker settled back in her chair and peered at him over the rim of her mug. "Call it whatever you want, darling."

Max crossed his arms. "Besides, I have—how do they say it? More fish to fry?"

Goshawk chuckled. "Bigger."

"What?"

"Bigger fish to fry. It means—"

"I know what it means."

Digging in his pocket, Max removed the small device Spencer found in Spartak's leather bag and held it up for Goshawk to see. He thumbed the on button so the screen lit up with the numeric keypad and PIN field. During their long trip, Max busied himself by attempting various number combinations, hoping to get lucky. The challenge was the PIN field didn't indicate the number of required digits and allowed Max to enter up to ten numbers, meaning there were ten billion combinations. All he succeeded in doing was to become frustrated. "What is this thing?"

Goshawk's eyes lit up as she took it from his hand. "Where did you discover this little gem?"

Max told her the story about finding the device in Spartak's case, how the former Russian army major denied knowing about it, and ended with his impression that Spartak was scared when he saw it.

She flipped the box over in her hand with an impish gleam in her eye. "This is a digital wallet. It's used for what's called cold storage of cryptocurrency."

"In English, please."

Goshawk laughed. "You look like I just spoke to you in Martian."

Max shifted in his chair. "Cut the crap. Just tell me what it is."

Another laugh. "You've heard of bitcoin, right?"

He knew bitcoin was an electronic currency that was used to pay for things on the internet but didn't know how it worked. "Yup."

"Bitcoin is a cryptocurrency, an electronic way of storing value. People can pay for goods and services with it, if the seller accepts it. There are various mediums of exchange for bitcoin on the internet, both legitimate and nefarious. Problem is, most online storage for bitcoin is terribly insecure. There are stories of people losing millions of dollars of bitcoin to hackers." Goshawk winked.

"So, let me guess. This is an off-line storage device, kind of like a bank book?"

"Sort of," she said. "It's more a wallet than a bank book."

Max pointed at the box. "If you lose this device, you lose your bitcoin."

"That's right."

"Can you break into it?"

Goshawk fingered the on button and fiddled with the keypad. "Ten-digit key. That'll take a while." She rose and padded into the cottage with Cerberus and Max following. "Spencer's on my main machine, but we can use my laptop." She tapped a few keys to wake the screen before plugging the device into a USB dongle attached to the computer. She settled into a modern-looking desk chair with her legs curled under her and typed at a speed Max didn't think was possible. The dog lay at her feet, her eyes tracking Max's movements. Spencer ignored them both, intent on his reading.

Max peered over Goshawk's shoulder, trying to make

sense of the string of yellow characters on the black screen. "What are you doing?"

Goshawk remained riveted on her work until Max gave up and strolled outside along the path to the ocean's edge. The sapphire water lapped at the amber sand and was clear enough to see through. He was about to pull his Blackphone from his pocket when he sensed someone behind him.

Goshawk's arms curled around his waist and spun him in a dance. He almost tumbled into the water but caught himself with a splash. Goshawk twirled away and removed her shirt with a flourish, revealing a smooth back covered with an intricate tattoo of a battle scene in different shades of blacks and reds. She kicked her shorts off into the sand, grabbed Max's waist, and pulled his pants down to his ankles.

"What about the—"

She tugged at his clothes until he was naked under the hot sun. "I'm running an algorithm that will try thousands of combinations every second. It'll break eventually. Meanwhile..."

He allowed her to pull him into the warm surf, and once they were a reasonable distance out and onto a sandbar, he pulled her close as she guided him into her warmth.

TEN

Corsica

"Uncle Max!"

The tow-headed ten-year-old boy on the other side of the video chat jumped up and down, while Max's sister, Arina Asimov, sat on the couch in the background with a laptop open and a glass of wine. Alex was hunched over his own computer keyboard, face close to the camera, brandishing a wide grin with gaps in his mouth where adult teeth were growing.

"Hey, bud, how's it going?" Max lounged in one of Goshawk's porch chairs with a view of the sand and water, while balancing a laptop on his knee and a coffee mug in his hand. The morning light changed the water to the color of cobalt.

Alex put his chin in his palms and leaned in to the monitor. "Good. Mom got me a skateboard. Wanna see it?"

"Of course."

When the ten-year-old disappeared from the screen,

Arina stood and approached the camera. "Hey, Max. Your face is looking good."

"Hey, sis. Thanks. You should have seen the other guy." He fingered the baggie of white pills in his pocket. "Everything okay?" Things were stilted between them since Arina pulled a disappearing act from the cabin in Colorado where Max hid them before they reappeared in Switzerland cohabitating with Victor Dedov.

"Yeah. Fine. Alex is finally being homeschooled, so that's good. He's doing well in math. Victor brought in a tutor to help out. The history books are different here than in Minsk."

"I'll bet." Victor was providing a more stable home life for Arina and Alex than he could ever hope to provide. *Don't get too comfortable, sis.* "Where is Victor? Is he home?"

Arina glanced over her shoulder. "No, he's away on business." Her voice was faraway.

"Do you know where he went? I was in the Middle East recently and thought I saw him."

Her eyes flashed. "How do I know? He said he was away on business."

Alex ran to the screen holding a large wooden skateboard gleaming with varnish. "Victor's gone a lot," the boy quipped.

What else do you know, Alex?

His mother patted his shoulder. "Shh... Show him your new board."

The youngster smiled wide as he held up the skateboard with amber-colored wheels and a black-and-gold logo in the center that read *Arbor Groundswell Series.*

Max gave a weak smile. "Wow, sport. That looks like a good one. Have you ridden it yet?"

Alex crinkled his nose. "Of course."

"Okay, don't forget to wear a helmet. You don't want to break your noggin."

Alex's eyes got wide. "What's a noggin?"

"It's your head, silly."

The boy tugged his ear. "When are you coming to visit?"

Max smiled. "I don't know, kiddo. Soon. Okay?"

"Sure."

"Put your Mom back on."

Alex yelled for his mother, who had retreated off camera.

When she reappeared, Max asked, "Do you have a way I can contact Victor?"

Her eyes narrowed. "Why do you want to—"

"It's nothing really. Just some business. Questions about when he and dad worked together. An operation they ran that might have something to do with this consortium thing."

She pinched her lip with her fingers.

Max grinned. "I promise. I'm happy that you and Alex have a place where you're safe, where Alex can get an education."

She crossed her arms. "Don't mess this up for me, Max."

Max held his hands up. "Wouldn't dream of it."

She rummaged on a table in the background and returned with a slip of torn paper. "I have an email address. He said he wasn't carrying a mobile phone."

Of course he's not. Max memorized the email address as she read it off. Based on the random mixture of alphanumeric characters, it sounded like an encrypted email server.

Arina pursed her lips. "I'm warning you, Max. Don't screw us."

Before Max could reply, the screen went dark.

Max thought a minute before writing a quick email to Victor using his own encrypted server.

I heard your recent transaction fell through. I have your olives. I'll give you a good price.

He chuckled as he closed the laptop and padded out to the beach where Goshawk sat nude in the shallow water gazing at the horizon.

———

"Who's next on your list?"

They lay on lounge chairs, letting the bright Corsican sun dry their salt-encrusted bodies. She ran her nails over his back, digging white lines into his dry skin and lingering on each of his three long-healed bullet wounds. Spencer had finished reading the sparse file that Goshawk accumulated on Kate Shaw and left to stroll along the beach.

Long ago Max memorized the file of the twelve men responsible for killing his mother and father and who put a contract on him, Arina, and Alex. "People tell me that I can't kill my way out of this problem. I've been wracking my brain to come up with a different strategy. So far, I'm drawing a blank."

Goshawk dug a nail into his back, drawing blood and causing him to flinch, before tracing a scar on Max's flank with her finger. "What about number six, Leoniod Petrov? I've got a partial file worked up on him."

"Isn't he the head of Rosneft? That gas huge company?"

"Yup. Controlled by the Russian government through a holding company. He's Rosneft's chairman."

"Close ties to the Russian president," Max rolled over and grinned at her. "Got anything good on him?"

"Not much. Typical Russian oligarch who made crazy money when the Soviet Union collapsed. Early on, he aligned with the Russian president, which saved him when the president went after the other oligarchs who called for reforms and challenged his power."

Max grunted. "I have no sympathy for those guys who made billions, but lost it when the Russian president forced them to sell back."

"That was a power play, right? Goshawk asked. "Those that failed to sell were either forced from the country or convicted for tax evasion on fake charges?"

The Russian president, a dictator in all but name. "Or outright killed." He rolled to his side, flinched as pain shot through his ribcage, and held his head up on one hand, taking in her long and bronzed figure. "By letting the mafia run wild, he's turned the towns of inner Russia into little criminal enterprises where the civilians are left with nothing. No jobs. No prospects. Not even the old Communist party benefits they used to have. Guys like Petrov are enabling the problem."

"The rich get richer."

"Exactly."

Goshawk rolled onto her back and shielded her eyes with a hand. "Petrov's got the usual stuff. Dacha in Sochi. Couple of mistresses. Dabbles in cocaine. Collects Ferraris. Owns part of an American hockey team. Houses in Italy and France. A few private jets."

Max's hand wandered across Goshawk's long bare thigh. "Sounds promising. Discovered an angle yet?"

"No. I'll keep digging."

His fingers drifted up to graze one of her apple-sized breasts. Her nipple became hard at his touch.

She snickered and dragged her nails down his chest,

drawing more blood. "You ready for another round, big boy?"

He bit back a yell from the pain in his rib as she swung a leg over him and arched her back until he was deep inside her. His eyes closed, and all he heard was the roar of the ocean and the crescendo of her moans.

———

It took six hours for Goshawk's algorithm to break the pin and another hour for her to fight through a firewall built into the device. While she worked, Max showered, shaved with Goshawk's pink razor and flower-scented cream, and fixed them a plate of meats, cheeses, and rice wrapped with grape leaves called dolmas. Spencer reappeared from his walk as Max set out the food.

Goshawk rolled her chair to the tiny coffee table and speared a hunk of chevre with a small fork. "This is weird."

Max shoved a prosciutto-wrapped chunk of cheese into his mouth. "What is?"

"Well, a ten-digit pin is rare on these things." She stabbed a piece of meat with her fork. "It requires a sophisticated code-breaking program. But the firewall was child's play. Any high school kid in his parents' basement could get through it. The only reason it took me so long was because I was watching for traps. Made me think there was some kind of trojan horse or trigger that might wipe the device."

Max tossed a fig into his mouth. "So, what was on it?"

Goshawk's eyebrows shot up. "This is where it gets interesting."

ELEVEN

Corsica

"For fig sake, just tell me." Max took a swig of green tea.

Goshawk squinted. "Are you trying to clean up your language?" The hacker rolled her chair back to her computer and brought up a webpage. "At today's prices, you found a little over a million dollars of bitcoin."

Max snorted. Money had never much mattered. He always seemed to have enough. Growing up, his father's position as assistant director of the Belarusian branch of the KGB meant they lived well. As an adult, he made enough through his freelance business or his jazz bar. If he needed money for an operation, he always found it. "Not bad."

"That's all you can say to finding a million bucks?" Goshawk let out a breath. "You might want to sell. The cryptocurrency market is crazy volatile and has rocketed up in the past couple of months. It's a huge bubble with tons of speculators."

Max glanced at Spencer, who avoided his gaze. "Fine.

Convert three quarters of it and stuff it into two of our operational accounts. Let's use Panama and Seychelles. Leave the remainder in bitcoin in case we need it for some reason."

A couple taps on her keyboard. "Consider it done. The device also has a flash drive."

Max ate a hunk of cheese. "And?"

"And you need to see this."

Spencer's eyes followed Max as he got up and made his way over to her machine. Displayed on the black command line window was a long list of files that included word documents, images, and several movie files. Goshawk clicked on one of the images. A window opened showing a stern-looking Caucasian male in his mid-sixties wearing the uniform of a general in the Russian army. The shoulder insignia showed the three stars of a colonel general, and his breast board was covered with rows and rows of colored accommodations.

Max sucked in his breath. "That's Sergei Fedorov."

Goshawk leaned closer to the screen. "Who is Sergei Fedorov?"

Max rubbed his chin. "Director of Russia's Federal Security Service, also known as the FSB. He's also number seven on the consortium. What is this file doing here?"

She folded her long legs under her. "Remind me what the FSB is and how it relates to the old KGB?"

He paced while he talked. "The FSB oversees a subset of the functions of the old KGB, namely internal security, counter intelligence, and border patrol. The SVR, or Foreign Intelligence Service, handles espionage outside Russia. But the FSB handles surveillance of foreigners while they're in Russia as well as media suppression and propaganda. The FSB also does the killing, when necessary, of the Russian president's enemies. In every practical sense, the FSB is the same as the KGB. They are the same people with the same goal—suppression of discontent to preserve a dictatorship. What else is in there?"

Goshawk clicked on three files. One revealed details of Fedorov's financial assets, one outlined particulars of his wife and children, and one showed intimate specifics of his daily routine with logs of his daily appointments.

Max leaned close to the screen while he read through the material. "It's similar to the information we received on Spartak. Same file structure, same level of detail, same organization." Max stretched his arms.

The thin hacker opened more files. "Whoa. Here we go."

Max leaned over her shoulder. The screen was filled with pictures of Sergei Fedorov in compromising positions with other men. "Whoa is right. If these get out, Fedorov's career is over. Being gay in Russia, especially at his level, is a big no-no."

Goshawk looked at him with furrowed eyebrows. "Why?"

"Homophobia is rampant in Russia—part Christianity, part Stalinism, part Western decadence. And since the Russian president has positioned Russia against the West, voila. It's in vogue to be anti-gay."

She opened more files, and they skimmed the documents.

His pulse quickened as he read. The documents were assembled in the style of an old KGB hit file and were obviously designed to provide someone—Max guessed himself—an opportunity to get to Fedorov. Details of the times, locations, and identities of dozens of men with whom Fedorov had liaisons. Memos speculated about his future tête-à-têtes. The file included intimate narratives of Fedorov's romantic interludes that resembled sting operations using male honeypots. There were blueprints and maps of the hotels and dachas Fedorov frequented with his boyfriends. Max couldn't ask for a better set of files with which to plan Fedorov's assassination. Once again, he was given the perfect setup to kill a member of the consortium. He sat back and rubbed the stubble on his chin, trying not to smile. *But why? And who was providing this information?*

A squeal from Goshawk. "Holy shit, you gotta see this." Her nose was pressed to her screen.

Both men stepped over. "What now?"

Goshawk angled her screen revealing a video player on the large monitor. "Found this in an encrypted folder." She hit play.

The video was short, and the grainy recording was made with a low budget camera. It showed a tall woman in a track suit and a stocking cap jogging down a city street. A wisp of blond hair escaped from her hat and waved in the wind as she ran. Two beefy men, also in track suits, pounded behind her, struggling to keep up. As the woman ran up the street and turned left onto a tree-lined trail, she disappeared behind a long hedgerow, followed by the bodyguards.

Max gaped at Spencer and pointed at the screen. "Is that who I think it is?"

She played the video again.

The video finished and Goshawk tapped to open a .jpg file that revealed a headshot of Piper Montgomery, the director of the Central Intelligence Agency. She was an attractive woman, smugly confident, with ivory teeth and a pair of fashionable glasses perched on a pert nose.

Spencer grunted and pointed to another file in the directory. "What's in that text file?"

A tap by Goshawk revealed two pages of detailed information about Montgomery's security detail—the weapons they carried, how they rotated in six-hour shifts, and detailed surveillance logs of her movements accompanied by her bodyguards.

Max whistled. "Whoever assembled these materials is preparing to either assassinate or kidnap the director of the CIA."

Spencer tapped Goshawk's shoulder. "Can you send me that?"

The hacker looked over at Max, who shrugged. She clicked with her mouse a few times. "Okay, sent. But I don't understand. Why is this important?"

Spencer stood and walked to the kitchen and deposited his empty beer bottle in the sink before returning to the living room. "Montgomery is the one most likely to know where Kate is."

The hacker's eyes widened. "You don't mean you're going to—"

Spencer hooked his thumb into a belt loop. "Got any better ideas?"

The three of them looked at each other while Max's thoughts jumped between the file on Fedorov and the separate dossier on Montgomery. They were different in tone and structure, with the Fedorov file matching something he might assemble himself while the Montgomery information was hastily compiled and limited in scope. The former was KGB style—thorough and complete. The Montgomery file didn't inspire confidence.

Spencer disappeared from the room and reappeared minutes later with his bag slung over his shoulder. "You coming?"

Max leaned against the table with his arms crossed. "You sure that's what you want to do?"

Spencer spread his arms. "Montgomery was the one who ordered Kate's arrest, and she's the one who's keeping her prisoner. The best way to find Kate is to ask Montgomery."

Max shook his head. "Best way to join Kate in the brig."

The ex-CIA operator walked to the door, his boots pounding on the wooden floor. "I'm not hearing any alternatives."

Max shook his head. "That dossier is thin. Better odds with Fedorov."

With his hand on the doorknob, Spencer frowned.

Everything slowed while the faces of Max's nephew and sister flashed through his mind. *Kidnapping Montgomery is a bad idea.*

Goshawk sat frozen in her chair, watching the two men.

Before Max thought of something to say, Spencer opened the door and disappeared.

As the heavy steps on the wooden deck faded away, Max ran outside. "Spencer! Let's talk about it."

But the lanky operative was gone, leaving behind only a set of boot prints in the sandy path.

TWELVE

Vatican City

The throngs of tourists and Pope-sighting hopefuls in Piazza San Pietro were thick despite the chilly temperatures. A dull sun shone overhead in a cloudless sky that took the edge off a crisp wind, but most of the visitors to the historic square were bundled in jackets and hats. Saint Peter's Basilica rose majestically on the western end of the plaza, the large dome dominating the skyline and the fourteen statues decorating the roofline like sentries. Maderno's fountain was to the right of St. Peter's Basilica, its trickling water sparkling in the sunlight.

Victor Dedov's choice for a meeting spot was a good one. A busy plaza in the heart of a secure location with little chance of being noticed or overheard. Max took a fast boat ride with Carlu to the Italian port town of Ostia. A hired car took him to the center of Rome, where he performed an hour-long surveillance detection route before jumping on the metro and exiting at the Cipro station. Nothing odd jumped out at him except a raven-haired woman in a black watch cap wearing wraparound sunglasses on a pale winter day. The girl appeared twice in his SDR.

Probably nothing. Another hour of meanderings revealed no sign of the girl, so he made his way on foot to Saint Peter's Square.

While he walked, he reflected on Victor Dedov. When Max's father and mother were killed by a large chemical bomb hidden in a truck that mysteriously penetrated his father's security team, Max suspected the job was planned and executed by inside operatives of either the Belarusian KGB or the Moscow FSB, and that Victor —former director of the Belarusian KGB—must have had a hand in the operation, either overtly or tacitly. Max's suspicions grew when Victor publicly stated that Chechen extremists were behind the bombing, an assertion lacking factual support. The perpetrators of the bombing remained a mystery, although Max now knew that the consortium had pulled the strings behind the killing. He just didn't know who had planned and carried out the attack.

As Max spotted Victor across the busy plaza, he was reminded that he didn't trust the man despite his sister's attachment. What she saw in him Max didn't know, although he guessed it had more to do with stability than love. He grudgingly admitted appreciation for the secure and safe home Victor provided for Arina and Alex at great cost to himself. But the now-retired KGB director was always scheming on something, and now Max found Victor in the middle of the Turkish desert attempting to purchase weapons illegally from a high-ranking member of the consortium.

Is he still running clandestine operations with some

nefarious or illicit ambition? My instinct is he's involved in this somehow. But how? What is he up to?

"Victor." Max nodded once.

Dedov greeted him in return using Max's given Belarusian name. "Mikhail, how are you? Imagine my surprise when I received your message."

The former director wore a down jacket with a Western logo, wool trousers, and a flat cap to keep his balding head warm. His eyes were slits, and his face wore a hard expression.

Max smiled. "Arina says you've been traveling a lot lately. I assume now that you're retired, you're out seeing the sights."

Victor raised his arms and gestured at the buildings around them. "Is there anywhere more splendid than this? We're standing among some of the world's most marvelous architecture." He grinned and cocked his head. "So you want to make a deal? Something about olives?"

While the two men strolled to the basilica, Max took out a soft pack of Italian cigarettes and ripped off the plastic wrapper. "I have some goods you might be interested in. Something I think you tried to buy recently?"

Dedov gave him a sideways glance. "So it was you out there in the scrub. Why were you there?"

A scan around at the milling tourists revealed nothing alarming. No one was in earshot. "It should be obvious," Max said. "I could ask you the same question."

A smug smile from Victor. "Well, I supposed our aims are each our own. Mine is simple—I need to protect something extremely valuable."

Max stroked his chin as he pictured Arina and Alex going about their daily life in a castle full of armed guards, a necessary by-product of their fight to remain alive. "Quite, which is something I'm also interested in. I have the...er... shipment of olives and would like to donate them to the cause. Assuming we can come to an arrangement."

They reached the broad stone stairs leading to the front entrance of St. Peter's Basilica where there was a line of visitors waiting to enter the church. Dedov stopped and turned. "Are you suggesting a deal?"

Max lit a cigarette using the lighter with the burnished Belarusian flag that he received from his grandfather. "I might be. Two questions."

Dedov shoved his hands in his jacket pockets. "I'm listening."

Max blew out a plume of smoke. "How did you come to be out there in a transaction with him? You know my objectives."

"Not beating around the bush, are we?" Victor stared across the enormous plaza at the Via della Conciliazione, the road leading east into the heart of Rome. "I have to be honest, Mikhail. I didn't know who I was dealing with until the last minute. One must go where the fish are, so to speak. I was as surprised as anyone. But by the time I knew, it was too late. I had to go through with the transaction."

Anyone who says they have to be honest means they're not being honest.

Victor faced Max. "As you probably know, there aren't a lot of options when it comes to getting a hold of...um...that flavor of olives. We need more of them around the house." Victor shrugged. "What was I supposed to do?"

Max flicked ash from his cigarette. "How did he know I was out there?"

The former KGB director faced the front of the basilica. "How do I know? When the shooting started, we got out of there. I thought it was the Turkish military."

Max exhaled a large plume of smoke. "Any speculation?"

While slowly shaking his head, Victor pursed his lips. "I'm as stumped as you."

Max ground the cigarette out on the ground. "Right. Just thought I'd ask. How about I have the olives delivered directly to you? My contribution to the...um...household."

A wide smile appeared across Victor's face. "I was hoping you'd see it that way. This can be a win for both of us after all."

After discussing delivery arrangements, the two men parted ways. As Victor walked east at a brisk pace across the plaza, Max couldn't shake the feeling that the former KGB man was playing him.

He put his Blackphone to his ear. When Sammi's voice cackled through, thick with an accent and garbled from the transmission, Max said, "Remember that thing we discussed yesterday?"

"That's an affirmative, sadiqi."

"We're a go." Max disconnected the call and picked up his extinguished cigarette butt and put it in his pocket before joining the crowds exiting the piazza.

Time to find out what Dedov is up to.

THIRTEEN

Rome, Italy

Two things struck him while he strolled along Via della Conciliazione to the Tiber river, his hands jammed in his jacket pockets. The first was a haunting vision of the exquisite Katrina Zabat who he first met during a post-job vodka bender in a rose-lit bar in Rome's Monti neighborhood. He couldn't walk the streets in this city without thinking of her. The second was a glimpse of the raven-haired girl.

The woman strode along the opposite side of the street, dodging pedestrians, on a beeline to somewhere. Not fast, but not slow either. Slightly ahead of Max, traveling in the same direction. A leather backpack bounced on her shoulders as she walked. *It's the boots. The same boots. Western style, chunky heels. American's call them harness boots.* He scanned the sparsely populated streets but recognized no one else. Dodging a woman riding a motorcycle and bundled in a scarf, he crossed the street and matched steps with the raven-haired woman.

It's probably nothing.

His long legs easily kept up. They passed a café where a couple sat in a window enjoying foam-topped coffees, crossed Via dell'Erba, and continued past the Brazilian embassy. The woman gave no indication she knew she was being followed.

As the Tiber came into view, she darted left, bounded up four concrete steps, and disappeared into a church. Max slowed to decide his next move—lose her or risk exposure by following her into the building. His need to get a good look of her face settled it. He took the steps two at a time and yanked open the heavy oaken doors.

His eyes grew accustomed to the dim interior as he made his way through the foyer and into the nave. Gold gilded walls towered a half dozen stories over his head, and arched passages led to transepts on both sides of the altar. Caramel-colored pews with maroon cushions stood empty on either side of a wide aisle. Dark and light tile in concentric squares led to an ornate altar. The church was empty.

Pretending to admire the intricate frescos lining the walls, Max strolled through the nave and toured the transepts while searching for the raven-haired girl. She had vanished.

Side doors led to interior sections of the church. He opened one to reveal a set of descending stairs. A second led to a storeroom packed with hymnals, cushions, candles, folding chairs, tables, paper goods, and other church accoutrements. A third door opened to a short hallway with a closed door at the end. No sign of her. She was probably a student late for a Bible study or had a job working in the church kitchen. Strolling the length of the center aisle, he stopped long enough to dip his finger into the holy water in the stone font by the door, crossed himself, and pushed open the double doors.

And ran smack into a tall woman, her face and hair covered by a cream scarf.

He stepped back. "Excuse—"

She grabbed him by the jacket and pushed him back into the church's entry foyer. Another shove sent him sideways into a darkened corner.

Catching himself, he brought his hands up in hiraken, knuckles outstretched, and looked for his attacker.

She appeared wraithlike in the shadows, her beige overcoat flowing in the sparse light. With a flourish, she removed her scarf to reveal a familiar face.

"Julia. What the—"

She grabbed his wrist. "No time. We have to go. Follow me."

Light flashed as she went through the double doors with Max on her heels.

What on earth is this all about?

A white motorcycle rested on its kickstand next to the church steps. Julia swung her leg over the leather seat and fired up the engine and he slid on behind her. *Wait, isn't this the motorcycle he dodged while he pursued the raven-haired girl? What the hell is going on?*

They sped away from the church at top speed. He leaned into the curves with her and held lightly onto her hips as she dodged lorries, weaved around pedestrians, and missed bumpers by a hair's breadth. They crossed the Tiber and were soon lost among the mazelike streets of central Rome. He stole several glances back but saw no one following. After another thirty minutes of navigating traffic, Julia stopped under the portico of the Palazzo Manfredi. She tossed the keys to a bellman, and Max followed her through the lobby, up a set of sweeping stairs, and down a hall.

Once they were in the hotel room, she flung her overcoat onto the king-sized bed and whirled to close the curtains. "You're getting sloppy, Max."

The furniture had a pleasant patina, like someone had worked hard to remove its newness without it looking dingy. Max stepped to the bar cart. *Fancy hotel, someone put fresh ice in the bucket.* "Good to see you too, Julia."

Although raised by his father Andrei and Andrei's wife, Max's true mother was Julia Meier, a women he met only months before. His father left a picture of Julia in a go-box buried in the dirt floor underneath a butcher's shop in Minsk, knowing Max would find it. Julia, an agent of the German BND intelligence service, and Andrei had a long and stormy affair while she ran Andrei as a double agent. It was this betrayal that Max surmised had led to the consortium's contract on the Asimov family.

"Come on, Max. You have to watch yourself."

"The raven-haired girl?"

Julia adjusted the drapes. "She's been on your ass the whole time you've been in Rome."

Max examined each of the bottles on the cart. "And you know this how?"

Feet planted, her arms were crossed over her chest. "I've been following you, waiting for you to finish talking to that pecker-head Dedov."

"How did you find me?" It dawned on him. "Goshawk. She's the only one who knows where I am."

A corner of Julia's mouth curled up. "Except, apparently, that girl in the leather jacket."

Max grabbed two tumblers, poured gin into a shaker, added ice, splashed in some vermouth, and shook. He clinked ice in the glasses and poured a measure of the alcohol mixture in each. Tossed two olives in each and handed one to Julia.

They clinked glasses, and Max asked, "Who is she?"

Julia peeked between the curtains. "Never seen her before."

"Was she alone?"

Still looking through a slit in the curtains, Julia took a minute to respond. "Best I can tell."

"You spooked her." Max tried to look past her shoulder out the window. "Which is why she disappeared through the church. Any sign of her?"

A shake of her head. "She's not what I'm looking for." As Julia held the curtains closed, the butt of a pistol protruded from her open sport coat.

For the first time since the flight from the church, Max got a good look at Julia's face. Deep lines creased her brow and dark circles hung below her eyes. Her makeup, usually applied perfectly, was smeared in places. "Julia, what's wrong? Why are you here?"

Her eyes welled up and she brushed away a tear before taking another peek through the curtains. She talked while looking out the window. "I can't stay here."

He stepped around the bed. "What do you mean? Stay where? What's going on—"

A gasp and her drink fell to the floor, splashing alcohol onto the carpet. "Shit. They're here."

He moved to the window, but she held the curtain closed with a tight fist. "Julia, who's out there?"

She pulled out her pistol, her eyes wide. "I have to go."

He grabbed her wrist. "Talk to me, Julia. Who's down there on the street? Why did you want to see me? Who's after you?"

Julia resisted his grip, and fought to keep the curtains closed. "I only have a few seconds. I can't tell you now. You'll learn everything in due time. You have to trust me."

His grip tightened on her wrist. "Who is it, Julia? I can help." He strained to release her fingers from the curtain.

"Max, stop."

He let go. *Why was she preventing him from seeing outside?*

She blocked him from getting to the window. "I have to disappear."

"What do you mean, disappear? Why?" He set his glass on the bar cart.

A tear rolled down her cheek. "Things have taken a turn for the worse. Things I can't control."

He spread his arms. "What things? What are you talking about, Julia?"

She wiped at the tear. "I wanted you to see me with your own eyes, to see that I'm well and fine. And to tell you that I'm disappearing. My choice. I want you to know I'm alive, but I'm going away for a while." She placed her hand on his shoulder. "Okay?"

His eyes welled up, a sensation he hadn't experienced in a long time. "Have they added you to the list?"

Her eyes cleared as she smiled. "Mikhail, I've always been on the list."

"So, what is it?"

Julia smiled again. "At some point, you'll know. Or we'll both be dead and it won't matter."

She let go of the curtain and, gun in hand, wrapped her arms around him in a tight hug. As she did, she whispered in his ear. "Your father had a secretary. Her name was Raisa. Last I heard, she's in Moldova. Find her. If anyone knows what your father was up to, it was her."

Brushing his cheek with a kiss, she pushed herself away and disappeared out the hotel room door.

When the door slammed shut, Max glanced through a slit in the curtains and saw an empty and quiet street. He exited the room, took the stairs down two at a time, pausing at each landing, but saw no one. In the lobby, an elderly couple argued with the valet while a young blonde in a short skirt fiddled with her phone. After exiting through the front door, two boys ran past him chasing a dog. Cabs blared their horns, trucks trundled by, and commuters on bicycles wove through traffic. Julia was nowhere in sight, nor were any pursuers.

Was she lying about being chased? And if so, why?

FOURTEEN

London, England

Freezing rain spit from a gunmetal sky and the occasional gust of icy wind cut through Max's thin leather jacket as he made his way along the darkened city street. He wore a black scarf around his neck and lower face and a flat cap on his shaved skull. Black leather gloves—he called them his mafia gloves—completed his meager winter wardrobe. A Walther PPK was snug in a shoulder holster. One could never be careful enough, especially because the last time he was in London, he was the most wanted fugitive in the world.

He ran a long surveillance detection route that took him through half a dozen London neighborhoods while he sampled some of the city's heartiest food. Roast with gravy. Yorkshire pudding. A couple pints of ale. His brief encounter with Julia ran through his head dozens of times, but he was unable to make sense of her behavior. *Was she just paranoid? Or was it all a trick?*

Here in London, three pedestrians braving the storm stuck in his mind during his SDR. A mature man in a stocking cap and wool overcoat carrying a newspaper, a student toting a backpack, and a woman of indeterminate age in a Burberry jacket. None of them resembled the raven-haired girl. None of them reappeared during his long and meandering route through central London.

Icy water sloshed on his boot as he stepped into a vacant street. Spencer's abrupt departure from Corsica concerned him, and he questioned his decision to let him go on his own. The former CIA man was a capable operative, and even though he might be distracted by his love and paternal tendencies toward Kate, he knew how to take care of himself. There was still no word from Spencer. *I hope you can forgive me, my friend.*

Victor Dedov was a distraction. Max had supplied Sammi with specific instructions regarding the shipment of weapons, and now he waited. He put it out of his mind.

Julia's whispered instructions were another matter. That his father might have left a clue with his secretary matched the elder Asimov's method of operation. The photo in the box underneath the butcher shop floor. The thumb drive hidden in the family picture. The elder Asimov had established a pattern from beyond the grave.

For the first time, he felt lost among the swirling tide of events. A much larger conspiracy was underway, the events of which he only had an inkling. With Spencer's disappearance, Kate's incarceration, and his birth mother running for her life, he had few places to turn, which is what brought him to London in the middle of an ice storm.

From the dawn of his training, from the very genesis of his evolution into a spy, agent, and KGB-sponsored assassin, Max always operated alone. His father drilled into his head the folly of faith and how he should trust no one, no agency, no government, and no individual. *Everyone has their own agenda,* he liked to say. *Laugh with many, my son, but trust no one.*

Agitation niggled at the back of his neck as he made his way through the frozen rain, splashing through slush puddles, his hands jammed into the pockets of his leather jacket. He tightened the scarf over his face and tugged on the brim of his cap in a futile effort to protect himself from the frozen pellets that hit his face. Turning sideways, he slipped through a hedge, darted across a dark backyard, and stopped in front of a wooden fence as tall as his shoulders that looked new and smelled of fresh pine. Tall oaks and junipers grew in front of the fence, and a row of trimmed jack pines towered on the far side. A warm glow emanated from the other side of the wall, as it had the previous night when he cased the neighborhood.

His agitation was replaced by an edginess he didn't understand. He was alone, his surveillance detection route had ensured that. *So why the unease?* He hunched by the wall and waited. Nothing moved.

In addition to the new wood aroma of the fence, he caught another odor—the acrid stink of feces. Max withdrew a small cylinder from his pocket which he clenched in his teeth before grasping the top of the fence and vaulting over. When he landed, his feet sunk into mud, and he grasped the cylinder and readied it for what he knew was coming.

Movement disturbed the stillness in the yard. He whirled and raised the metal canister as a dark blur sailed at him through the air. He depressed a button, and a mist of capsaicin mixed with propylene glycol hit the moving blur. Max shifted his weight enough so the flying hunk of fur and muscle deflected off his arm and into the mud, where it landed and turned on him, snarling. Max gave the dog another dose of pepper spray, and she whined and rubbed her face in the mud. When he stood, he found a shotgun stuck in his face.

Beads of water clung to the gun's matte black barrel, and it was held rock steady. The voice on the other end of the gun was pinched. "You came prepared, I see."

The man behind the double barrels wore a disheveled yellow slicker, and his goateed face dripped with freezing rain.

Max put his hands in the air. "Hello, Callum."

The shotgun didn't waver. "Look what the cat dragged in." Callum Baxter poked Max in the chest with the double barrel.

"Callum, it's me. Max. You can put the gun down."

The man's eyes squinted at him through the rain, bushy eyebrows furrowed, the finger tight on the trigger. "I'm picturing the headline now. Famous Russian assassin gunned down in London. MI6 officer awarded knighthood."

Max rolled his eyes before waving his hands in the air to disguise a slight shift to a more athletic stance. "How about MI6 officer overpowered in his own backyard while his attack German shepherd dozed in the flower bed."

Baxter's face slackened, but he took a step back. The gun was steady, while the rain came down in sheets. "You burned down my office and almost took the house with it. You obliterated my files, my life's work. You and your computer hack somehow erased terabytes of information stored on MI6 computers. You can't just waltz in here—"

Max hit the barrel with the heel of his left hand while turning his body sideways, sweeping Baxter's feet from under him, and plucking the shotgun from the MI6 agent's hand. Baxter thumped down on the water-soaked lawn as a splash drenched Max's boots. Ejecting the shells from the gun, he stuffed them in his pocket before offering Baxter a hand.

"Got any tea in that new office of yours?"

FIFTEEN

London, England

Baxter's yard was large and well landscaped, and even in the encroaching winter months, the care with which the trees, shrubbery, and tended flower beds was evident. A hulking ivy-covered brick and stone Tudor home sat in darkness on the far end of the yard, while a deck jutted into the yard. To his left was a small outbuilding, also built of brick, its style matching the house. A row of windows ran under the outbuilding's eaves, casting light over the yard.

The newly built office offered a warm respite from the weather. Inside was appointed with new leather furniture, and a modern desk chair sat in front of a big desk piled high with books, files, and papers. A laptop computer was perched on a stack of notebooks, and a large ashtray held two pipes and a pile of ash. The inside smelled of Frog Morton tobacco and smoke from a woodstove. Along one wall were two large monitors showing video feeds of the yard from security cameras, and a third monitor showed muted news from the BBC.

Max shed his jacket and plopped down on the leather couch, resting the shotgun across his knees. "I like what you've done with the place. Quite an upgrade."

Callum Baxter, senior officer in Britain's Secret Intelligence Service, also known as MI6, knelt to pour bottled water on the German shepard's face to rinse off the pepper spray. She curled up in front of the fireplace, snout on her front paws, red eyes blinking at Max. Baxter hung his rain jacket on a coat-tree and fiddled with a pipe, all the while keeping his back to Max. When he finished and faced Max, unlit pipe clenched in his teeth, his face was red, and his eyes blazed. "Something tells me I should have shot you while I could."

As Baxter cast around for something to light his pipe with, Max dug into his pocket and tossed him the beat-to-hell Zippo lighter with the burnished Belarusian flag on the side. It was the last reminder he had of his grandfather, the man he now suspected of putting this entire conspiracy in motion. Max leaned the shotgun against the couch. "How about that tea?"

The MI6 man didn't speak until he had his pipe lit and he had blown a plume of woodsy smoke into the air. "It's after midnight. Eve is long gone. If you want tea, you can go in the house and fix it yourself." Another cloud escaped his mouth. "Why don't you tell me why you trespassed in my backyard and assaulted my dog. And how on earth did you know I have a dog?"

Max crouched in front of the fire, where he savored the warmth and petted the German shepherd's head. "Easy. Dead spots on the grass from dog pee. Weren't there last time I was here. What's his name?"

"Her name is Quinn."

Max stroked Quinn's back. "I want to make a deal."

Baxter grunted. "That's what phones are for."

Max considered lighting a cigarette, but decided against it. "I wanted to see your new office."

The MI6 man looked around. "Turned out better than I expected, but I can't replace all the files you burned."

"Trust me." Max rubbed Quinn's belly. "It's better this way."

Another grunt. "Better for you, maybe. What kind of deal?"

On his journey to London, Max rehearsed his pitch to Baxter, a man who might be reluctant to work with Max after the events of the prior fall. The straight approach was best, so he began with the operation to take out Spartak Polzin, Victor Dedov's appearance, and finished with the discovery of the file on Sergei Fedorov. He left out many details, including Julia's flight and the intel on the CIA director, but gave enough information to cause Baxter's left eyebrow to twitch.

When he was done, Baxter puffed on his pipe, sending plumes of blue smoke billowing to the ceiling. He finished the bowl, tapped out the ash, and repacked a new one. "Someone gave you enough details of Spartak Polzin's plans for you to put together an operation. Here's a target, set up for you like a bullseye. An offer you can't refuse."

"Something like that," Max said. "Whoever compiled it and gave it to me knows I couldn't ignore it. And they are right. I have to find out what's behind the curtain."

Baxter puffed. "And now they've given you a second file to tempt you into action. A pattern."

"Right." Max scratched Quinn behind the ears.

Baxter lit the pipe with the Zippo. "Makes me wonder if whoever gave you the file also tipped off Spartak to your presence. Otherwise, how did he know you'd be there?"

Max shrugged. "It could have happened like that, but he died before I found out."

Leaning back in his chair, Baxter chewed on his pipe stem. "What if someone on the inside of the consortium supplied you with that information to distract you, from, say, more important tasks?"

Max held the dog's gaze while he petted her between the ears. "How do you mean?"

Callum eyed his dog and resumed puffing. "Since you torched my hobby, I had to come up with another pastime." Baxter cleared his throat and walked to the fire and added a log. "I suppose it was you that sent me that untraceable wire of cash?"

Max's brow furrowed. "Don't know what you're talking about. Is that how you built this place?"

Baxter snorted. "Anyway, like I said, I needed a new hobby, so I looked into this consortium group of yours." He took a drag and blew out a thin plume of smoke.

Outside, frozen rain pellets blew against the windows with a sharp crackle. Max eyed the panes while he waited for Baxter to continue.

"Wasn't able to dig up much more than you'd already shared with me, but what I had was enough to open a case file at MI6 and put a team on it."

Quinn rolled over on her back again, and Max scratched her chest.

With his legs crossed, Baxter tapped the tip of the pipe on his teeth. "As you know, the consortium is highly secretive. We know the names. We believe the ringleader uses an alias to conceal his true identity. We're unsure of their true aim, although we have corroborated that part of their objective is either a countermeasure to OPEC's price setting power or a play to corner as much oil and gas as they can to benefit Russia and China. Securing a long-term supply of the black stuff is on everyone's agenda, and those two countries have been partners on such endeavors in the past. What's not clear to us is why the secrecy. OPEC is out in the open, so why not the consortium? That leads us to believe they have other intentions." He puffed his pipe. "We've learned three things about the group. The first, as you know, is they are targeting you, Arina, and little Alex. We've corroborated the operation, or should I say the contract, through other channels. We don't know why, but there is an extraordinarily high price on your head."

Max snorted. "Tell me something I don't know. Every two-bit killer with a peashooter is after me."

The MI6 man cleared his throat. "Right. The second thing is—" Callum huffed out three smoke rings. "Are you familiar with the Government Communications Headquarters here in London, also known as the GCHQ?"

Max rubbed the back of his neck. "Vaguely. Like FAPSI in Russia, or the NSA in America?"

"Right." Baxter tapped his pipe over an ashtray. "Well, my task force liaised with the GCHQ, who launched a systematic and broadly scoped surveillance operation on the names on the consortium list. Phone, mobile, email, text, everything. They have this crazy computer program where they can feed all that data into algorithms and form assertions and conclusions about certain things. Pattern recognition and whatnot."

Max smirked. "It's called machine learning."

"Whatever. It's remarkable what these kids can do."

The pipe smoke made him want a cigarette, but Max held off. Instead, he dug into his pocket and found the baggie of pills and swallowed one dry. "I'm guessing they came up with something you're dying to tell me."

Baxter nodded as he refilled his pipe bowl. "The second operation... or activity—" He stopped and used Max's lighter to restart his pipe. "It's curious, but the whiz kids are steadfast. They claim they've detected some patterns that indicate the consortium has a rift. Two factions that are at war with each other. One school of thought is it's a power struggle for control."

Max kept his face blank as his mind churned through the possibilities. "That fits. One side is supplying me with dossiers on members of the other side."

Baxter nodded while he stroked his goatee.

"This may work to my advantage," Max said.

Again, Baxter nodded, puffed, and pulled on his goatee. "When do I get to hear this offer of yours?"

Max paced back and forth in front of the fire and didn't speak.

A grunt from Baxter. "You can't even ask it, can you?"

"I need... Well, I'm curious."

Baxter smiled. "You want our help, isn't that it?"

Max spread his arms. "You don't have to make it sound so... well, so desperate."

Baxter covered his grin with a hand. "This is what people do, Max. They ask for help. They make partnerships. They—"

Slapping the desk, Max startled the dog. "I'm not most people."

A chuckle from the MI6 man. "Obviously. Why don't we call it a consultation? Will that make you feel better?"

After shoving his hands in his pockets, Max moved back

to the couch. "My head tells me to go after the next one on the list, even if it is a setup."

"Take out Fedorov," Baxter said. "But it may not get you any closer to the answer you seek."

Outside the wind howled. "Someone told me once that even if I kill every one of the consortium members, I may not solve my problem."

"Wonder who that was?" Baxter set his pipe in the ashtray. "Let's hear the other idea."

Pacing in front of the couch, Max gave him a brief description of Julia's suggestion to track down his father's former secretary.

"Right. So going after Kate is off the table?"

Was that a tic in Baxter's eyebrow? Max said nothing.

Turning away, Baxter refilled his pipe. Facing Max again, he chewed the pipe's lip.

Max stroked the dog's back. "Taking down Fedorov might uncover useful information. The more of them I kill, the more pressure I put on them, the more discontent, and the more leverage I have."

Baxter grimaced. "Or the trap might spring."

"Right. And at this rate, it's going to take me years to kill all these guys, and longer as they replace the empty seats."

Baxter chewed his pipe stem. "My counsel, which is worth what you're paying for it, is to go after the secretary. The key to this whole thing is uncovering your father's actions that led to his death."

"My father did have a habit of hiding clues in places only I can find."

The MI6 agent talked as he rummaged in a desk drawer. "And what about Spencer?"

"Spencer can take care of himself."

Baxter still rummaged. "Can he?"

Why does Baxter's voice sound off? "What are you not telling me?"

Baxter knocked the ash from his pipe and ran a pipe cleaner up the stem. "The third finding of the GCHQ."

Max raised one eyebrow. "What?"

"I haven't told you the third finding of the GCHQ." Baxter shook his tobacco pouch. "Remember the data wonks—"

"Yeah, yeah. I remember. What about them?"

A glint appeared in Baxter's eye. "Here's where we talk about a deal. Quid pro quo."

"You haven't told me what it is."

A pained expression took over his face as Baxter shifted in his chair. "I'm not sure how to explain this, or even make sense of it myself, but I'm hoping you can help me. Believe it or not, I was looking for a way to contact you when you walked through my door."

Baxter stomped up and down the tiny office as Quinn's eyes followed. "The GCHQ produced another finding that surprised me."

Max moved his hand in a circle. "I don't have all night—"

Baxter gestured with the pipe as he walked. "While their algorithms churned through all the data on the consortium, they got some alerts they didn't understand at first."

Max rose from the dog's side to stretch his knees. "What kind of alerts?"

"I'm getting there for Pete's sake." Baxter stopped walking long enough to thump his pipe on an ashtray. "They found some communication information that correlates to activity around the time the CIA snatched Kate."

Max plopped down on the couch. "How is that possible? Are you saying the consortium and the CIA are working together?"

"Not exactly. What I'm about to tell you is highly confidential."

Max rolled his eyes. "I think we're in the nest here."

"Right." Baxter shuffled through some papers on his desk before turning around empty-handed. "They're not in cahoots. In fact, they're working against each other."

"Cahoots? I don't know that word."

"It means to collude. Work together."

"Okay. So are they working together or not?"

Baxter smirked. "Listening in on the CIA is delicate."

Max glanced at his watch.

Baxter cleared his throat. "Based on the GCHQ's assertions, after triangulating on intel they picked up from the consortium and from the CIA, it looks like the consortium is looking for Kate while the CIA is keeping her location a secret specifically from the consortium."

Max cocked his head. "Why does the consortium care about Kate? Maybe they view her as a way to get to me?" He pointed a finger at Baxter. "Wait. You want to find Kate too, and you want my help to do it. You think because the consortium and the CIA want her, there must be a reason."

Baxter shrugged. "That's MI6's assessment. Aren't you interested in why the consortium thinks finding her is important, and don't you want to see that justice is done and Kate is released?"

Blood coursed through his face as Max stood, shrugged on his jacket, and made for the door.

Baxter held up a hand. "Don't go yet. That's my deal. I help you with Raisa, you help me find Kate."

Max put his hand on the door knob before facing Baxter. "Lives are at stake, Callum. My family's lives. I'll go it alone. I've done it before." *I'm tired of being manipulated by so-called intelligence agencies. MI6 wants to find Kate, they can find her themselves.*

He wrenched open the door and disappeared into the hail and wind.

SIXTEEN

London, England

The precipitation made his meandering surveillance detection trip through the quiet city less agreeable, but he didn't mind the frozen rain, even considering his poor choice of outerwear. The weather drove everyone from the streets, which made it easier to spot a tail, and the cold helped clear his mind.

There wasn't a night that went by since Kate was taken into CIA custody when his heart didn't go out to her. He often wondered at the viability of a rescue attempt but knew it might take weeks, if not months, of planning and a dangerous operation to snatch her, followed by an even riskier period when she would need to recover and hide from a government that would be hell-bent on recapturing her. Even with the help of MI6, the effort would be enormous and extraordinarily risky. Meanwhile, his sister and nephew were vulnerable. As much as it pained him, he needed to stay focused.

Baxter's deal would be a huge distraction. *Still, why did MI6 want to find Kate?* The question nagged at him as he stomped through puddles of slush.

He was about to duck down the grimy stairs of a tube station when a fleeting vision, a momentary connection between one recent memory and the present, jolted him from his thoughts. A woman dressed against the weather with a black wool cap, black plaid scarf pulled up over her face, and a long dark wool coat was on the opposite side of the street. Her head was down, her hands were jammed into her pockets, and she looked to be in a hurry as she scurried along the empty sidewalk. *Something about her.*

While he took the stairs down to the tube, he wracked his brain for the connection. He cleared the turnstiles and jumped aboard a train that had ground to a halt. When the subway pulled away from the station, he strode the length of the sparsely populated train looking for signs of the woman, all the while chastising himself. She couldn't have possibly run down the tube station stairs to make the same train.

It came to him as the tube screeched to a halt at Piccadilly Circus. Her boots were the giveaway—knee-high with tall block heels. Not stiletto, but thick, like cowboy boots. Harness boots. They stuck out because they reminded him of their cabin in Colorado. The raven-haired girl from Rome.

His eyes were alert for any sign of the woman while spending another hour riding the tube, exiting at one station, popping up to the street to walk to another, and jumping aboard whatever train appeared first. He saw no further evidence of the woman. He exited at Embankment Station and emerged into the rainy, sleety chill before making a beeline for The Savoy, where he had a room under the name of Winston Binch.

Ice pellets stung his cheeks as he walked with his head down. *Am I walking into a trap? Is something larger happening that I can't see now? What did you leave me with, Dad? What kind of puzzle did you concoct? And why?*

Tired of the endless surveillance detection routes, fatigued from walking, chilled from the weather, he ducked into the hotel, showered, and put on dry clothes. After a hot meal from room service, he packed his small backpack and left the hotel through a service entrance, stepping back into the howling storm.

Time to unravel the mystery. As much as it pains me, I need help.

SEVENTEEN

London, England

"Change of heart?"

Baxter was dressed in the same rumpled clothing as the night before and looked as if he hadn't slept, which given the early morning hour, was probably the case. He admitted Max with a smug grin.

This time, Max had called ahead. After performing yet another exhaustive surveillance detection route that included eating a stale croissant and drinking weak coffee at an all-night diner, he made his way to Baxter's backyard. There was no sign of the raven-haired woman with the boots.

The sun hadn't yet risen as the two men sat sipping black coffee. A fire sputtered in the woodstove. Quinn lay on the couch next to Max, accepting head scratches while keeping two wary eyes open.

Max shrugged at Baxter's question.

A grin from the MI6 agent. "So why are you here? I assume it's not to drink my coffee."

Max sipped and grimaced. "That's for sure. This is worse than the piss they served in the Red Army." He took another sip. "Someone once told me that I can't kill my way out of this mess."

"You said that yesterday."

"I'm getting there." Max tasted the coffee again. *Don't admit weakness.* "This intelligence game is full of number crunching. I can't do it all myself, and Goshawk doesn't have the processing power."

The real reason is too painful to admit. His father's face floated through his mind. *Once is happenstance. Twice is coincidence. Three times is enemy action.* The thought of the pursuer, on top of everything else, shook him to the core. *It's too much.*

"So, you need us." The corner of Baxter's mouth went up. "What happened to change your mind?"

Standing, Max refilled his cup from the pot. "This thing is bigger than me. There's a much larger conspiracy behind the consortium." *I can't say it.*

"What leads you to conclude that?" Baxter tugged on his goatee.

The coffee in Max's cup, though weak in flavor, felt good as it slid down his throat.

Baxter crossed his arms. "This thing, if it's going to work between us, has to go both ways."

Max studied the surveillance monitors mounted on the wall. The yard was grainy and dark. Nothing moved. "You wouldn't understand."

"Try me."

I can't do it. Max shook his head.

The MI6 agent ambled to the stove and stoked the fire

with a metal poker before tossing in a fresh log. "For the record, I agree with you. There's a lot to this we're not seeing. An obvious trap set for you in Turkey. The introduction of the Fedorov file, hidden in such a way that surprised Spartak. It smacks of something deeper, as you say."

Quinn yawned, rolled over, and Max rubbed her belly.

Baxter tugged on his goatee. "What's the best course of action—"

The dog's ears perked up. She jumped from the couch and stood poised at the door while emitting a low growl. Startled, Max retrieved the shotgun from where it leaned against the desk, and Baxter stepped to the door, his head cocked. A minute went by. Quinn growled, motionless. Baxter moved to the wall and examined the security monitors.

Max positioned himself next to the door.

Another minute went by.

And another.

Without a sound, the dog relaxed her ears and padded to the couch where she curled herself into a ball and closed her eyes.

The two men locked eyes while Baxter retrieved a pistol from a desk drawer. "The benefit of you burning down my office is that it enabled me to rebuild with modern security measures. Bulletproof glass and walls reinforced with steel plating."

Max pointed at the door. "And a doggie door."

Baxter plopped into the chair and checked the gun's magazine. "Right."

Max sat on the edge of the couch, shotgun across his lap. A vision of the raven-haired woman entered his mind. *Was she outside? Crazier things have happened.* "You don't happen to have a bug scanner, do you? A wireless signal detector?"

Baxter's bushy eyebrows knit together. "You think someone's tracking you?"

Max shook his head. "I'm probably just being paranoid."

With a scowl, Baxter rummaged in a drawer before finding a cellphone-sized black box with a beefy antenna. He flipped on the device and approached Max. "It has a one-meter radius." He waved it around Max's legs, arms, and torso before shaking his head. You're not giving off any signals." Baxter flicked it off and stowed the device back in the drawer. "So we have a deal?"

Max cocked his head. "What deal?"

A chuckle from Baxter. "You already forgot. MI6 will help you. In return, you help us find Kate Shaw and beat the consortium to the punch."

The coffee mug was empty. *Why did everyone want to find Kate?* "Is the search for Kate a sanctioned MI6 operation?"

Head bobbing, Baxter grinned. "Of course. The chief approved it. He'll be glad to hear you're on board."

The chief was the head of Britain's Secret Intelligence Service, a peer of the director of the Central Intelligence Service, and Callum Baxter's direct superior. Max swallowed on a dry throat as he watched the dog. Her eyes scanned the room, but otherwise she was calm.

Baxter cleared his throat. "We have a deal?"

At that moment, Quinn's ears perked up again before she jumped off the couch, approached the door with her neck stretched out and growled.

Baxter spun in his chair to look at the monitors, while Max set his mug on the desk and stepped next to Quinn, who was frozen while pointing her snout at the door, a rumble coming from her throat. "Anything on the monitors?"

The MI6 agent peered at a grainy black-and-white screen showing the backyard where the fence intersected with the home's brick wall. "Thought I saw something, but I get a lot of false positives on this thing. The cameras have motion sensors that are supposed to ignore small animals and branches blowing in the wind."

"Does she jump at every animal?"

The only sound in the room was Quinn's low growl. "Negative."

As the dog's growl grew louder, Max shoved shells into the shotgun while Baxter watched the monitors. Seconds ticked by.

Baxter leaned against the edge of the desk, his eyes roving from monitor to monitor. "You sure you came alone?"

Max nodded once. "I took the usual pains to make sure I wasn't followed."

When Quinn sat back on her haunches, her growl became a whine.

"I just saw movement." Baxter jabbed at a monitor. "Right corner of the main house."

Max put his hand on the doorknob. "I'm going out." Gripping the Mossberg with two hands, Max slipped out of Baxter's office. The foul weather had kicked up again, and snowflakes swirled in the air and melted into little spots of water as they hit his leather jacket. He ducked around the office walls where a line of young plum trees ran along the fence between the outbuilding and the main house, his feet sinking into the wet earth. He kept to the darkness between the trees and fence, the shotgun held up, cheek against the stock, his senses tuned. When he got to the end of the row of trees, he stopped, crouched, and waited. Aside from the waving branches, he saw nothing.

Maybe the cameras picked up the moving trees.

Across from where they thought they spotted movement, he hid in a stand of shrubbery. Rows of honeysuckle sat in stony silence devoid of their leaves. This part of the fence was lower to allow gated access to the side and front of the house. His eyes were accustomed to the cloudy gloom, and no shadows moved among the shrubbery.

While avoiding the splash of light from Baxter's office, he followed the vegetation to the gate. As he approached the stand of honeysuckle, he stopped and pulled a penlight from his pocket and shined it on the ground. His heart skipped a beat.

Footprints.

Small, with a thick heel.

The gate was open a fraction of an inch. Max flicked off the light and gave his eyes a moment to adjust before prodding the gate open with his foot. Mossberg up, he walked along the side of the house.

The ground here was gravel and devoid of vegetation, so he had no trouble picking up the footprints again in the sodden front yard. He followed them along a short hedge of conifer and out to the street, where they disappeared on the wet pavement.

In this part of the city, the streets were narrow with one row of parking along either side, leaving barely enough room for a Mini Cooper to pass. The cars were all dark, and nothing stirred. He returned to Baxter's office, reported what he learned, and leaned the gun against the desk.

Baxter took the gun with a grunt. "I never leave that gate open. Can't have Quinn wandering the streets."

Collapsing on the couch, Max accepted a cup of steaming coffee.

"So, the deal?" Baxter stood, arms crossed.

"Yes. We have a damn deal."

The MI6 agent chuckled. "And?"

Max groaned. "And I need your damn help."

EIGHTEEN

Salzburg, Austria

"Sir, your phone."

The giant calling himself Nikita Ivanov accepted the device from his assistant and barked into it. "Go."

He listened as he marched down the corridor. Outside, a bitter arctic freeze settled on the eastern side of the Alps enveloping the city in a layer of frost. Inside, the massive home was toasty thanks to a thermal heating system under the floors. Still, the mansion's stained glass windows were rimmed with ice. He had many homes, including the castle in Germany and a sprawling estate in Greece, but this was his favorite.

His wide network of spies and informants—ranging from old men who did nothing but tail people to young career-minded professionals at all levels of government and industry—were arranged in a reporting hierarchy with mid-level managers who collected the intel and doled out payments and reported up to higher bosses. One of those higher bosses was on the other end of the call. "Sir, it's just as you expected. Stepanov met with Spartak two weeks before the aborted gun deal. While we don't know all of what was said, we do know Spartak expressed doubts about going ahead with the transaction. He suspected a trap, but Stepanov forced him to go ahead with it." The caller added a few more details before hanging up.

Ivanov tossed the phone back to his assistant without breaking his pace. His suspicions were confirmed—a group of men were conspired against him. A group of men on his council. Men he had trusted.

A thumbprint scanner opened a set of double doors, and he left his assistant behind. A long corridor of stone, its walls decorated with neoclassical art works of heroic warriors and soft nudes, stretched in front of him. He pounded down the hallway, ignoring the art, and used his thumbprint to open another set of doors. After enduring more corridors, stairs, and security checkpoints, he marched into a room buried deep beneath his mansion.

His team was already in place. Felix, his wiry body-guard and jack-of-all-trades, sat nursing a mug of coffee. The wavy-haired Sophia, a disillusioned American from somewhere in Texas, was hunched over a computer working a mouse and speaking rapidly into a headset. Whiteboards around the room were covered in diagrams, schematics, and images, while three large monitors showed news feeds from around the world. These two were the only people he trusted to root out the conspiracy against him.

He didn't bother to sit, and his voice was a bark. "Where are we?"

Sophia ended her call, tapped a few keys, and the picture of a man in a Russian army uniform appeared on a monitor. Broad shoulders but a sallow face with a hard look in his eyes. Endless rows of medals, tape stripes, ribbons, and insignia on his breast.

She stood. "Ruslan Stepanov, head of Russia's Main Intelligence Directorate, known as GRU. Former standout Spetsnaz, now oversees the department with twenty thousand of the elite troops. Rumored to command a hundred retired Spetsnaz as his personal bodyguard unit." A clicker advanced through dozens of images of Stepanov in various military uniforms, some showing him in suit and tie, a few catching him in social moments with a drink in his hand. Most images showed him shirtless and engaged in feats of strength, bare-fisted boxing bouts, and men striking his midriff with steel bars. "He once claimed that he'd retire if any current member of the Spetsnaz bested him in a physical contest. He's still in office."

Ivanov grunted. "Keep going. I know all this."

Sophia advanced the slides until an organizational chart showed on the screen. "As number two on your petroleum council, Stepanov is next in line to the Chancellorship should you become...ahem...deceased." A slide advanced to show a financial statement. "We know Stepanov's personal finances are highly leveraged. He invested in a few deals that went south. For example, he underwrote Spartak's recent failed gun sale, and his personal spending habits are atrocious. Cars, houses, jets for his personal use."

Felix chuckled. "Oligarch wannabe."

"He views his ascension to the chancellorship as a financial windfall," Sophia said. "A way to get out of his current jam. He sees his peers building wealth while he flounders."

She advanced to another slide that showed Stepanov shaking hands with the current Russian president. "We've uncovered evidence that he's providing intelligence on your council's actions to the president in direct violation of the council's bylaws. There isn't anything that your council does that the president isn't informed about."

"Stepanov is angling to be the next Russian president," Felix said.

Sophia nodded once. "That's our assumption. The president isn't getting any younger—he's sixty-eight—and there will need to be a replacement soon."

Ivanov grunted again. This was a topic which he discussed many times with his superiors, although he wasn't about to inform Sophia or Felix of that. "Besides his link to Spartak's weapons trafficking, what evidence do we have of their conspiracy against me?"

The muscles in Sophia's normally stoic face tensed. "So far, nothing. Only conjecture and speculation."

"What about his links to other council members? I need to know what other council members are aligned with him and against me."

Sophia crossed her arms. "Nothing concrete yet, sir. Electronic chatter and surveillance reports indicate he has at least one other member on his side. We're working on an identity."

Felix set his mug on the table and stood. "Let me at Stepanov. I'll get it out of him."

Ivanov's deep laugh filled the small room. "Soon, Felix." He gestured for Felix to sit. "For now, we tread lightly. The operation with Asimov and Spartak went off just as we planned. I need evidence of Stepanov's treachery before we take drastic action otherwise my people will be very upset. Keep on him. Trace the money. Get evidence."

"Yes, sir." Felix dropped back into the chair.

"Now what of Asimov's movements? Any indication of Kate Shaw's whereabouts?"

Sophia shook her head. "So far, nothing. We lost him for three days. He showed up in London and met with MI6 twice. He traveled to Rome and met with Victor Dedov before eluding us again. We speculate he's joining up with MI6."

"Makes sense, given the Brompton bomber thing." Ivanov paced and rubbed his chin. *That was an outcome I didn't predict.* "Do we know why he met with Dedov?"

"Only a guess, sir. Maybe Asimov wants to know why Dedov was buying weapons from Spartak—"

"I'd like to know that also."

"Right." Sophia set the clicker on the table." We believe Asimov arranged to sell the weapons to Dedov during the Rome meeting."

That brought Ivanov's pacing to a halt. "Interesting. Why?"

Sophia pursed her lips. "Unknown, sir."

Felix lifted his mug. "Perhaps to arm Dedov's men who guard the castle in Switzerland where Asimov's sister and nephew are holed up?"

"Perhaps," Ivanov pointed at them before leaving. "Okay, keep on it. Call me the minute you know something."

NINETEEN

Unknown Location

They don't look like locals, do they? The natives have brown skin, sweaty faces. These guys are white jarheads with coarse skin, square jaws, and muscles bulging through sweaty T-shirts. Dark beards laced with gray. Tattoos of bloody daggers and skulls. A gold chain. Leather holsters with secured pistols. That rules out a grab. Guess I'll lie here and see what they do.

Pain radiated to her spine as two of them grabbed her bare arms, lifted her like a doll, and propelled her through the door and down the hall, her bare toes dragging on the dirty tile. She fell into a wooden chair caked with feces and blood where her arms were secured with hard leather straps.

Some of that blood is mine, isn't it? All of it, I guess. That chair was clean when I got here. When was that? Can someone please wipe the mucus off my chin?

Two of the men filed from the room. Two others remained by the door.

I have to pee. What's taking so long? A wet warmth appeared on her bare legs. Great, guess I'll just pee here. As good as anywhere. Her gaze grew hazy and her head became difficult to hold upright so she let it loll to the side. *That's better.*

She lost all concept of time until blurry humanoid forms filled the room, lurching, shuffling, crawling. *What was that children's book Andrea used to read to me? About the wild things? Yes, that's them.* A giggle sounded in the room. *Whoops, was that me?*

Hunger gnawed at her stomach, which she ignored. *Easier to be weak than to eat.*

Long ago she fought them. Clawing, biting, kicking. Guttural screams. Tears. Yelling. Begging. That was before the beatings. Before the drugs. Before the hunger strike. Now she couldn't make her muscles work, and oddly she felt no emotions. Just a dull haze. So she rocked back and forth, held up by the leather straps, waiting for what, she didn't know.

I held out, that's for sure. That's for damn sure. Just like they taught me. But shit babe, that pain. It didn't end. At some point, I didn't care. I stopped caring. It wasn't worth it, so I told them. So why am I still here? When does it end? The end has to be better than this.

Sounds came from the blobs. More questions. Those damn questions. Fuck the questions, the never ending questions. Where is Mikhail Asimov? Who is Nikita Ivanov? Where is Spencer White? What is the Komissariat for the Preservation of State?

I don't know, damn it. If I knew, I'd tell you. There's nothing left, don't you know that? Idiots.

A fuzzy white blob materialized in front of her. A prick on her arm, near a set of veins that were peppered with needle marks, and a surge of euphoria flooded her mind, followed by a moment of clarity.

Aah.

The room crystalized, and the white blob became the fat man. His white lab coat was stretched over a massive girth. Beady eyes peered into her eyes with a penlight. "Welcome back, dearie."

Latin accent. High pitched for his girth. That kind of weight can't be healthy, can it?

A video camera stood on a tripod in front of her with a blinking red light. The two guards remained near the door, their arms crossed. The doctor, as she called him, took a step back. A hypodermic needle clinked as he set it on a silver tray.

The doctor's words were slowly enunciated. "You know the drill by now. Tell me where we can find Mikhail Asimov. Or maybe you know him better by the name you gave him, Max Austin."

What is he saying?

The doctor bent so his face was directly in front of hers. "Aw, dearie, you don't want to disappoint me, do you? How about Spencer White? Tell me where he is."

What's a spencer white?

The fat man mopped his brow with a dingy handkerchief before retrieving another hypodermic needle and filling it with a clear liquid from a vial. "Why do you persist, my dear?" His big gray teeth flashed. "Such a lovely gal. If you'll only tell us what we want to know, we'll set you free. Give you some food, let you clean up, take a rest. Now tell me. Who is Nikita Ivanov? What is his real name? What is the Komissariat for the Preservation of State? We know you know. All you have to do is tell us and all will be forgiven."

Nikita Ivanov. Wasn't her cat named Nikita? No, it was Otis. The cat she had when she was a girl. What happened to that cat? A tear slipped down her cheek. *The kitty cat is dead now. Was Otis buried somewhere nice? With a little gravestone?*

More words, but they faded into the distance while the doctor slowly dissolved into a white amoeba.

Had her cat been white? No, not white. Calico, perhaps? Or brown with white paws. Yes, the white paws... Like little white boots.

The fuzzy white ghost dissolved into darkness. She woke later curled on the cold ground, shivering, the vision of the cat's white paws consuming her. When the tears flowed, her body wracked with sobs, mourning the cat she loved, until she was cried out.

TWENTY

London, England

Max bounded up the Lear's stairs and ducked to enter the cabin, stopping short when he saw a young blonde wearing an off-the-rack suit. She read a dossier through a pair of black horn-rimmed glasses while holding a glass of soda water or perhaps a gin and tonic. The remaining leather seats were empty. Something about her triggered a vague memory. "Pardon me. I must have the wrong plane."

As he turned to depart, the door to the lavatory opened and Callum Baxter stepped out.

"Ah, Max. There you are. You're late. The trains run on time in Her Majesty's secret service, you know."

"Who's—"

Baxter brushed by him on his way to the cockpit, so Max took a seat facing forward with a clear view of the blonde. Her eyes left the folder and she smiled at him before returning to her reading. There was a flash of knowing intellect and self-assuredness behind the glasses despite the young face.

The Lear's external door was shut and latched by Baxter before he took a seat. "Limited service on this flight, I'm afraid." He nodded at the galley. "Fix your own refreshments. Plenty of gin and Scotch. None of that American whiskey you like. Did you forget something?"

He tossed something at Max, who caught it, relieved to see his grandfather's lighter. He removed the inner case from the external shell, noted it was filled with lighter fluid, and reassembled it.

Baxter rubbed his nose. "Don't worry. I didn't muck with it." He handed Max a thick manila envelope as the Lear sprinted down the taxiway.

Opening the envelope, Max dumped a pile of cash on his lap.

Nodding at the bundles of euros, Baxter said, "Benefits of working for MI6."

Max stacked the bundles and flipped through them with his thumb. "Who said I was working for you? That wasn't part of the agreement. It's a partnership."

Baxter chuckled. "C's orders."

"C?"

"The chief goes by the initial C." Baxter shrugged.

He glanced at the blonde. "Not M?"

Baxter rolled his eyes. "No. That was Ian Fleming's fiction."

The blonde groaned without glancing up.

Max snickered. He read a lot of spy novels during his Western indoctrination by the KGB. "What about The Circus? Is MI6 still referred to as The Circus?"

This time the blonde's eyebrows rose, and she nodded her head.

Baxter groaned. "A fabrication by le Carré."

Max glanced at the blonde. "Didn't le Carré work for MI6? Shows you what he thought of it." The blonde concentrated on her reading.

Baxter glared at him. "You remember Cindy, don't you?"

It came back to him. Cindy was in the van the day Baxter's men took him captive in Cambridge. It felt like years ago, but it was only two months ago.

Cindy offered a well-manicured hand.

Max took the firm grip before catching Baxter's eye. "What exactly does C think I'm consulting on?"

The MI6 man cleared his throat. "I didn't specify. But let's be clear. Officially, MI6 doesn't kill people. We let the CIA and the Mossad do that kind of stuff. Our Savile Row suits are spotless."

Max scrutinized Baxter's rumpled pants and jacket. "That's Savile Row?"

Baxter sighed. "It's a figure of speech."

"Officially?"

Baxter recrossed his legs. "Our culture is to never confirm nor deny, but I can tell you that in my twenty-plus years of working for the secret intelligence service, I've never seen nor been party to an agency-sanctioned killing. So keep your pistol in its holster while you're on our dime. Officially." He laughed at his own joke and glanced at Cindy, whose head was buried in the dossier.

Max thumbed through the stacks of cash again, guessed it was about twenty thousand euros, and tucked them into his inside jacket pocket. "You let consultants do it for you. Plausible deniability."

The MI6 agent shrugged again. "We use a lot of consultants when it suits our needs, just like any agency. Surveillance, black-bag jobs, counterintelligence."

As the plane leveled out, Max studied Cindy from the corner of his eye. Her pantsuit was a dark wool that contrasted against a snowy-white blouse with wide lapels. The neck was open, and a silver pendent hung against her pale skin. Golden hair in a modern cut ended at the shoulders and curved around her face. A complexion that suggested Scandinavian. Diamond studs in each ear. Eyes showing a hint of crinkle, putting her age at mid- to late-thirties. A bare ring finger.

She raised her head, and Max caught her eye. She grinned, revealing a row of perfect white teeth. Her smile went all the way to her eyes before she shuffled the papers and bent down to resume her task.

Baxter cleared his throat. "Cindy is one of our senior analysts over at Vauxhall Cross. Since our...ahem...first operation together, she's led the team looking into this consortium of yours. She's got six analysts on lockdown, and we're not letting them out of the room until they find everything they can about the group."

Max raised his eyebrows. "And? What have we found so far?"

"She's here to give us a brief."

Cindy closed the dossier she was reading, the cover of which had the words *Top Secret* stamped across the top in red. She stuffed it in a metal briefcase and snapped the lock closed.

Straining to hear over the Lear's drone, Max leaned on his elbows.

Referring to another file, Cindy bent over the armrest. "When Russia annexed the Crimea back in 2014 and the conflict with Ukraine ignited, we decided we should once again pay attention to Mother Bear, as I like to call her. It's not that we weren't watching before, but Crimea was the first overt move since Yeltsin and the fall of the Soviet empire. The Russian president's actions signaled a resurgence in imperialism, or at least a desire to reassert himself. That triggered a realization that the era of the left-leaning oligarchic rule, and perhaps the emergence of a freethinking democracy in Russia, had been replaced by a resurgence of the old-guard policies that we can trace all the way back to the Russian revolution and Vladimir Lenin." She lifted her drink for a sip.

Max cocked his head. "Explain."

Cindy adjusted the pleat on her trouser revealing a bare white ankle. "As you probably know, the Russian revolution in 1917 was a watershed. Frustrated by years of famine and hardship from Tsar Nicholas II's participation in World War I, the country was primed for a new idea. The Bolsheviks, led by Vladimir Lenin, presented this opportunity. The Tsar was tossed out and assassinated, and Lenin and the Bolsheviks took over, eventually creating the Communist party and the Soviet Union. Lenin also created a secret police organization called *Cheka* back in 1917. The Cheka was responsible for quelling uprisings against the Bolsheviks, sometimes in brutal and oppressive ways. Over time, that group took more and more power, and eventually morphed into the agency that became the KGB."

The Chekas weren't in the history books Max studied in school. "Quelling?"

"It means to pacify," Baxter said.

Cindy consulted a paper in her file. "Although the Soviet intelligence agency shifted and morphed over time and the term Cheka—meaning secret police—disappeared, the word chekist has come to mean a member of the secret

Russian ruling class. The KGB, as you know, evolved to become one of the largest secret police organizations known to modern man, enforcing a rabid style of repression against its own citizens that allowed the Communist party to stay in power. Some scholars say that the KGB is the true source of power behind the Soviet Union, and even now in Russia. The fact that the current Russian president—a dictator in all but name—came from the ranks of the KGB isn't lost on anyone."

Max grimaced. "Makes you wonder who's really in charge in Russia. The president or the KGB."

A bright smile from Cindy. "Now flash ahead to the fall of the Soviet Union in 1991 that was tied to Gorbachev's *perestroika*, or political and economic reforms—"

Max held up a finger. "I know this part."

Cindy held up her hand. "What you may not know is that while the west and NATO celebrated a victory, there was an obscure theory going around—"

"A conspiracy theory," Baxter said.

Cindy frowned at her boss. "Right. A conspiracy theory that the fall of the Soviet Union was a ruse concocted by the hardliners in Russia to let the West think they had won. The conspiracy theory even has a name—the Perestroika Deception."

This wasn't the first time Max had heard the term, but the phrase was usually accompanied by scoffs and jeers. "Big price to pay, losing thirteen colonies. Tax revenue. Control over oil and other natural resources. Seems like a stretch. Why would they do that?"

Cindy toyed with a pen and glanced at Baxter, who tapped on his Blackberry with his head down. "Some think it was to allow the chekists to regroup after the populist uprisings," she said.

The MI6 man stopped typing. "In hindsight, seeing what's going on in Russia now, it's hard to argue with the theory."

"The theory doesn't get much play in academic circles." Cindy crossed her ankles. "But the intelligence community agrees that certain Communist leaders wanted three things: to distract the West from communism's true aims, to reduce the threat of NATO, and to attract Western capital to the country to rebuild its crumbling infrastructure. A little-known analyst at the CIA wrote a paper that got leaked that made over a hundred predictions about the evolution of Russia as a result of the Perestroika Deception. Almost all of his predictions have come true."

Max glanced at Baxter. "What's all this got to do with the consortium?"

The pen flipped around in Cindy's hand. "Think of the chekists as a shadow government or a kind of deep state. You know what that is right?"

He nodded, although he wasn't sure.

Her pen twirled in a blur. "It's a group of politicians, military, or business leaders, who effectively run government functions while the outward facing politicians act as stand-ins without knowing. The intelligence community believes that Turkey has long been run by a deep state of nationalist hardliners dating back to the Ottoman Empire."

Max sat back and studied the young analyst. "You're going to tell me that the consortium is a Russian shadow government made up of these checkers? Callum, do you believe this?"

"Chekists." Cindy nodded. "And yes, that's our working theory, albeit with several complications."

"Tell him the main one." Baxter said.

Cindy sat back and tapped the tip of her pen against the

armrest. "The consortium is made up of Russians and non-Russians, including Chinese and members from former Soviet satellite states like Ukraine and Latvia."

Max leaned on his elbows. "Maybe their intent is to remake the Soviet Union."

"We're considering that theory. But the consortium is solely focused on the control of oil production, supply, and distribution, which is hardly a recipe for domination over the Russian people. One component, perhaps. But they won't get there by simply controlling natural resources. We dove into the backgrounds of the men on the consortium, and they're a mix of liberal oligarchs, Russian domestic and foreign intelligence types, and business men. There are only a couple members that we can trace back to chekist and KGB origins."

Max glanced at Baxter, who was examining his nails. "You must have another theory."

Cindy eyed Baxter, and Max caught a shake of the senior MI6 agent's head. "We do," she said. "The theory is tangential—"

"Well done, Cindy." Baxter stowed his phone and handed each of them a sheaf of papers. "Shall we go over the operation in Moldova one more time? Make sure we all know our lines?"

She frowned as she accepted the papers.

What is it about the chekists Baxter doesn't want him to know?

TWENTY-ONE

Dubāsari, Moldova

The color of the Soviet-era van had faded to a mottled gray. It listed to the left, requiring Popov, the portly Moldovan taxi driver, to keep the wheel wrenched to the right to keep the van straight, which was more difficult because of the potholed pavement of the border town. Despite the frigid temps, perspiration coated Popov's brow as he coaxed the vehicle to the crossing leading into Transnistria. Every few minutes, he flicked his eyes to the rearview mirror to check on his passenger. The man made him nervous.

During the hour-long drive from the private terminal at Chisinau International, the man didn't utter a word. He traveled light—one backpack—and paid cash in advance using leu, Moldova's local currency. His dusty black T-shirt was worn under a weathered leather jacket. Jeans, boots, and wraparound sunglasses completed his outfit. The clothing was unremarkable, except for the ball cap that was pulled low in a way that made Popov think military. Not military in the officer sense, but special-ops like he saw in the American TV shows. *Didn't Bradley Cooper wear a similar hat in that movie about the sniper?*

As Popov's eyes flickered between the passenger and the smog-choked road, he tried to place his nationality. Caucasian but darkly tanned. Maybe American, or German. High cheekbones, strong jaw, and broad shoulders. Dark eyes like obsidian. No hint of a smile. *I don't want to see this man in a dark alley, that's for sure.*

At the border crossing, the taxi driver showed his papers and waited while the agent, a bored man flanked by two Russian peacekeeping troopers, studied his passenger's passport. He caught a flash of maroon with gold lettering that might indicate Russian or Romanian. Not Ukrainian—those passports were blue. As the border agent handed back the papers and Popov nudged the van over the cracked concrete bridge leading across the Dniester river, the unofficial border between Moldova and Transnistria, he settled on Romanian. *Romanians are some bad dudes.*

A tap on his shoulder and he choked back a scream. The passenger held out a wad of the pale green, yellow, and orange Moldovan currency. "Pull over here."

As Popov swerved to miss an old man on a motor scooter while searching for a spot to stop the van, the man jumped out the sliding door and disappeared into the crowd. The driver calmed his breathing before turning the van back in the direction of Moldova.

———

While posing as a tourist and using his mobile phone to snap pictures of local landmarks, Max meandered through the streets of Dubāsari looking for tails. After a quick bite of a sour beef soup known as *ciorba* and some ravioli-like squares of pasta filled with mushrooms called *burechiușe*, he hailed another taxi and offered the driver enough cash to take him an hour south to the region's capital, Tiraspol. The last driver made him nervous, causing him to make the switch.

This wasn't Max's first visit to the small self-proclaimed republic hewn from the collapse of the Soviet Union. Unrecognized by most of the world, the symbols of the old Soviet regime were everywhere—on signs, on buildings, and especially on the locals' faces. The region's flag still displayed the hammer and sickle, and imagery of Stalin was visible in murals. The republic of Transnistria was a sliver of land trapped between Moldova and Ukraine jammed with Russians and Ukrainians who wanted nothing to do with a post-Soviet world and who saw no reason Moldova should be independent.

The local Transnistrians chafed against Moldova's edict to recognize only the Moldovan language, and bristled at Moldova's anti-minority, ethnocentric, and chauvinist positions that called for the Slavs, especially Russians and Ukrainians, to leave or be expelled. And so they formed their own republic. Although unofficial and unrecognized, the region had its own currency, police force, military, de facto government, and even its own elections. Max operated in this portion of Eastern Europe several times as a junior KGB agent and knew the area well. He empathized with the locals and admired their chutzpa at daring to form their own government rather than suffer at the persecution of the ethnic Moldovans. The region represented an example of the folly of a small number of governments trying to corral a high number of minorities. While Max had little sympathy for hardline Soviets, he had no patience for persecution.

Live and let live.

Apologizing for his lack of local currency, Max pressed a stack of Moldovan leu into his new driver's hand, pulled his cap over his eyes, and pretended to doze as the sedan took off down the M4 highway.

His new partnership with MI6 was getting off to a rocky start. To monitor the operation, Baxter had insisted on a mic, a GPS transmitter, and continuous MI6 satellite coverage. At one point, he referred to protecting his investment. Max refused, not wanting to get caught with the incriminating equipment. The row got heated, with Baxter's face blossoming to a crimson red and the venerable agent almost ripping out his goatee in frustration. Ultimately Max won the argument by threatening to leave MI6 altogether. Baxter had stormed out of the room, leaving a shaken Cindy alone with Max to finalize the operation's details. Max was entering Tiraspol, a bastion of old Soviet hard-liners and former chekists, under a Russian identity and without any tethers to MI6. *If you knew Transnistria, it was safer this way.*

Max exited the cab near the botanical garden, hitched his backpack to his shoulder, and took off along one of the wide dirt pathways that meandered among a late fall landscape of browns, tans, and muted greens. To his left, a wedding party was bundled in coats and scarves as the bride and groom exchanged vows. A student with a purple streak in her dark hair squatted and studied a placard next to a stand of bushes. Otherwise, the park was empty, except for the two men that followed him, keeping their distance, making no attempt to disguise their presence.

Similar to Moscow, any stranger entering Tiraspol should expect to be followed. The two men resembled retirees, with white wisps of hair escaping their caps and large bellies protruding over belted pants straining to contain their bulk. Maybe the two men were simply out for their daily constitutional. But after Max made a series of unhurried turns through the park, pausing in strategic locations to watch behind him, the two retirees stayed with him.

It was a chilly day, no precipitation, but an occasional wind from the north blistered his face. While the two men strolled without conversing, their track jackets flapped in the breeze. When Max left the gardens to walk along the town's pedestrian mall that teemed with tourists, they stayed with him. The message was clear: The Transnistrians were watching.

Had they identified him, or were they simply tagging along behind a stranger?

As he made a show of glancing into store windows along the mall, he weighed his options. He could pull a few tricks out of his bag and ditch the two men, but a sophisticated move might signal Max's status as an operator, something he wasn't eager to do.

After reaching the end of the pedestrian mall, he made a right turn in the direction of the hulking brown and tan parliament building that resembled an American college dormitory. Standing in front of the structure, towering over a smattering of pedestrians, was a regal statute of Vladimir Lenin, his back ramrod straight, cape billowing out behind him.

Tells you everything you need to know about Transnistria.

He made a left, away from the parliament building, and turned down a side street with alleyways running behind the stores and restaurants on the pedestrian mall, looking to duck through a back entrance. The retirees had disappeared. He made another left, zigzagged around two dumpsters, and opened the door leading into the kitchen of a family restaurant. Several men in white uniforms, with sweat pouring off their faces, looked up as he wormed his way through the kitchen. Avoiding a waiter, he pushed through the swinging door leading into the dining room and ran directly into the muzzle of a pistol.

Three large Slavic men with white faces and red lips blocked his path. Two held guns while the third waved a piece of black material. The man in front, who resembled a lineman on an American football team, pushed the gun into his stomach while a second man shoved the black material over his head, sending his world into darkness.

"Took you guys long enough."

TWENTY-TWO

Tiraspol, Transnistria

With a pistol jammed into his back, they hustled him through the restaurant and shoved him into the back of a van, his shins barking on the bumper. Through the hood, he caught the foul odors of decaying food and mold. His arms were secured in front of him with duct tape, and he was relieved of his backpack, phone, and wallet. No more words were spoken by his captors, and he kept his mouth shut.

The ride was jarring but short. Little effort was made to avoid the potholes and broken pavement along the city streets, long neglected since before the fall of the Soviet Union. By the time they came to a screeching halt, he was bruised and battered from rolling around on the van's metal floor.

When they stopped, Max was pulled from the vehicle's rear and dragged through what he assumed was a dirt lot, catching smells of motor oil and animal manure. After entering some kind of structure with a concrete floor, he was pushed into a chair. The din of power tools sounded in the distance, and voices carried from far away. A pneumatic whir was followed by the release of compressed air. Closer was the sound of tape unspooling before he felt his torso secured to the chair. Crude but effective.

Muffled voices receded into the distance. Hoots and guffaws in Russian came from somewhere behind him. A waft of cigarette smoke he recognized as a Russian brand. An engine roared to life and receded.

The takedown was crude but distinctly Russian, rough but efficient. No one talked. The only thing non-Russian about the snatch was that no one had beat him.

Yet.

Russians liked a good beating thrown into a kidnapping for good measure. Maybe a bullet would end his life without warning. Except Russians didn't mess around. He was alive because someone wanted him alive.

Approaching feet clicked on concrete. More cigarette smoke and a low scratchy female voice in Russian. "Unhood him."

A gun muzzle was pressed into his neck as the hood was yanked off. He blinked in the dim light, his eyes adjusting to the murk. The room contained rows of decrepit metal shelving holding stacks of auto parts, some in boxes, some corroded with rust. Through an open door, a late model German sports sedan, out of place in the exceptionally poor republic of Transnistria, was on a lift. A man in dirty overalls was in the process of removing the vehicle's exhaust. The silhouette of a woman stood before him.

A fist slammed into his face, followed by a second punch that might have broken his nose. Warm blood and mucus dripped down his lip and seeped into his mouth. One of the retirees wound up for another strike but held back when the woman touched his arm. "Enough. For now."

A halo appeared around Max's eyes, and his head pounded. "Why the fuck did you do that, Raisa?"

"Hello, Mikhail. Been a long time, no? I think you were heading off to the military academy the last time I saw you."

The statuesque brunette in her early fifties wore a white blouse open at the neck to reveal a deep dove-white décolleté. Except for her high cheek bones and Slavic features, she looked like a Western business woman with expensive shoes. A thin cigarette was held between hooked fingers with glossy nails, and she regarded him through a pair of fashionable glasses.

Max flashed a smile despite the ringing in his ears. "Not the reception I was hoping for, Raisa."

She pursed her lips. "You're a hot commodity these days, Mikhail. One has to take precautions. Call this insurance."

Max managed a small shrug despite the bindings. "Anyone finds out I was here, at least you're covering your ass."

"Something like that." Raisa waved away the thug. "Don't stray too far, Igor. This one was trained by Andrei himself. He'd kill you just as soon as look at you."

Max rolled his eyes. "I would never do that. Raisa, what's with the drama here? Why the mugging? I just came to talk."

"I don't know, Mikhail. Call it instinct. The only thing that's kept me alive all these years has been my gut, and something told me it's not safe to invite you in for tea."

The noise from men working continued in the background, and Max projected his voice to be heard. "You and my father go way back. He looked out for you. He took care of you."

She snorted. "That was a long time ago. Now he's dead, and he left me to take the fall."

A lanky man appeared from the garage with a metal tire iron hanging from a fist. Tall enough to be a basketball player, his thick curly hair was hidden under a greasy knit cap. Max recognized the young man as Raisa's son Dominik. Dominik set the tire iron on a table, leaned against a metal shelf, and lit a cigarette.

Working his muscles to try to loosen the tape, Max smiled. "Getting into the family business I see."

A laugh. "The disavowed secretary of a KGB traitor has to make a living."

He shook his head. "Andrei would be disappointed."

Her face flushed a dark shade of red, and Raisa slapped him. "You think I give a fuck what Andrei thinks? He left me to take the heat. When someone defects in the KGB, who do you think they interrogate first? I spent two months in a hole in the basement of Lubyanka before they decided I didn't have anything to do with Andrei's...um...extracurricular activities."

The sting in Max's cheek subsided. "He didn't defect."

Another snort. "He might as well have. You know what I'd be doing if I were a few years younger?"

Max looked away. *Yeah, I know.*

"That's right. They'd kill my son and evict my parents from their apartment in Moscow, leaving them homeless." She banged her fist on the table, making the tire iron rattle. "Fucking those fat men in the Kremlin would be my only option."

"So instead you run this chop shop and funnel part of

your profits to the Kremlin," Max said. "It's protection—as long as you're paying, you're safe."

Raisa snorted again and turned her back on him. "You don't know what you're talking about."

"It's not hard to figure out. My guess is you're part of Victor Volkov's network—"

She spun around to face him. "We were, until you took him out."

"The first of many, Raisa. So who do you pay now?"

She looked away as she took a drag on her smoke. "Fuck off, Mikhail. Why are you here, anyway?"

Are you angry at being left to fend for yourself? No, I don't think so. You're bitter because he never loved you like you wanted him to.

Slowly, Max flexed his muscles and loosened the tape around his arms. "Andrei left something with you. I've come to collect it."

Her brow furrowed. "Left something?"

Max's heart sank as Raisa searched her memory. He envisioned a warmer homecoming to a woman who was close to his father.

"He didn't leave something with you and ask you to hold it in case I came looking?"

The former secretary shook her head. "Why—"

"Think. Was there anything you took from his office? A book, or set of files, or some kind of keepsake?" *Like the memory stick hidden in the back of the photograph?* "A picture maybe?"

She turned away from him again. "There's nothing. The day after he was killed..." She wiped her cheek and faced him. "I was escorted from the building. The next day, two men in suits showed up at my apartment and took me into custody. They said evidence was found that Andrei gave information to a foreign government, and they needed to talk to me. Two months later, I was released. They said they didn't find any evidence that I had helped him." Tears streamed down her face. "It was horrible. I couldn't believe it about Andrei. I never saw the inside of my office again. A few of my things were sent to my apartment, but I was already packing to move here to be with my son." She glanced at Dominik, who was cleaning his nails with a pocket knife.

Max's eyes widened. "What happened to the stuff they sent?"

Raisa shrugged. "I guess it's in our flat somewhere." She looked at Dominik again, who concentrated on his nails.

"Let me look through it." Max shuffled the chair in her direction. "After that, I'll leave you alone."

She finished her cigarette and flicked the butt into the corner in a shower of sparks. "How do you know he left something?"

He kept his face blank. "The less you know, the better. Trust me."

A snort from Raisa. "Trust the son of a spy accused of treason who is also wanted by the SVR for treason. If they find out you're here, I'm a dead woman. What's stopping me from turning you in? Lots would be forgiven if I marched you into Moscow wearing cuffs."

Max raised his eyebrows and smiled. "In your heart, you know Andrei is innocent. Just like you know I'm innocent. Otherwise, I'd already be dead."

With a sneer, she turned on a heel and marched from the room.

TWENTY-THREE

Corsica, France

Goshawk sat back and reflected on her work. In the world of the Dark Web, it was becoming harder and harder to maintain her status as an individual hacker for hire. After the notorious Bluefish discovered her location and launched a massive cyberattack on her firewall defenses and forced her to flee her Paris home, she linked up with a formidable fellow hacktivist named The Monk who offered her refuge and resources. Eventually The Monk would demand repayment for providing the safety of his network of firewalls, proxy servers, and dark networks.

The cost of doing business.

Since settling into her cottage at the south end of Corsica, she spent every waking hour working to determine Bluefish's true identity. Using the hacker handles of 6URU, or Guru, and Z16Z46, or Zigzag, she established herself as an anti-NSA pro-whistle-blower railing in defense of Edward Snowden and WikiLeaks in order to attract attention. As her activity was noticed by what she assumed were NSA and other US government watchers, she deployed clandestine bots and secret spiders programmed to roam the internet and report back to her secure remote servers.

Her tactics followed an electronic version of traditional human surveillance. It took months, but she assembled a map of identities, connections between those players and remote electronic locations, and networks used by those players. She wrote and launched an artificial intelligence machine-learning neural network that she called Grant after Grant Green, one of Max's favorite jazz musicians, and put it to work on the vast database she was collecting. She searched for patterns in the data and kept a running list of curious anomalies in the results. Until this point, she had uncovered little, other than the identification of a few low-level actors tied to the NSA who watched her, not unlike how Russian spies often tracked Western business men visiting Moscow.

Using another established pseudonym, oDD17Y, or Oddity, she took a bolder approach. After several weeks of research and establishing her bona fides by performing pro bono hacktivist operations, she was led to a chat board in the Dark Web named The Jimmy Road. Jimmy meant to unlock, and Road was a knockoff from Silk Road, the first modern darknet marketplace. It was only after she agreed to break into a French police database and forge the parole acceptance affidavit of a former member of the hacktivist group Anonymous, who was imprisoned for stealing bitcoins, that she was finally granted access. What she saw made her grin for the first time in months.

Like any chat room, there were a handful of moderators with names like Sphinx, Catch-22, and Tr@ce. Dozens of other identities offered up sporadic posts. Each one of the posters was someone seeking the identity of a fellow hacker, which was taboo among her brethren. Hackers guarded their secrecy with the utmost rigor. One can find anything on the Dark Web if they know where to look, and this board focused entirely on revealing identities of hackers.

After ten minutes of browsing posts, she moved to the bounty section where posters offered to pay in exchange for an identity. The real business of the forum took place here. A quick search for Bluefish yielded no results. *No surprise there*. With an imp-like grin, she created a new post and entitled it One Fish, Two Fish.

Wanted: Identity, IP, geolocation, and other particulars for a person or group calling themselves Bluefish. Likely government. Name your price.

She hit Enter, got up, and made herself some tea, her mind wandering to Max, his predicament, and her role in helping his cause. Something in her heart fluttered, something she didn't expect. With effort, she pushed it away, tossed the tea in the sink, found a bottle of Corsican rosé in the icebox, and punched in Carlu's number.

Only one way to cure love.

TWENTY-FOUR

Tiraspol, Transnistria

The mechanic shop fell into silence when Raisa walked out. Dominik followed her a second later. Max sat in the chair, arms secured, torso taped to the wooden slats of the chair's back. The retirees stood guard, each with a Makarov pistol clutched in their meaty hands, track jackets stretched over protruding bellies. Requests to use a bathroom were ignored. A plea for a cigarette went unanswered. "How about some water?"

No response.

Eventually Raisa and her son reappeared. Dominik carried a cardboard box which he dropped at Max's feet. It was one of those moving boxes sized for books, and it was sealed with clear tape and displayed the name of a moving company in Cyrillic text.

Raisa motioned at one of her men to cut the tape, and she pried open the box.

Max craned his neck to see better. "Can you untie me?"

One by one, Raisa removed the items. An ornate candle in a glass jar. An old-fashioned desk clock. Several books along with a framed picture of a much younger Raisa alongside Dominik as a boy. "That's it, except for a stack of papers."

"The picture." Max pointed his chin at the framed photo. "Open up the back of the picture."

Raisa glared at him before she removed the cardboard and the picture from the frame. She held it all up to show him there was nothing there.

"Try the clock." Max squirmed to see better. "Open the back where the battery is."

She opened the back of the clock and took out the batteries. "Nothing."

Max wanted to pull the entire clock apart, cut into the candle, and shake out each of the books, but he couldn't move.

Raisa tossed the books into the box, followed by the candle and the clock. She reassembled the picture and gazed at it before carefully setting it in the box. As she did, a locket on a chain fell from her blouse and dangled from her neck. She shoved it back into her shirt and fastened a button.

The flash of the precious metal caught Max's eye. "What's in the locket, Raisa?"

"Nothing. Just an old picture."

"Of who?" Max arched his eyebrows.

"No one."

He strained at the tape violently enough for one of the guards to move closer. "It's my old man, isn't it?"

"Don't be ridiculous." She pulled the blouse tight around her neck.

"Did he give it to you?"

She stepped away. "Leave it alone, Max. These guys are going to drive you back up to Dubāsari and take you over the border into Moldova. They might have to rough you up some to make it look good. From there you can grab a cab up to Chisinau. Don't come back here, Mikhail. There's nothing here for you, and the people we answer to won't take kindly to your return." She strode from the room.

The heel clicks faded into the distance leaving only the sounds of the mechanic's shop. A deep breath escaped his lips. *Hiding something in a locket was just like his father. Raisa may not even know it's there.*

One of the guards produced a switchblade and the other held a gun to Max's face while the tape holding him to the chair was cut. He stood and stretched his shoulder muscles by moving them in circles, until a guard grabbed him and wound duct tape around his wrists. "You guys ex-KGB? Moscow Centre? What directorate?"

No answer. The one with the gun waved it at the opened roll-up door where the van was parked.

Max walked. "How's retirement? Tough? Finding it difficult to pass the time?"

They ambled behind him. Max abruptly turned and held his two wrists up. "Seriously. I have to pee before the car ride."

One of the men lowered his gun to keep from running into Max. The second was in the process of digging in his pocket for the van keys. Max made an abrupt downward motion with his hands, while pulling his elbows back, and used his body as a wedge that severed the duct tape. With his wrists free, he stepped in, trapped his opponent's gun arm in his left armpit, and drove his right fist into the man's throat, choking off a yell. A wrench of his left arm and the other man's arm bent in a way it shouldn't, forcing him to loosen his grip on the gun. Max snatched the pistol.

Spinning, Max fired the Makarov. Two rapid bangs filled the warehouse, and two red holes appeared in the second retiree's chest. The man staggered, gun halfway out of his holster, his eyes wide. Max whirled and fired point-blank at the first man, putting two 9mm bullet holes in his broad chest. He sank to the concrete floor with a surprised look on his face.

A quick pat down of the first man revealed Max's Blackphone, wallet, and passport. He shoved the second Makarov into his belt before melting into the dimly lit racks of car parts.

TWENTY-FIVE

Tiraspol, Transnistria

The warehouse was quiet. The workers had disappeared. The overheads were snapped off, leaving only the dim glow from security lights to illuminate the endless shelves of boxes and car parts. Max crept from row to row, watching for movement and looking for Raisa.

A faint scrape to his left caused Max to flinch, and he shifted in time so the iron bar whistled past his head and bounced off his shoulder. Pain shot up his neck and down his arm.

Corroded steel flew at Max a second time, aimed straight for his face. He stepped back, bumping a metal rack of exhaust pipes, and the bar missed him by a hair. Instinct prevented him from firing his gun as Dominik's rage filled face materialized out of the darkness. The young man wound up for another swing.

Snatching a piece of chrome exhaust pipe from the shelf, Max used it to parry the next strike, sending a ringing sound reverberating through the warehouse. He blocked another attack and poked Dominik in the neck with a weak jab. His opponent recovered and swung the tire iron, his eyes flashing.

Max struck him with the pipe and caught his forearm, which forced Dominik to let go of the weapon. The tire iron clanged off the concrete floor and Max stuck the gun in his face. "On the ground. Now."

With a sneer, Dominik stretched his long frame on the floor. Max patted him down and tossed away a knife before using electric cords he found on the shelf to secure Dominik's arms and ankles. "You're lucky I didn't shoot you," he hissed at the younger man. "Where's Raisa?"

"Go to hell." Dominik squirmed and tried to move away.

Max kicked him in the ribs. "Stay still. Keep quiet."

With the Makarov in front of him, Max threaded his way out of the shelving and into an open area where metal stairs led up to a set of offices a story above. To his right were the mechanics' bays, and to his left was an open space for unloading tractor trailers. The ground was cluttered with boxes, and the concrete was stained with grease and oil.

"Mikhail!"

His name rang through the building. The thin form of Raisa stood at the top of the metal stairs, a pistol clenched in her two fists and aimed at him.

"Hello, Raisa."

She yelled through clenched teeth. "My son? Where's Dominik?"

"He's fine. Bruised ego, but fine."

Her face relaxed.

"The locket, Raisa. I need the locket."

Her eyes darkened as a tear slid down a cheek. "I loved him, you know."

Max nodded once. "I know. A lot of people did. He had that way about him. Toss it and I'll leave you be."

She sniffled as she stepped down the stairs, the pistol wavering. "I would have done anything for him. I tried so hard to make him love me. I would have gladly given myself to him. He treated me like a queen. He was such a good man. He didn't deserve to die that way."

When she stopped at the bottom step, Max let his gun drift lower.

She wiped a tear from her cheek. "He gave me the locket the week before he...it's all I have left. My only memory."

Max held out a hand. "I know, Raisa. Just let me look at it. I'll give it back. I promise."

"Why, Mikhail? What is this all about?"

"I wish I could tell you. All I know is he uncovered something that got him killed, and now the same people are after me. I think he left me a message. Something that will help me save Arina and Alex."

She wiped another tear away, unfastened the top button of her blouse to remove the locket, unhooked the clasp with one hand, and held it out. "Take it. If it helps you. If it helps your nephew. I don't need to cling to the past. I don't need to hang on to something that never was."

She threw the locket at him.

TWENTY-SIX

Tiraspol, Transnistria

The locket arced through the air.

As if in slow motion, it soared at Max, and he held out his hand.

A barrage of bullets pounded into the wall, shattering the stillness in the mechanic's shop.

Raisa staggered, and a spatter of blood sprayed on the wall behind her. She faltered and stumbled but caught herself on the railing. Her gun fell from her hand and clanged off the metal stairs before clattering to the ground. A bullet flew into her brow, and her head snapped back. She held herself upright by a death grip on the handrail, suspended on the stairs, before sinking to her knees and collapsing against the bloody wall. More bullets clanged off the metal staircase.

Max whirled and dropped to a knee, pistol up in two hands, searching the murky darkness for a target. The locket hit the floor with a clink while hurried footsteps sounded on the concrete. A shadow fell over the floor near the rear of the warehouse, and Max fired twice, causing a black-clad commando to fall to the concrete.

Who the hell are these guys? Did someone alert the Russians?

Max held his pistol with one hand while he searched the ground for the locket with the other. From behind the far row of shelving came a storm of bullets that plinked off the exhaust pipes behind him.

Where's the damn locket?

His hand touched the metal chain. He grabbed it, stuffed it in his pocket, and backed into the shadows as another volley of gunfire hit the concrete where he just kneeled.

Stealing around a shelving unit, he peered through the gloom for movement. He turned around another shelf and scanned the darkness in all directions. Nothing. He came to a center aisle with rows of shelving units on both sides and stuck his head out to look both ways. The corridor opened into the mechanic's bays, and beyond that was the front door. The commandos would have left a team waiting to take down anyone who tried to escape out the front. The main warehouse area and an open roll-up door were to the rear.

There. Something flickered in the shadows near the open door. A human shape bristling with armor and weapons moved near a stack of fifty-five-gallon drums. Max aimed and fired three times. The shape stumbled and fell.

Five steps took him around the end of one shelving rack to another closer to the front of the building. Another couple of steps and he almost tripped over Dominik's inert form. In a hushed whisper, Max told him about the intruders before cutting his bonds. "Is there a way out of here other than the front or back?"

Dominik looked at the ceiling while he whispered. "Ladder running up the wall leading to the roof. Another ladder outside goes to the ground."

"That's our way out. If I give you this pistol, do you promise not to shoot me? Your mom's dead. Her killers are out there somewhere. There's a team. I don't know how many. We need each other to escape alive." He held out a pistol.

Dominik's bulging eyes filled up with water before he scrambled to his feet and accepted the weapon.

Max patted the man's shoulder. "I'm sorry about your mom. She was a good woman. Let's split up and head for the ladder. I'll cover you while you climb. You cover me from the trapdoor. Cool?"

TWENTY-SEVEN

Tiraspol, Transnistria

He saw the movement almost too late.

A pair of black-clad arms came up, rifle held out, and fired as Max propelled himself into Raisa's son. A rain of bullets spit from a suppressor and sailed by his ear as he and Dominik went down in a tangle of arms and legs. Max landed on his back and fought to bring his gun around to fire, but the shooting stopped. Jerking his head in several directions to find the target, he saw a man wearing black combat gear on the ground a dozen meters away, partially hidden behind shelving, not moving. The warehouse was still.

What the heck? Who shot that guy?

"Make for the ladder," Max hissed as he pulled Dominik to his feet. The shooting started up again as bullets sang over their heads and plinked into the metal shelves. Instead of returning fire, he crouch-ran with his arm around Dominik's shoulder until they came to the ladder.

Dominik stopped and spoke in a whisper. "It's too exposed."

The shelving units towered over their heads but didn't reach up to the high ceiling. Someone on the ladder would be exposed for a few seconds to a shooter below. "Start climbing when you hear the distraction, and don't look down until you're through the trapdoor. Got it?"

While Dominik crept around the end of a shelf, Max stole through the shadows to the end of the shelving. Freezing for a few beats, he watched for movement. The room was still. No gunfire. Holding the Makarov, Max put his shoulder against the tall metal scaffolding and pushed with all his strength. The shelving moved, teetered, but remained upright. He pushed again, this time using a rocking motion to get the tall unit swaying. A final shove sent the boxes crashing to the ground as the shelf tipped over and fell against the next set of shelves. The whole row toppled like dominos, and a deafening roar filled the room as the shelves hit the ground.

A long shadow darted up the ladder while Max held his breath. No gunfire sounded. As Dominik reached the top, he stopped to wrench open the trapdoor before disappearing into the night. A moment later, the young man's head appeared through the trapdoor followed by his hand holding a pistol.

Don't shoot me. Don't shoot me. Max darted across the open warehouse to the wall. He gripped the Makarov in his teeth and grasped a metal rung. No shots. He crept up two rungs of the ladder. Two more rungs would expose him to anyone below with a gun. Still no gunfire. He scampered up the ladder and popped through the trapdoor and into the nighttime air.

What happened to the attackers?

————

The stolen Dacia Logan sedan sped west along the empty highway in midnight darkness. Max chain-smoked and flicked butt after butt out the open window while replaying the scene in the mechanic's shop in his mind again and again.

Something didn't add up.

A group of commandos stormed the warehouse, killed Raisa, and tried to kill him and Dominik. The two men barely escaped, aided by an unseen party who killed at least one bad guy. It didn't make sense.

How did the commandos know about the locket? Had Max led them there? And who was this mystery helper? I'm missing something.

He flicked a cigarette out the window in a shower of sparks and dug out his phone, turned it on, waited for a secure connection, and dialed Baxter while bracing himself.

"Where in bloody tarnation have you been?"

Max mashed the accelerator to the floor. "Tell you later. Coming in hot. Twenty minutes out. Get the jet ready."

TWENTY-EIGHT

In the Air Over Romania

Max settled into the Lear's wide leather seat and fought off a deep fatigue as the takeoff's g-force pushed him back. The plane leveled off, and he managed a smile as Cindy handed him a cup of steaming black coffee. He sipped and held the cup in both hands, staring straight ahead.

Cindy had sucked in her breath at the sight of Max's bruised face and broken nose when he appeared in the hangar before their departure. His shirt was dusty and the sleeve of his leather jacket was torn, but he brushed off her concerns and urged them to get the plane in the air.

After takeoff, he let her apply a cold washcloth to his face and fuss over his wounds until Baxter shooed her away.

Popping two hydrocodone and chasing them with water, he glared at Baxter. "Why'd you do that?"

Baxter blew on a mug of tea while Cindy settled herself on the arm of Max's chair. "Debrief time."

How much should he divulge?

Bone-tired, all he wanted to do was sleep. Using as few words as possible, he described his talks with Raisa and the subsequent attack on the mechanic's shop but left out the evidence of the mysterious third party.

Baxter played with his goatee. "Describe these commandos."

"Well equipped. Russian military-grade rifles. All black. Helmets. Professionals, but didn't know the layout of the interior."

"Four of them?"

Max nodded. "I think so."

"And you took out all four of them before escaping up the ladder to the roof with this Dominik fellow?"

"Correct."

The MI6 man's bushy eyebrows twitched.

Max reached into his pocket and withdrew Raisa's locket and gave it a once-over. The chain was thin silver with an ordinary clasp at the neck. The locket itself was also sterling silver, about the size of an American quarter and as thick as three quarters stacked. The monogram AA was scratched into the back with jagged and amateurish etching. Max tried to work the clasp with thick fingers but gave up.

He gave it to Cindy, who held it up to the light. "Is this what all the fuss was about?"

Max pointed at the locket. "Open it."

Cindy pried open the two halves of the locket with a fingernail. After a glance at the contents, she handed the open locket to Max.

Whatever was inside caused Raisa's death and might give him the clues to unravel the mystery of his father's actions. He took it with a mixture of unease and hope. One side of the locket's interior was empty. The other held a picture. The image was grainy and old. It showed a man and a woman in an embrace, facing the camera, but the details were faded by time.

Baxter handed him a magnifying glass.

Max took the implement. "You carry this around with you?"

Baxter leaned to get a closer look. "Trust me. When you reach a certain age, you'll carry one too."

The lines of the woman's face, now clear through the glass, looked familiar. Shifting his attention to the man, he wasn't surprised to see his father's face as a younger man. He handed the locket and the magnifying glass to Cindy.

She inspected the image for a moment before squinting at Max. "The man looks just like you. Except for the hair."

He smiled. "It's my father when he was about my age."

Cindy scanned the photo again. "Who's the woman?"

"Pretty sure it's Raisa."

She smiled. "She's beautiful."

He drank the coffee, which had grown cold. "Was."

Another casualty.

"See if you can dig out the picture," Max said, still gazing out the dark window.

Cindy scraped at the image with her fingernail until Baxter handed her a pocketknife. She used the tip of the blade to pry up the photo, which she cradled in her hand. "Aha!"

Max accepted the locket and looked inside. Staring back at him was a black micro SD memory card with white lettering that read *Sony, 16GB*. He dug out his Blackphone. Along the side of the heavy device was a tiny slot that accepted a micro SD card. He shoved the memory card into the slot and turned on his phone while remembering how his father had hidden a similar memory card in the frame of a family photo. *The clues are slowly falling into place.*

Using the phone's navigation, he tapped his way to the folder showing the memory card's contents. There was only one file—*Mikhail.mov*. Max inserted earbuds. "Sorry. Might be private."

Baxter sat back in his seat and grabbed a file to read while keeping one eye glued to Max. Cindy moved to a chair across from Max.

Tapping on the .mov file, Max's stomach flipped when his father's image filled the screen. The view was taken from the chest up as his father sat behind his desk in the secret office he kept underneath their barn. Andrei looked relaxed, as he always did, dressed in a faded denim work shirt open at the collar, revealing a thatch of gray chest hair. His stubble was laced with white, and his thick hair was pushed to the side and held down with some kind of product. As was his habit in his latter years, he clenched a thick cigar between the fingers of his anvil-sized fist and used it for emphasis as he spoke.

"Mikhail, if you're seeing this, it means I'm dead and you've succeeded in tracking me this far. I'm proud of you. Indeed, my son, in some ways, this moment was preordained. I knew in my heart that your childhood training would prepare you for this very moment."

Max rolled his eyes. *You always liked the melodramatic, papa.*

Andrei took a puff on the cigar. "I pray that some members of our family have survived. You must do everything in your power to keep them alive. More on this in a minute, but you'll need their help. Especially your half sister, Arina. If she dies, all is lost."

What's this, more melodrama?

Another puff on the Havana. "By now you've figured out that Julia Meier is your birth mother. I wish I could tell you to trust her. Asking a son to spy on his own mother is difficult to do, but ask it I must. We had a beautiful love affair, and I adore her to this day, but I never knew her intentions. Eventually the mistrust and the nature of our professions drove us apart."

Max looked up and Cindy raised an eyebrow at him. He flashed a smile at her and directed his attention back to the movie.

"I hope someday you will forgive my indiscretions. Your mother—I mean your surrogate mother—is a wonderful woman who deserves a far better man than I. She stuck with me through the relationship with Julia, for what reason I'll never know. Maybe she realized men are fallible, imperfect. Maybe she had her own affairs. I'll never know, and I don't want to know. Regardless, you must forgive her for the way she treated you while you were growing up. You didn't deserve it. It's not your fault you were born out of wedlock. She did the best she could."

Andrei Asimov blew smoke at the ceiling. "And Raisa. Ah, Raisa. What can I say? A beautiful woman, but a lost soul. I wanted to help her, but she wouldn't let me. I pray she's found peace."

A lump formed in Max's throat.

His father coughed and sipped clear liquid from a tumbler. "Now on to the business at hand. This information is for your ears only. While what I'm going to tell you is not the full breadth of my knowledge of the consortium, it is a key piece of the puzzle. I hope you understand that for my safety and yours, I'm required to break my knowledge into multiple parts. I've hidden those parts in ways only you can find. Others cannot hope to assemble this information without your help. Putting the entire puzzle together will tax your brain and your stamina, but you must stay strong, as I know you will. Despite our differences, I know you've become a far better operative than I ever was."

"The forces aligned against you are vast with many resources at their beck and call. They will not tire; you must outlast them. They will rest at nothing less than putting the entire Asimov family into the ground, a result that you cannot let happen for reasons that will eventually become clear. Trust me when I say it's more than just vanity or patriarchy. They know I've assembled this dossier. They know that the keys to unraveling its mysteries lie within the Asimov family. They know that by eliminating us they can bury the information forever. You must not let that happen."

Max's stomach turned over at the thought that his patriarchal instincts for keeping his family alive served more than just a familial desire to keep their blood line alive.

Another puff of smoke from his father. "With that said, let me get to the subject of this missive." His father took another drag on the cigar and let the smoke trail from his lips while staring at something off camera.

"Kate Shaw."

Max dropped his Blackphone on his lap.

Cindy put her hand on his knee, where it remained longer than necessary. "What is it?"

Max waved her away as he retrieved the phone.

On the video, Andrei waved a meaty hand clenching the cigar. "By now you've met Kate. You must forgive her for concealing our partnership, but I implored her to reveal it only at the right time."

Max's fatigue-addled brain attempted to process what he was hearing as his father continued. "When things fell apart with Julia and German intelligence, the nature of the information I uncovered meant I needed to find another partner. There was only one other group I could think of, even if my contact with them might spell my own demise. As you know, traitors to Mother Russia are treated with harsh punishment."

"Before contacting the CIA, I considered following in Edward Snowden's footsteps and using an outlet like Wiki-Leaks to expose everything to the public. But the information I uncovered is only useful to an organization that will know how to use it. Simply airing it to the public would be ineffective, especially in this day and age of the public's tendency to believe anything their leaders tell them. So I decided to go through an intelligence agency."

"I considered the Mossad, but I had no contacts there." Another puff. "Despite us being on opposite sides, I've known Kate since her days on the Soviet Desk in Moscow and at the embassy in Minsk, in Budapest, in the Czech Republic, and in Belgrade. I found her to be a straight shooter, someone I could trust. She was a natural choice when it came time to divulge my findings."

Misty smoke from his cigar swirled around his face, obscuring his eyes. "I cannot overstate the sensitive nature of the information I uncovered. It's enough to take down a regime and expose conspiracies that illuminate the very core of Russia and the Soviet Union before it."

"Despite my best efforts, there are factions that know about various pieces of the puzzle. I couldn't assemble this amount of information and hide it without some of it seeping out. The Russians are the most aware, and I believe the Germans are after the dossier to gain the upper hand over Russia, as is a rogue faction in the CIA, who probably learned of it through a leak in Kate's team."

Max hit pause on the playback. *No wonder everyone*

wants to find Kate. Cindy caught his eye, but he ignored the glance and hit play.

"You're probably wondering how much Kate Shaw knows." His father winked. "The answer is only some. I tested her by giving it to her in bits and pieces, some of it is true, some of it is false. Turns out, while I could trust Kate, some of the information leaked out through her team. A leak I have only recently uncovered. If you follow the clues, the leak will eventually be revealed."

"Due to the leak, there are various groups looking for it —the Chinese, for instance—as well as others. You must act with all due haste, my son, before a competing group puts the picture together. If that happens, all is lost."

"Your job, should you choose to accept it"—his father winked again—"is to reassemble the various pieces of this file. Once you do, you will know what to do." His father's eyes darted to something behind and above the camera before he glanced at his watch.

Who's in the room with you?

Andrei Asimov leaned close to the camera and gestured with his cigar. "I have to wrap this up, Mikhail. Your first task is to find Kate, if you haven't already. You must earn her trust. She has a piece of the puzzle you need. A piece I hid in Kate's mind using a method we developed in the KGB back in the fifties."

Max's eyebrows shot up.

His father spoke to the camera. "I embedded some information in Kate's mind using a hypnosis technique. There is only one way to unlock this information, Mikhail. Find Kate and get the information. With the right trigger, Kate will reveal the information buried in her mind. I can't reveal the trigger. You must discover that for yourself. To reveal that here is simply too dangerous in case this video ever falls into the wrong hands."

His father leaned two beefy arms on the desk. "Get with Kate Shaw, Mikhail. She is your ally. Find her. Trigger her memory. You'll know what to do."

The video screen went black.

TWENTY-NINE

Unknown Location

Heavyset was too kind a word for the obese man making his way along the dirt corridor. His tent-like white Oxford shirt was drenched with sweat and was translucent where it clung to his pale rolls of fat, and a leather bag was slung over one massive shoulder. As he lumbered along the passageway, he mopped his brow with a handkerchief while muttering to himself in Spanish between loud raspy breaths.

The man walking behind the fat man was as thin and gaunt as the lead man was rotund. Dark skinned and bookish, wearing a neat suit despite the heat, the slim man carried a medical bag and nothing else.

The procession was watched through one eye by a craggy-faced man wearing an eyepatch. He called himself the warden, and knew his staff called him the pirate behind his back, a moniker he found appealing. The warden stood with feet planted in the middle of the dank hallway. "You're late."

The thin man said, "Traffic was hell."

The warden addressed the fat man. "Clock's ticking, Diego. Is today the day?"

Diego shrugged his massive shoulders and spoke in Spanish. "These things cannot be rushed. The subject was close to catatonic when you brought me here. I cannot work miracles."

The gaunt man with the medical bag cleared his throat, and the warden signaled with his hand. A jangle of keys was followed by the clunk of a door lock and the metal door swung open. The man with the medical bag disappeared into the room flanked by the two guards, leaving the other two men in the hall. Diego kept his eyes on the ground.

"How much longer, Diego?"

Again, Diego shrugged. "It depends."

The warden clenched his fists and stepped so his chest touched the interrogator's immense stomach. "We're out of time. My people want results."

The fat man fell against the cinderblock wall. "You cannot rush the artiste. You refused my request for a cleaner, more comfortable place in which to talk. You torture her when I'm not here. You—"

"Nonsense! We do no such things."

"I know what you do. I can tell. These things that you do undermine my abilities." He dropped the leather bag in the dirt. "I've submitted my report to—"

The warden's knife was out and pressed against Diego's fleshy neck. "You did what? You'll get results, fat man, or I'll cut you into tiny pieces and feed you to my prisoners. You hear me?"

Before Diego could react, the man with the brown skin

returned to the hall and the warden made the knife disappear.

"No change physically," the tiny man said. "Blood pressure is low. She's dehydrated. Other vitals within normal range. She looks thinner than before, if that's even possible, and I understand she's not eating. You should get her to eat. Maybe some fresh fruits and vegetables instead of the—"

The warden held up his hand. "Enough. We'll handle the food. Your job is to keep her alive."

"If you want her to stay alive, she needs fruits and vegetables—"

"You're done. Now get outa here."

The little man shook his head as he walked away.

The warden followed Diego into the interrogation room. The chamber resembled something out of an insane asylum. The walls and floor were covered in dingy and chipped tile. Mold covered the grout, and moisture dripped from somewhere. Dried and crusted fluids made the floor tacky to walk on. Rust stained pipes crisscrossed the ceiling, and a drain was centered in the floor. Fluorescent lights buzzed overhead casting the room in an icy blue luminance. The patient, as Diego called her, sat in a chair, head lolled back, eyes closed, chest moving with a shallow breath. She was naked, and her mottled skin was splotched with blood and dirt.

Diego spun. "I told you to get her some clean clothes."

The warden shrugged. "We haven't located any yet."

The interrogator's face turned beet red before he reeled off a string of Spanish expletives. "I can't work in these conditions. If you want results, you will follow my instructions. Do I make myself clear?" Diego shuffled to the table and set his leather case down, where he opened it and removed a syringe and vial of clear liquid. He turned to glare at the warden. "Do you mind?"

With a bow of his head, the warden left the room and walked to a room several doors down with a desk, chair, a coffee maker, and a set of monitors, where he settled in to watch.

———

The Ferris wheel cranked and sputtered in what felt like a fruitless effort to turn. Around them, getting smaller as their basket rose higher and higher, the fairgoers enjoyed hot dogs and cotton candy while wandering among decrepit rides and food stalls. The air was warm and heavy with that damp Atlantic Ocean salt while the aroma of boiling grease and sugar wafted up from the fairgrounds.

Her hands gripped the safety bar with white knuckles, but she sat on the edge of the seat to get the best view. Her stepmother sat rigid next to her and stared straight ahead. Kate wanted to yell out in excitement. It was only the reprimand that would come from her stepmother, a tightly wound woman of stern comportment named Andrea, that held her back.

Instead she bounced in her seat and hoped her friends saw her. That summer she enjoyed the growth spurt that the other kids experienced the previous winter, which allowed her to ride the Ferris wheel for the first time. After weeks of pleading, Andrea finally relented. Now Kate wanted everyone to see her in all her glory. Unable to control herself, she let out a whoop, attracting the attention of several kids on the ground.

"Kathleen Shaw. Hush, now. Hush your voice."

She wanted to stick her tongue out at her stepmother but

didn't want to risk the inevitable slap—the slap she dared not tell her father about. She leaned far out over the bar so her torso hung in midair and waved to her friends. Her wave was greeted by hoots and hollers from the ground.

"Kathleen Shaw, by Jove, sit straight in the seat. I will haul you off this ride in an instant if you don't behave."

By this time their passenger car was at the top, high above the ground. Kate scooched back an inch, but her waist was hinged over the bar. She was intent on seeing her friends and showing them what a big girl she was.

Her stepmother grasped her by the belt loop and yanked. "Kathleen! I swear—"

As Andrea yanked, two things happened at once. The Ferris wheel shuddered, and her belt loop ripped. As her stepmother lost her balance, the rickety contraption shuddered again, and the basket tipped. Her stepmother, without a firm grip, tumbled from the basket. Kate, who grasped the basket's safety bar with both hands, flew out into the open air before she was jolted back into her seat by the momentum of the basket. She watched in horror as her stepmother plummeted through the air and hit the ground.

"Andrea!" Kate screamed. "An...dre...a!"

———

Diego had just jabbed a third needle into his patient's right deltoid when the yelling began.

"Andrei, Andrei! Andrei!"

The screams made the hair on Diego's arm stand up. He staggered but held the needle in her shoulder and forced the plunger down. Pulling out the needle, he dropped it into his open briefcase, and fell into a chair. The screaming stopped, and the patient opened her glassy and unseeing eyes.

"Welcome back, my darling," Diego said. "How was your sleep?"

———

In the room with the monitors, the warden slopped hot coffee into his lap when he sat up at the captive's screams.

"Andrei, Andrei! Andrei!"

The name meant only one thing. A breakthrough.

He grabbed his mobile phone and touched a preprogrammed number. It rang twice before it was answered. "Do we have progress?"

Breathlessly, the warden relayed the information until the voice cut him off. "Excellent. It will only be a matter of time now before she breaks and we have the information we need. I'll send a team."

The line was severed.

THIRTY

Corsica, France

Unlike the hacker world portrayed in the movies, where alphanumeric characters stream across colorful screens and cybercriminals sweat profusely while they pound on keyboards and utter angsty expletives, the real hacker world is much more mundane. It's more hurry up and wait than nonstop action. The hacker writes some code that gives instructions to a bot or spider and sends the agent into the internet. Often the hacker has time to kill while waiting for a result, which is why many are also voracious computer gamers.

Goshawk didn't play computer games, because she wanted her mind sharp, not addled by the kaleidoscope of blinking lights and colors that make up modern online games. She preferred long walks along the beach or following a faint trail through the maquis, letting the Corsican sun warm her tan skin. Stripping down and wading into the warm Mediterranean surf or taking a long soak in her outdoor tub with a glass of wine.

With sunburned shoulders and sand between her toes, Goshawk entered her tiny cottage to the urgent dinging of an alarm on her computer. Ignoring the chime, she padded into the kitchen, made a cup of hibiscus tea, dropped ice cubes in it, and perched in her desk chair. After waking the screen saver, she entered a twelve-digit security key, checked the status of her firewalls, and activated a virtual private network. Only after she was satisfied her systems were secure did she read her messages. A chat window blinked at her.

Achurincro: I know this Bluefish

Goshawk, who received dozens of false positives, people fishing for information, or quick-buck artists, rolled her eyes and tapped the keyboard with one finger while sipping her tea.

oDD17Y: Prove it

Her tea was almost gone by the time she received a response.

Achurincro: 100 BTC

A quick calculation in her head told her 100 bitcoin was a little more than $400,000 US dollars at today's prices. A ridiculous bounty to pay, even for this kind of job.

oDD17Y: Fuck off

Goshawk was about to shut down her computer when the chat window dinged again.

Achurincro: 80 BTC via Occam's Escrow

She tapped a nail against her mug. $300,000 was more reasonable, but the escrow idea intrigued her. Most smaller Dark Web transactions were made on the honor system—honor among thieves, if you will. But a neutral middleman was helpful with large amounts. Occam's Escrow was a service on the Dark Web made for just this sort of thing.

oDD17Y: Prove you know Bluefish

Goshawk tidied the kitchen, fed the dog, and refilled her tea before a ding sounded. When she saw the response, she sat up.

Achurincro: His office is down the hall from mine I'm on his team

Goshawk chewed on her lip.

oDD17Y: Why do you want to give him up?

Achurincro: Ever tried to raise a family on a government salary?

oDD17Y: That the only reason?

Achurincro: My reasons are my own

oDD17Y: 50 BTC

Achurincro: I'm not risking my life for less than 80 BTC. How will you use this information?

Everyone has their price.

oDD17Y: That's my business, especially at 80 BTC

Achurincro: How do I know it won't blow back on me?

oDD17Y: You don't, that's how these things work

Goshawk left her chair to use the bathroom, change into a flowing silk robe, and touch up her toenail polish. She was tossing a romaine salad together with a Dijon vinaigrette when the ding sounded again, so she carried the wooden salad bowl to the computer and munched on the greens while she read.

Achurincro: Okay, we're on.

A long string of characters and a web address allowed Goshawk to access an encrypted private escrow account.

She made the bitcoin transfer and sent Achurincro a confirmation.

The salad was gone, the kitchen tidied, and a bottle of

Domaine Abbatucci General de la Revolution Blanc, whose herbal notes brought to mind the maquis, was half gone before Achurincro got back to her.

A long string of numbers appeared in the chat window that was a web address in the Dark Web, one that didn't have the domain name service associated to make it recognizable by a human. She copied the URL and pasted it into a secure browser and was presented with a folder on an Apache web server. After clicking it, she was presented with a series of .txt files with names that indicated encryption.

Another ding sounded, and a long string of alphanumeric characters—an encryption key—appeared in the chat window. She clicked on the first .txt file and copied the string of alphanumeric characters into the resulting pop-up window, which decrypted the file. When the contents of the .txt file appeared on her screen, she sucked in her breath. After decrypting the rest of the files, she saved them to her own secure server before sending the password to release the escrowed funds.

Achurincro: Nice doing business with you, stay in touch

oDD17Y: I just might

Goshawk sat back in her chair, a mixture of elation and raw fear pulsing through her. If Bluefish was indeed who Achurincro said he was, the eighty Bitcoin was money well spent. Rising, she walked into her bedroom and fished the Glock pistol from underneath her pillow. She racked the slide and checked the magazine before chambering a round.

I think I'll carry this around for a while.

THIRTY-ONE

London, England

Cindy's voice cut through the cabin. "Look at this!"

Max jumped, now awake. Cindy pointed at her laptop screen, and both Max and Baxter got up from their chairs to get a better look.

She turned the machine so they could see. "This was in my Twitter feed, where I track a bunch of hashtags."

The Daily Mail @MailOnline
Breaking: Piper Montgomery, US CIA director, has been declared missing. A spokeswoman confirms that the Agency's head has been missing for three days. Foul play is suspected.

A recent image of Piper Montgomery in a pantsuit with her hair pulled up under a broad-brimmed hat, walking next to the American president, accompanied the tweet. Cindy turned the computer back around and clicked the link in the Tweet before reading aloud.

CIA DIRECTOR MISSING

Tom Bower for the Daily Mail
Published: 18:00 EDT, 6 November 2018

WASHINGTON - The director of the Central Intelligence Agency, Piper Montgomery, has been reported missing. The story broke in the New York Times and was confirmed by an Agency spokeswoman but offered no additional details, citing national security concerns.

According to the New York Times, two members of Ms. Montgomery's security detail were found dead from gunshot wounds. Their bodies were discovered at the entrance of Whitehaven Parkway on a path frequented by the director on her morning runs. The director's body was nowhere to be found, leading investigators to believe she was kidnapped. It is unknown whether any contact between the kidnappers and officials has occurred.

The article went on to describe Montgomery's long and distinguished career as a six-term Maryland senator and chairwoman of the Senate Select Committee on Intelligence before her recent appointment as director of the CIA. She was hailed as a reformer, a no-holds-barred fighter for what she believed, and a skillful administrator who enjoyed the ear of the president.

Max smirked. "Looks like Spencer got to her."

Baxter held one of the Lear's secure telephones to his

ear while he talked in a hushed voice. Cindy was busy clicking and reading.

After picking up one of the Lear's secure satphones, Max dialed a long string of digits and put the phone to his ear. A series of clicks came through the headset before a droning ring sounded.

After three rings, Goshawk picked up. "Go."

"Nice. How about great to hear your voice—"

A snort. "I'm busy. What do you—"

"Did you see the news? What do you know that the newspapers aren't reporting?"

Rapid typing in the background. "Yeah, sugar. That's why I'm busy. I can't raise him."

"He's probably just busy interrogating that bitch. You know how—"

A huff in the phone. "No. That's not it. He disappeared."

"What do you mean?"

"They made the snatch—"

Max held up a hand. "Wait. Who's they?"

"An old war buddy of his. Drove the getaway van."

The back of his head hit the headrest. "An amateur. Great."

In the background came more clacking on a keyboard. "You wouldn't help him. What else was he supposed to do?"

He frowned. *Everything's my fault.* "Fine. Go on."

"Had her under interrogation for two days and made all his check-ins until about two hours ago. He missed that one, and now I can't get a signal on his mobile phone."

"What about this accomplice? Do you have a name?"

The typing stopped. "Working on it."

Standing, Max paced the Lear's aisle. "I'll stay on. See if

you can roust the guy."

Baxter took the phone from his ear and typed on a small laptop.

Max waved at him. "Anything?"

Baxter talked while he typed. "I called an old friend at the CIA who sounded rattled. Apparently, this has never happened before. Protocols are in place, but he's afraid to talk to me right now. Said he'll call back."

Max put his phone on speaker so Baxter and Cindy could hear. "Can this plane get us to the States?"

Goshawk's voice came through. "Sugar, I got the accomplice. Name's Knuckles. I'll conference him in."

Max groaned. "Knuckles? What kind of name—"

Clicks and whirs were heard through the headset before a crusty voice came on the line. The man talked at such a pace that Max had trouble following. "Whoa there, partner. Slow down. Start at the beginning."

"We had her in a safe house," Knuckles said. "Spence was... Wait. Is this line secure?"

Goshawk sighed. "Of course."

The man's voice broke several times as he talked. "Spencer was getting through to her. He had her on the ropes, man. On the ropes. We stopped to give her a rest, and that's when it happened, man. Four paramilitary dudes stormed the safe house. I thought they were going to mow us down, like they were CIA or FBI or somepin'. But they took 'em both, man. This was no leo raid."

"What's a leo raid?" Max asked.

A groan. "Law enforcement, man. Shit."

Max leaned his elbows on his knees. "How did you escape?"

Knuckles sucked in his breath. "One minute I was staring at blank screens, the next minute the house was full of commandos. I was conked on the head and went out. When I came to, the house was empty. Everyone was gone."

Baxter rolled his eyes.

"Describe what they were wearing," Max said. "Any markings or insignia?"

Rapid breathing came through the phone. "All black uniforms. Negative on the insignia, man."

Max eyed Baxter. "Okay. Knuckles, right? Slow down and breathe."

Two deep breaths were heard through the phone. "Okay."

"What were their skin color?"

"Masked," Knuckles said. "Gloves. I couldn't tell."

"Helmets?"

Siren's sounded in the distance, and Knuckles took a minute to answer. "Yes, sir."

"Did you search the safe house after?" Max asked.

"Negative. I got the hell outa there, man."

Max leaned back in his chair. "How long ago was this?"

Silence for a beat. "Twenty hundred Eastern, sir."

Max looked at his watch and did the math. Three hours ago.

The million-dollar question. "Did you learn anything from Montgomery? Anything at all?

"Naw, man. But she was breaking, man. I know it. Spence was close. I could feel it."

"Where are you now?"

He mentioned the name of a no-tell motel in Northern Washington, DC. "Not sure if I can go back to my place. Not sure what to do."

Max waved at Baxter, who got up and disappeared into the cockpit. "Sit tight. We'll be there in ten hours."

A moment later the Lear made a hard bank to the west.

THIRTY-TWO

Washington, DC

"The American's call this thin ice." Baxter scowled at the dark city through the vehicle's window. "And we're on it."

Max looked up from his mobile phone, which he had used to try to raise Knuckles since they landed. No luck. Buildings flashed by in the darkness, their lights twinkling in the raindrops on the vehicle's window. They were in the rear of a SUV speeding through the rain-soaked streets of the American capital. Baxter sat in the middle bench while Max and Cindy were in the third row, the latter typing furiously on a laptop tethered to a secure cellular connection. The driver was standard livery from the British Embassy, while a young MI6 man rode shotgun. They were ten minutes out from the Crown Motel located in Washington's Brookland neighborhood.

Max removed an MI6-provided Glock 9mm from a shoulder holster and checked the mag before slipping it back underneath his leather jacket. "How so?"

"We're violating about a hundred different intelligence protocols and probably a few laws. Starting with failing to inform our counterparts at Langley."

Max scoffed. "We had a protocol at the KGB. It was called never alert the locals that we were there."

"And how'd that work out for you?"

Leaning forward, Max held Baxter's gaze. "We got a lot done without interference and red tape. Besides, about the worst thing we can do is alert the CIA to our presence. They've got Kate."

Baxter's toe tapped a fast rhythm on the SUV's carpet. "Second on the list of offenses is bringing in a rogue agent—"

Max dismissed him with a wave. "As my father used to say, this is what's for dinner."

The MI6 agent in the passenger seat, an Oxford man named Harris, who was still fighting a rash of acne, turned around. "Two minutes out, sir."

The team was quiet until they turned into the empty parking lot of the Crown Motel. Two letters on the neon sign were out so it read Crow M tel. The pavement was in disrepair, and the roof sagged over the inn's tiny office. A yellow light glowed from one office window. A Harley Davidson motorcycle was parked outside the door of room 221, but otherwise the parking lot was empty. Max pointed to the motorcycle. "Over there."

They piled out, except for the driver, who left the SUV running, and Cindy, who was glued to her laptop. As Max walked by the motorcycle, he put his hand near the exhaust pipe and found it cold. He hoped his failure to raise the former marine meant he was sleeping or had stepped out to get food. As he approached the door of room 221, he drew his pistol out of habit. Sirens rang in the distance.

When Max touched the handle, the door creaked as it swung open on dry hinges. "Knuckles?" *Don't fucking shoot me.*

Chemicals, raw sewage, and heavy perfume, along with moist and fetid heat hit him in the face. *Did someone leave the shower on?* He stepped in with his gun drawn while Harris was behind him, similarly armed.

The hotel room only had space for a queen-sized bed, a chair, and a credenza with a television. The bed was stripped of its sheets, and a muted television displayed a grainy image of a war movie. A window air conditioner hung askew at the back of the room, and a chair with ripped upholstery lay sideways on a threadbare carpet. A steam radiator chugged and rattled in one corner on its highest setting.

Harris groaned. "Oh, man."

Oh man indeed.

In the center of the bed was a naked man, between sixty-five and seventy years old, a faded tattoo of the POW*MIA symbol on one shoulder, his chest unmoving. A length of rubber tubing was wrapped around his elbow, just below his bicep, and a syringe was stuck into his forearm. More drug paraphernalia was on the round Formica table within the dead man's reach. His prick was limp but encased in a condom. A canvas duffle bag overflowing with clothing sat on the floor near the bathroom.

Max checked the bathroom while Harris looked under the bed to make sure the room was empty.

"Latex gloves?" Max asked while he stuck his face near to the dead man's mouth to ensure there was no breath.

Harris disappeared out the door while Baxter stuck his head in the room. "Oh, bloody hell. We shouldn't be here."

Harris returned and tossed Max a pair of black latex

gloves. "Pretty obvious what happened here, don't you think? Heroin and a hooker. Man overdoses. Hooker bolts, leaving the door open."

Max snapped on the gloves. "That's what they want you to think." He examined the man's arms and looked closely between his fingers before raising each foot to check between his toes.

Harris stooped next to Max. "What are you looking for?"

Max let a leg drop back to the mattress. "This man was not a drug user. Junkies like to hide their needle marks between their fingers or in the webbing between their toes. I see no evidence of drug use, other than the needle stuck in his arm." He rooted through the contents of the duffle bag. "Search the room, Harris. Look for a mobile phone or a computer or anything of that nature."

The sirens grew louder as Baxter rapped his fist on the doorjamb. "We can't be here when the cops get here."

A quick but thorough search revealed no devices. Max gazed around the room but saw nothing else of interest. "This smacks of a professional job."

Baxter snapped his fingers. "Let's go. Now!"

The three men piled into the SUV and the driver floored the accelerator and spun the wheel, sending them over a curb and onto a dark side street. As the hotel disappeared behind them, three DC patrol cars roared into the Crown Motel's parking lot, lights flashing.

"Poor Knuckles," Max muttered. "He deserved better."

THIRTY-THREE

Fort Meade, Maryland

The soldiers on duty at the south gate of Fort Meade didn't blink twice when, at zero three thirty on a blustery November morning, a figure jogged toward the gate, his distinctive jerky gait marking him as Lieutenant General Vincent "Vinny" Brown, USMC. The squad guarding the gate came to attention while their team leader gave the order to raise the barrier. As the three-star general lumbered through on one of his legendary early morning ten milers wearing nothing but shorts, a general issue sweatshirt, a stocking cap, and a small hydration pack on his back, the soldiers all shook their heads in amazement.

South of the tangle of government buildings, the rows of stark dormitories, and the forest of white satellite dishes that populate the US Army base and the National Security Agency's headquarters lay the Patuxent Research Refuge, a 12,800-acre wildlife area managed by the US Fish and

Wildlife Service. Gusts of snow, blown by a harsh Maryland nor'easter, swirled around the general's feet as he ran south and ducked onto a trail that disappeared into the hickory and dogwood thicket of the refuge. Even though his combat boots were quiet on the dirt trail, he spooked a snowy egret from her perch next to a frosted pond.

The general had been stationed at Fort Meade long enough to remember when the north tract of the reserve was US Army property. This was before President Clinton exercised a general reduction in army bases and 1,800 acres were given to the refuge. As General Brown exited the army base proper, he picked up his pace and beads of sweat formed on his forehead. The trail stretched straight west from the gate, covered in places by a thin layer of blown snow, and he soon left the army base behind.

As the deputy commander for Support of the United States Cyber Command (USCYBERCOM), Vinny Brown had intimate knowledge of Fort Meade's security systems. His daily runs through the refuge over the years gave him a detailed familiarity of the wildlife area's hidden nooks and crannies. He switched the headlamp off and allowed his eyes to grow accustom to the dusky moonlight as he followed a trail he knew well.

An hour into his run, the general halted when the trail paralleled a small stream. Shrugging off his hydration pack, he pretended to rummage while looking in both directions. Convinced he was alone, he ducked off the path and scrambled up a rocky incline. If one looked closely, they might notice the vegetation and limestone scrabble was recently disturbed.

The top of the bluff allowed him an unimpeded view over the tops of the trees. The lights of the base to the north and Washington, DC to the south glowed in the gray morning sky. He squatted on his haunches and removed a small satellite telephone from a compartment in his hydration pack and touched the ON button. As the satphone warmed up, he took out a small device from the pack, about the size of a cigarette box, with a mini USB dongle attached. This he plugged into a port on the satphone and toggled a switch on the box. Lastly, he connected a small tablet computer encased in a protective covering to the phone via a cable. After the gear was warmed up and connected, he dialed a long string of digits on the satellite phone.

It took a while for the signal to bounce through three orbiting satellites, connect to a ground station in Germany, and speed through six firewall-protected servers in Iceland. While the general waited, a northern long-eared bat darted and weaved above him.

Not for a moment did General Brown think his actions were treasonous. He was a patriot to the core, a lifelong marine, and he loved his country, having demonstrated a willingness to put his life on the line for her through a dozen deployments in Afghanistan, Iraq, and Somalia. *Someone's gotta fight for this country. The damn president sure isn't.*

The voice that came over the satellite phone was scratchy and garbled. *"Ni hao?"*

General Brown spoke into a microphone located on the small box attached to the satellite phone. The box scrambled his voice, turning it into a metallic drone, making it impossible for either a recipient or a recording device to discern his true voice pattern. Brown answered the Chinese salutation in English. "I believe you and I have a common query."

Static came over the transmission. "Who the fuck is this?"

Brown grimaced. "You may call me Bluefish."

Silence.

"I believe you are hunting for a woman named Kate Shaw," Brown said. "We can help each other."

"How do you know that? Who is this? How'd you get this number?"

He glanced around the bluff. Nothing moved. "Doesn't matter, but you'd be wise to listen."

A string of expletives filled his earpiece. General Brown narrowed his eyes at the cursing but did not interrupt. When it was over, he said, "I take it that is a yes?" Brown didn't wait for an answer. "As a show of good faith, I'm willing to provide you with some information that will help you."

The other end of the line was silent for so long, he thought she'd hung up.

When the voice answered, it was surprisingly strong. "I don't need your help."

A throaty chuckle erupted from deep in his sternum. "Of course you don't. You're a highly effective and well-trained operative. I've followed your career with interest for many years. You're secretive, but I know some things. I know where you call home. I have access to your bank accounts. I—"

"Enough. You made your point."

"I know a few other things. I know where Kate Shaw is."

"So stop yammering and tell me so I can get on with it."

"I need something in return."

"Tell me." Her voice was urgent.

"Mikhail Asimov dead. You make that happen, I'll give you Kate Shaw's location."

"No problem. How do I get ahold of you?"

General Brown tapped his finger on his thigh. "Stay by your phone. I'll be in touch." He severed the connection, stowed his gear, and resumed his run, his grim expression having nothing to do with the exertion from his exercise.

THIRTY-FOUR

Washington, DC

"We should get rooms at a Hampton Inn instead." Baxter paced the plush carpet of the expansive three-room suite. "They watch my damn budget like a hawk."

Fresh from a shower, Max shrugged on a T-shirt. "Forget it. Life is too short to stay in crappy hotels. Besides, I paid cash so there's no paper trail."

Three knocks rapped on the door and Cindy entered carrying a cardboard tray with three coffees and a bag of breakfast sandwiches from a trendy coffee shop. She handed the cups around and settled onto a settee next a tall window overlooking Georgetown.

Max peered at the muddy liquid in the cardboard cup. "What is this crap? Can't I get a normal black coffee?" Cindy frowned, so he took a sip and faked a smile. "Not bad, actually."

Baxter tasted his coffee and grimaced. "My CIA contact is nervous, partly because we're off-protocol and partly because the agency is in shock over Montgomery's disappearance."

Hoping to spot a coffee maker, Max scanned the hotel room. "Understandable."

Baxter nibbled at a breakfast sandwich. "He agreed to meet with me alone."

"Fine," Max said. "I'm happy to listen in."

The MI6 agent shifted in his chair and dabbed at his goatee with a napkin. "How do you expect to do that? We're stateside, without access to gear, with our tallywacker hanging out for everyone to see. One false move and we're in a vat of hot water."

Max shrugged. "I'm sure your embassy has something we can use."

"I'm sorry, Max." Baxter stood and threw his napkin down. "This time I draw the line."

"You have two choices." Max sipped his coffee. "You can let me listen in or you can watch while I nab him, strip him down, cover his head with a sack, and pour water on his face until he tells us what he knows." He set his cup down while holding Baxter's gaze.

Cindy's eyes darted between the two men. Baxter fumed and paced, yanked his goatee, muttered to himself, and threw his arms in the air. "Bloody hell, Max. Fine. I'm sure the embassy has something we can borrow."

———

The meeting was to take place on a park bench on the National Mall near the Lincoln Memorial Reflecting Pool, in full view of the World War II Memorial. The reflecting pool's fountains were turned off for the winter, but the water hadn't yet frozen solid. The National Mall's lawn was various shades of brown this late in the fall, and only a few hearty souls bundled in wool or down braved the November bluster. Baxter was wrapped in a thick overcoat, scarf, and wore a flat cap that made him look like a bootlegger from the twenties as he sat on the specified bench bobbing his leg up and down to stay warm.

The MI6 SUV was parked on Constitution Avenue opposite the Academy of National Sciences building. Max and Cindy sat in the rear, both wearing headphones, while Harris sat in the driver's seat. The transmission from Baxter's hidden mic ran through Cindy's computer to record the conversation. Max pointed a digital SLR with a telephoto lens through the darkened windows to watch Baxter and snap pictures of the mysterious CIA contact.

The appointed time came and went. They had only the mic, buried in Baxter's wool coat, and no two-way communications.

Max focused the lens on Baxter's face as the minutes ticked off his watch. *Hang in there, my friend.*

Fifteen minutes past the appointment, Baxter glanced at the SUV and shrugged. A moment later, when Baxter rose to his feet, a burly man in a parka sat down on the far side of the bench. The camera's motor whirred as Max snapped pictures, and the images flowed to Cindy's laptop over a secure Wi-Fi connection. The man had a fleshy face with a bulbous nose, heavy eyebrows, and an unkempt beard. His jacket was blue with some kind of logo on the sleeve and a hood trimmed in fur. His pants were wool, and his shoes were scuffed wingtips.

"Looks like the CIA's version of Baxter," Max said under his breath. "Ever seen him?"

Cindy laughed. "No, I haven't. Want me to see if I can

get into the CIA mainframe and pull down their organizational chart?"

Max kept his eye glued to the camera. "Sure, but be careful."

Their voices were low, but Cindy amplified the audio feed.

The CIA man spoke first. "What brings you over the pond?"

Baxter tightened his scarf. "Oh, bits and bobs. You know, the usual."

"We're off the record, right, Callum? You have to give me your word."

"Absolutely, Stephen. We've known each other too long."

The CIA agent gazed out over the reflecting pool. "This thing is a real mess, Callum. Langley is in total chaos. In all my years, I've never seen anything like it."

"Doesn't the agency have a succession plan in place?"

Stephen sputtered. "Of course, but I'm not talking about the abduction. Most of the old guard is quietly drinking a toast to her disappearance to the point where I wonder if it isn't an inside job. And I'm not the only one."

Baxter's shaggy eyebrows darted up. "Good God. You can't be serious?"

"No one wanted her," the CIA man said. "No field experience. No empathy for the man out running agents, putting their butts on the line to generate intel so she can fluff it up with the White House. We're an ass hair away from another attack on US soil, for Pete's sake."

His face placid, Baxter leaned back and crossed a leg. "Not to mention she's a she."

"That doesn't help with the old boys. But the mess I'm talking about is the agency's relationship with the White

House. She fucked that up to the point where I'm told the president didn't even meet with her. The old director used to give the president a briefing every morning."

"So, Wodehouse is now the acting director?" Baxter referenced Chester Wodehouse, the deputy director, a man who came up through the ranks and spent time as bureau chief in Afghanistan, Iraq, and Libya and enjoyed the support of the CIA's rank and file.

"For now. He won't last. They'll put another bureaucrat in there who can pander to the DC policy wonks and budget hounds. Someone who doesn't know shit about running an op."

Stephen pulled a cigar from his pocket, snipped the end, and lit it with a wooden match. "Hoping you have some intel for me on this one. I could use a break. That's why you're here, right?"

Baxter shook his head. "I was in town. Thought I'd get the scoop."

"Bullshit, Callum. You can't bullshit a bullshitter. You're never just in town. What gives?"

Max held his breath.

Cindy tapped on his shoulder and pointed to her screen. It showed an image of a man in a suit jacket and tie who resembled a much younger version of the man sitting on the bench next to Baxter. Curly red hair, face freckled from the sun, and a glint in his eye. In contrast, the man on the bench looked tired and gray. Max returned his eye to the camera. "Who is he?"

"Stephen MacCulloch. Director of the Counterintelligence Center Analysis Group. Pretty senior guy."

His eye still glued to the camera eyepiece, Max nodded. "Counter intel, huh? Interesting connection." He directed his attention back to the conversation.

"We've known each other for a while, Stephen. I think our relationship has been mutually beneficial over the years, don't you agree?"

MacCulloch glanced at Baxter. "You're not going to pull this on me again, are you?"

Baxter took his hands out of his pockets and gripped the edge of the wooden bench. "You do it to me. I do it to you. What comes around goes around. Our countries are stronger and better off for it."

The CIA agent rolled his eyes. "Fine. What do you want to know?"

"Any details about her abduction that aren't in the press?"

MacCulloch shook his head. "Why are you asking?"

Baxter lifted one eyebrow.

"Fine," MacCulloch said. "But if you find out anything—

Baxter grinned. "You'll be the first to know."

"It was a straightforward snatch," MacCulloch said. "Two bodyguards were shot twice each at midrange with a 9mm. The shots were accurate enough to avoid the vests. Shooter probably waited in the bushes to the left of the path. So far, we've got nothing—and I mean nothing. No abandoned getaway vehicle, no weapon, no eyewitnesses. It's as if she disappeared like a ghost."

"What else?"

"Another reason we think it's an inside job? They knew her route and the exact timing of her run. They knew her security detail."

"That information might have been generated through surveillance."

The CIA man snorted. "Doubt it. She changed her route often and randomly. Even her security detail didn't know the route until the night before. The CIA is good at protection."

"Not good enough." Baxter said. "What else can you tell me?

MacCulloch shifted on the bench. "You must know something or you wouldn't be here. This is serious, Callum. You can't hold out."

Baxter stretched his arm along the back of the bench. "You have my word. The moment we do, I swear we'll let you know."

Atta boy.

Max snapped a few more pictures of the two men. Before getting into the SUV, Max had routed the camera to deliver the images to two locations—Cindy's laptop and his own Blackphone—and programmed his phone to send the images through a secure connection to a server Goshawk could access.

The long silence made Max worry that the mic had cut out.

MacCulloch cleared his throat. "This doesn't make sense. I should be the one asking you for information. This is going to even the score, you know."

Baxter smirked. "That's why I'm here."

The CIA man grimaced and scanned the area around them. "We found where they held her. At least initially."

Both Baxter's eyebrows shot up.

"In a house. More of a mansion, really, up in Chevy Chase, north of DC."

"And?"

With a quick glance behind them, MacCulloch kept his voice low. "Our theory is there was a second incursion. The safe house looked like it had been invaded. We found evidence of a battering ram similar to those used by law enforcement on both the front and back doors. The room where the director was held looked like a team swept in, grabbed her, and left. Chairs knocked over, a table upturned, that sort of thing. There was interrogation paraphernalia left behind but no electronics. It's a damn mystery."

A wind ruffled the stiff hairs on Baxter's chin. "Can you trace any of the gear?"

MacCulloch sucked on the cigar and blew out a puff of smoke. "Working on it. A lot of stuff was left behind, so we'll find something eventually."

"I need one more thing," Baxter said.

MacCulloch let out a long breath. "Are you going to tell me what this is all about?"

"Someday."

Silence from MacCulloch.

"I need to know where you're holding Kate Shaw."

MacCulloch frowned. "Who?"

"Come on, Stephen, it's cold out here."

The CIA agent's eyes roved around the park before he answered. "That's the thing, Callum. We don't have her anymore."

A frown from Baxter. "Come again?"

"We had her at a black site. She was scheduled for transport to the Hampton Roads brig in Virginia, but she was nabbed en route. Once again, we think they had help from the inside. The mere fact that we had her was a closely guarded secret, let alone her transportation schedule. It was a commando team that looked and operated like SWAT or special ops. All blacked out. They used a small C-4 charge to blow the door to the van, tear gas canisters in the cab, zip ties to secure the guards, black bag over her head. The whole thing took less than forty-five seconds. Pro job all the way."

Baxter glanced at the SUV. "Jesus."

"Tell me about it," MacCulloch said. "No leads. Our theory is she's in the US. We've got the borders, the coast guard, and the airports on high alert."

Baxter stood and stretched his legs. "Something tells me you're wrong."

THIRTY-FIVE

Washington, DC

The MI6 SUV roared down Massachusetts Ave NW, made a left on Observatory Circle NW and another left into the driveway of the chancery building that comprised the working portion of the British Embassy. While guards checked credentials and used mirrors and bomb-sniffing dogs to examine the vehicle, Max scrutinized the building. Resembling a dormitory on a land grant college campus, it was a far cry from the Elizabethan architecture of the ambassador's residence next door. Square and squat, four stories high, with window-covered red brick walls, its utilitarianism was very un-British. Antennas, satellite dishes, and pipes covered the roof and security cameras dotted the walls and perimeter.

When the vehicle was cleared, they proceeded up a winding drive and disappeared down a ramp to an underground garage where they wound down two floors. After they parked, Max, Baxter, Cindy, and Harris filed through a security door and down a bland corridor covered by thread-bare beige carpet and lit by flickering fluorescent bulbs.

Max poked Baxter's shoulder. "I haven't seen this place in any James Bond movies."

Without slowing his pace, Baxter said, "Shut up and keep quiet."

An elevator took them deeper under the embassy proper, where they emerged into a concrete bunker filled with folding tables, dated laptops, and monitors hung on the walls. Two pink-faced men with loosened ties and rolled-up shirt sleeves sat at a table intent on their machines. Cindy found an open spot between them and opened her laptop. Harris poured himself some coffee.

Max stopped at the door. "What is this place? Who are these men?"

Baxter smiled and held his arms out. "Meet Task Force Middleton." He pointed at the two men, one after another. "This is Wood, and that's Kelly."

Max leaned against the door frame. "Sounds like a law firm. What's Middleton's mission?"

After hunting through his pockets for his pipe, Baxter gripped it in his hand and used it for emphasis. "You didn't think Her Majesty's secret service was going to give us a jet and an expensive cover and let us prance around the globe on her dime, did you? The task force produces intelligence briefings on our progress and serves as a support team."

Max glanced over Baxter's shoulder and into the room. Both analysts resembled overworked office staffers. One was balding, wore reading glasses, and hovered his face close to his screen while the other was younger, boyishly handsome, and talked earnestly to Cindy, who listened with squinted eyes. "What's Middleton mean?"

Baxter cocked his head. "Kate Middleton?"

Max shook his head.

The MI6 director slapped Max on the shoulder. "She's the Duchess of Cambridge. Wife of Prince William. You need to read your tabloids."

"What are they really working on? I mean, besides filing reports on our progress."

Baxter grinned. "Looking for Kate Shaw, of course."

Max looked in the situation room again. "This is it? Two guys and some old computers? You said there were six people on the team."

The two men glanced at Max and Baxter before resuming their attention on Cindy's screen while Baxter sputtered. "Keep your voice down. The rest of the team is in London."

Max's Blackphone buzzed, and he pulled it from his pocket. The caller ID read *Bluefish. What the heck?* He took two steps away from Baxter. "Who is this?"

A series of clicks proceeded the feminine voice in the earpiece. "Max, its me."

"Jesus, Goshawk. Why did you—"

"I know who it is."

Max cupped his hand over his mouth and the phone. "What are you talking about?"

"Bluefish. I know Bluefish's identity."

Max's mouth gaped open. "How—"

"Listen to this." The background was filled with rapid typing.

While Max walked down the hall, Baxter joined Cindy and the two MI6 men. "Okay, go."

The first voice that came over his earpiece was faint and scratchy but unmodified. "*Ni hao?*"

The voice sounded feminine. "Is that Chinese?" he asked.

Goshawk made a clucking sound with her tongue. "Yes. Hush."

The next voice was metallic and robotic. "I believe you and I have a common query."

The woman spoke in English. "Who the fuck is this?"

"You may call me Bluefish." Static crackled. "I believe you are hunting for a woman named Kate Shaw. We can help each other."

Max almost dropped his Blackphone.

More static. "I know a few other things. I know where Kate Shaw is."

Was he about to learn Kate's location?

"So, stop yammering and tell me so I can get on with it."

"I need something in return."

"Tell me."

"Mikhail Asimov dead. You make that happen, I'll give you Kate Shaw's location."

Max's skin crawled at the computerized voice demanding his death.

The recording ended, and Goshawk came back on the line.

"What was her response?" Max asked.

"He told her to think about it and he'd get back to her."

Max paced. "Who's the woman?"

"Don't know. I'm working on it." Her voice was distant.

"When's the big reveal of Bluefish's identity?"

"I put it on a secure file server for you." She once again sounded like her energetic self.

He memorized the server location she reeled off in his ear. "Were you able to intercept any other transmissions?"

"Negative. He's using a variety of randomized transmission protocols, and he's very careful. I'm not yet patched in to all his channels. It's possible he already made the deal with this woman, whoever she is."

"Or maybe not." His mind went to the Chinese names on the consortium list. "Continue monitoring, and let me know what you dig up."

"Of course, darling."

Max was about to end the call when Goshawk said, "Hon?"

"What?"

"This is getting real. Please be careful."

Max smiled into the phone. "Is this you caring about me?"

The line went dead, and he chuckled as he entered the situation room.

At the sound of his laugh, Cindy glanced up while Baxter hunched over one of the men's laptops in deep conversation. Max accessed a secure browser on his phone before navigating to the server Goshawk specified. When he saw the man's identity, he almost dropped his phone.

According to her intel, the man calling himself Bluefish was Lieutenant General Vincent Brown of the United States Marine Corps. The general was the deputy commander of an important-sounding group called the United States Cyber Command. If Brown knew where Kate was, he would not easily relinquish that information.

Max tapped Baxter on the shoulder. "I need to run an errand."

Baxter kept his eyes glued to the computer monitor. "Harris can take you in the car."

Max followed Harris from the situation room, up the elevator, and into the SUV. When they reached Franklin Square near 13th Street NW and K Street NW, Max stepped from the vehicle and turned to his driver. "Harris, you're a good man, so I'll make this easy on you. I'm going to walk across that park and disappear. You can try to find me or attempt to follow me, but you'll fail. Instead of chasing me, go back to the embassy and tell Baxter I gave you the slip. Cool?"

Harris opened his mouth to protest as Max vanished down a path through leafless oaks and poplars.

THIRTY-SIX

Washington, DC

His first stop was a restaurant on Dupont Circle called the Russia House. Outside, a set of red-carpeted steps ran up a sweeping stone staircase to an entrance covered with a green awning. The white stone baroque-style building sat among taller apartments and offices near the corner of Florida and Connecticut Avenues. An American flag flew to the left of the doorway, and red banners with the restaurant's name flapped in a breeze.

Inside was dark with more red carpet and mahogany trim, and despite the ban on cigarette smoke inside restaurants in the District, the stale odor of tobacco lingered. Red upholstered chairs and dark wood tables were filled with a variety of DC insiders enjoying cocktails and scanning menus. Max sidled past a pair of fresh-faced men wearing dark suits with red ties and found a seat at the end of a short bar. Glassware hung overhead, and a television with a sports news report was on in the opposite corner.

Catching the bartender's eye, he spoke in Russian. "Vodka. Cold, no ice."

The thin pale man with a black tie under a red apron perked up at the sound of his native language, so he made quick work of shaking the vodka over ice and pouring it into a tumbler. "Where you from, friend?"

Max surveyed the crowd using the mirror behind the bar. "Leningrad."

The bartender beamed. By using the old Communist name for St. Petersburg, Max signaled that he wasn't happy about the end of the Soviet Union and yearned for the old days of the party.

With a scrub of the bar using a dirty towel, the bartender smiled, showing a set of yellow teeth. "Born in Volgograd myself. Parents from Poland, just outside Kraków. Emigrated east when the Germans came. Shame what's become of Poland."

To Max's right, an American spoke with a demure young lady dressed in a modern-cut suit. The man towered over her and gestured with an unlit cigar in a big fist, reminding him of his father. "Rodion around?"

The bartender bent to wash glasses in the sink under the bar. "Who's asking?"

Max took a swig of the drink. "Andrei Asimov."

The bartender pinched his eyebrows together. "Bull-shit. You're too young."

Max leaned close enough so the bartender's breath wafted in his face. "Tell Rodion that Andrei Asimov is here to see him. Do it before I come over that bar and strangle you with your fucking tie."

Five minutes later, Max was ushered through the kitchen and up a set of back stairs where two gorilla-sized men frisked him and inspected his Blackphone. It took another threat and staring down one of the goons before he got his phone back. He was directed through a door into a cramped but luxurious office outfitted with shag carpet, a set of leather chairs, a massive desk, and a credenza housing an elaborate stereo system. Everything was red including the cherrywood desk.

Behind the desk stood a mountainous man dressed in a black shirt, black suit, and red tie. His skin was pale, and fat folds filled the area where his neck should be. A young woman wearing barely enough to create a hint of mystery was perched on the edge of the desk. When Max strode through the door, the man's face melted into a wide grin, and he raised two crane-sized arms while lumbering from behind the desk. "Look what the cat dragged in. Honey, get lost for a while."

The girl touched Max's arm as she slid by, leaving the lingering scent of cigarettes and an overpowering perfume.

The big man engulfed Max in a massive bear hug before holding him at arm's length. "Let me look at you."

With an effort, Max freed himself. "Rodion, I can't believe you're still alive."

The obese man laughed so hard his jowls shook like Jell-O and the small room was filled with his guffaws. "I could say the same thing about you, friend. Except we're plagued by different assailants. I'm under attack by sugar and oil and vodka, and you are chased by unseen assassins, no?"

Max grimaced. "How's your diabetes these days?"

A groan from Rodion. "Don't ask of such things." Opening a desk drawer, he pulled out a cigar box. "An occasion such as this calls for the best."

He offered the box to Max, who selected one and held it to his nose and inhaled the smoky aroma. "Cuban, no?"

"Of course. And my diabetes is fine. My little assistant

there manages to shoot me up with the proper amounts of insulin. Now it's my heart. A couple stents went in last month. Now the doctors say I need to become a vegan." Rodion pronounced it *vee-ghan*. "Of all the fucking things."

"You might like it." Max snipped the end from the cigar and dug his lighter from his pocket and tossed it at Rodion, who examined it before using it to light his cigar.

Rodion blew a thick cloud of smoke at the ceiling and tossed the lighter back. "I like a big steak is what I like. I heard about your mother and father. A real shame. I'm sorry for your loss, Mikhail. Andrei was good to me. You Asimov's are dying off by the truckload. I'm glad to see you standing in front of me."

Max lit his own cigar and fell into one of the red-leather wing chairs opposite the desk as Rodion picked up a phone and barked an order in Russian. A minute later, a different partially clad girl appeared carrying a tray with an ice bucket, a bottle of Green Mark, and two tumblers. The woman lingered, casting long looks at Max, until Rodion ordered her from the room. "Petulant little minx." Rodion poured two measures of the vodka. "None of that designer crap for an old friend."

Max held his glass up. "Just good old-fashioned pure Russian water. From the motherland."

They clinked glasses, and both men tossed back their drink.

The vodka went down Max's throat with a toasty warmth. It felt good to speak his native tongue to someone he knew and trusted. Despite not holding an official KGB title, Rodion had a long history of helping agents in the field. He was a loyalist, someone trusted to assist with the more mundane matters of an operation. For a price, of course. He also ran one of the best restaurants in Washington, DC, favored by US presidents and senators.

The two men spoke of Max's father and mother, and Max filled Rodion in on the events since the bombing in Minsk, glossing over details.

When the bottle was half empty, Rodion grunted. "What brings you to my little restaurant tonight? I'm guessing it's not the borscht."

Max walked to the credenza and flipped on the stereo. A Bill Evans riff made him sentimental for his old jazz club, *La Caravelle*. After turning up the volume, he stepped close to the desk so Rodion could hear his hushed voice. "I need two things."

"Name it," Rodion whispered. "I will do anything to avenge Andrei's death."

"My father left some things with you. For safe keeping."

Rodion's eyes lit up, and the rolls of fat around his neck shook as he nodded. "He did indeed."

"I need those things."

The big man spread his arms. "Of course. What else?"

As Max spoke, Rodion's eyes went wide and he fell into his chair.

Max leaned on the desk with his knuckles. "Will you do it?"

The big restaurateur poured another round of vodka and dabbed at his eyes. "You know what Andrei did for my daughter?"

Max poured another round. "I do."

Rodion banged his glass against Max's and tossed the clear liquid into his mouth. "I owe him, Mikhail. She is alive and at the head of her class at Johns Hopkins medical school. She's the apple of my eye, and I will do anything. You can count on me, my friend."

The two men talked in hushed voices as they worked through the details, and by the time they were done, the bottle was gone and the restaurant had long closed for the night.

THIRTY-SEVEN

Fort Meade, Maryland

"How does one capture and interrogate a Marine Corps three-star general?" Goshawk's voice came through an earbud attached to his Blackphone.

"Very carefully." Max sat in a rented silver sedan in the parking lot of the National Cryptologic Museum on the edge of Fort Meade, near the Baltimore-Washington Parkway.

"Funny," she said. "What's your plan?"

His eyes scanned the few cars in the lot. "The less you know, the better."

"Fair enough. You get the dossier I sent you?"

Goshawk had assembled dozens of electronic files on USMC Lieutenant General Brown and stashed them on a secure server.

"Very thorough. Anything in there stick out at you?"

"You saw his 201 file?"

"I did." The 201 file, also known as his personnel file,

contained all of Brown's promotion orders, mobilizations, decorations, evaluations, college transcripts from the general's undergraduate studies at the Naval Academy, as well as long lists of certifications from various technical programs specific to cryptology, computer science, digital security, and the like. "What about it?"

"Nothing. It's perfect. His record is unblemished."

"Maybe too perfect."

"Right. Did you read the details I sent on Bluefish's cyber activities?"

"Yes." Goshawk had also provided transcripts of various calls, posts, and other internet activity by Bluefish over the last six months, since Bluefish first appeared as an identity on the Dark Web. "It's not a lot."

"Right," she said. The sound of the ocean was in the background. "I'm still digging. He's good at covering his tracks."

"From my read, he had an exemplary record over a dozen deployments, with many commendations, awards and decorations. His disciplinary file is spotless. He's unmarried, with no children. Utterly devoted to the military his entire career. His parents died in a car crash before he entered the Naval Academy. No mention of siblings. So far, no skeletons or angles I can take to get to him. And the biggest mystery of all. Why did Brown adopt the Bluefish identity and risk a slam-dunk promotion to four stars?"

"It's a good question," Goshawk said. "I'm digging on that one. So far, not much."

Max scanned the faces of the men and women as they walked to their cars burdened by large computer bags and briefcases. "What's Brown's motive? His history points to a straight shooter and a distinguished soldier. What does he have to gain by all this? Why is he helping the same people who are out to kill me? Why does he care about finding Kate? What role does he play in all this?"

"Did you see the sealed files?" Goshawk asked. "The top secret ones?"

Blue light from the parking lot's vapor lamps glinted off cars as employees began their commute home from work. "The ones from his days in the Marine's Special Operations Command? What is that group, anyway? Like the Russian Spetsnaz?"

"Yeah. Sort of the Marine Corps' version of the Navy Seals. Elite squad of highly trained men. Most of his missions were in Afghanistan during the Russian occupation and again when the US fought against the Taliban, as well as numerous incursions into Iraq before, during, and after Desert Storm. Did you see the file about the op in the Ukraine back in '85 to sabotage the Urengoy–Pomary–Uzhgorod pipeline?"

He touched a rib and grimaced. It was still sore from the beating he took in Turkey. After digging in his pocket, he popped a painkiller and swallowed it dry. "Yes. That was only a couple years before the wall came down and just before Gorbachev took office."

"Correct," Goshawk said. "The op looked like it was meant to help cripple the Soviet economy, which was already struggling to keep up with the American's military buildup. The US figured the more they did to hurt the Soviet economy, the more likely they were to end Chernenko's hard line and help promote some kind of revolution in Russia that might lead to a democratically elected government. Question is, did that operation impact Brown in any way? What was his role?"

He toyed with a pack of cigarettes. "Captain. It was his show." Max eyed the *No Smoking* sticker on the rental car's dash as he fished a cigarette from the pack and fired it up. "Might be a connection there."

"You know what I think?"

"Tell me." He took a long drag.

"Why do people become traitors against their own government?"

He exhaled a cloud of smoke. "Money or ideology."

"Right. Or?"

Max shrugged. "No idea."

"Ego. Remember the story of Aldrich Ames?" The CIA guy they busted in '94 for spying for the Russians?"

"Vaguely."

"He married this gal named María del Rosario who bled him dry with shoes and vacations, so the FBI assumed he did it for the money. But he never got any respect at work. In fact, he was such a bad CIA agent that when he offered to spy for the KGB, the Russians initially ignored him. They thought it was a trick. Turned out once he started spying for Russia, he became a better CIA agent. He had a purpose. His purpose was to make his employer look bad. The same people that gave him such poor performance reviews."

He flicked ash through a crack in the window. "What's your point?"

"Maybe that's Bluefish's objective too."

"Except Brown is good at his job. Walk me through his routine again."

Goshawk sighed. "Medium-sized brick house in Odenton, Maryland. Ten minutes from his office at Fort Meade. Lives alone. Drives a maroon Buick. Leaves the house at three am. Usually home after dark. All his meals and PT are done at Fort Meade. Known for early morning runs through the park to the south of the base. That's about it. If he has a weakness for drugs or women, it's not showing up anywhere."

"What about money? What do his bank accounts tell us?"

"Nothing weird. He makes $178,988 annually as a three-star general. His house is paid off. He's maximizing his retirement savings. The rest of the money goes into an investment account. He's not a wealthy man, but he's well off and has frugal habits."

"Any offshore accounts?"

"Nothing I've found yet."

Max flicked ash into the passenger footwell. "Right. What about vacations? What does he do on leave?"

"Every year he takes a scuba trip to either the Caribbean or the south pacific. He's been to Okinawa, Hawaii, Belize. All the hot spots."

"And no evidence of a female companion? Or a male, I guess?"

"Correct," said Goshawk. "Why do you always look for the skeleton?"

"Everyone's got one."

"What's yours?" Her voice was a purr.

Max stubbed the cigarette out in the console between the seats and put the butt in his pocket before starting up the car. "You, of course."

———

For four days Max watched General Brown's garage door roll up at precisely three am. The maroon sedan rolled to Fort Meade, where the car arrived at the gate at precisely three-ten am. The evening trip was more flexible. One night it was nine forty-six pm, and the next it was seven fifty-two pm. Each night, the light in the general's bedroom went out at precisely ten pm.

On the fifth day, a cold, overcast, and blustery mid-November Friday, Max watched as the Buick motored off in the direction of Fort Meade. He followed to ensure the general entered Fort Meade before returning to his hotel for a nap. Later in the morning, he visited Chevy Chase Pavilion to do some shopping before taking another nap. As dusk descended, he drove to General Brown's neighborhood and went for a jog dressed in a dark track suit and stocking cap.

The general lived in a sleepy upper middle class neighborhood with classic brick houses set far apart on tree-lined lots. Foreign cars were parked in many of the driveways. The general's home, one of the smallest in the neighborhood, was bordered by a waist-high hedge of boxwood along his front yard.

As Max reached the front of the general's house, he slowed and looked around before vaulting over the hedge. He crouch-ran until he got to the side door, which was hidden in shadows. Using a set of lock picks that his father left among the gear at Rodion's restaurant, he opened the lock and slipped inside.

He worked fast, intent on reconnaissance. The faint odor of cigar smoke and dark roast coffee permeated the house. Stepping through a mudroom, bare of any boots or jackets, he entered a kitchen with granite countertops and honey-colored cabinets. The stainless steel sink was empty and clean, and the dishwasher looked unused. A drying rack next to the sink contained a bowl, a spoon, and a coffee mug. The pantry was full of canned beans, vegetables, and boxes of pasta and rice. A fruit bowl contained an avocado and a ripe banana.

He moved through the formal living room and dining room, both spotless. The walls were covered with reproductions of impressionist artists; there were no pictures of family members or friends. It looked and felt like a safe house.

In the rear he found a study with a scuffed but plush leather couch, several matching leather chairs, and a mahogany desk. The cigar aroma was strong here, with a large ashtray holding remnants of several cigars. A pair of reading glasses topped a stack of military history books next to a chair.

So that's what you do at night, General Brown.

The general lived in his study. Along one wall, underneath a large Monet print, was a mahogany credenza with more military history books, a stereo system, and a bar service consisting of a silver tray, three tumblers, and a crystal decanter. He opened the top and sniffed the unmistakable peaty odor of expensive Scotch. In the cabinet below the bar service were four unopened bottles of Macallan single malt. The general was a man of habit.

The credenza held a dozen framed pictures showing the general with groups of his military comrades. Max used his Blackphone to snap a picture of each photo and sent the lot to Goshawk.

Max checked his watch. *Ten minutes.*

He went through the desk drawers, taking care not to disturb anything, but found nothing of interest, and moved to the stairs. When he reached midway, he heard a sound and froze. A gentle tapping came from somewhere up the stairs. He took another step, and the sound got louder before dying off. He removed a compact Glock from his jacket pocket. Another step. The sound resumed.

The tapping grew louder. Two more steps and he peeked inside a room at the top of the stairs.

Tap, tap, tap.

He groaned when he saw the source. A tree branch outside the room's window was hitting against the glass. He stuffed the gun back in his pocket and resumed his search.

Two formal guest rooms and the master bedroom made up the second floor. Brown's bedroom was squared away with an alarm clock, another stack of military history books, another pair of reading glasses, and not much else. Max checked under the mattress and pillows but found nothing. The closet yielded a row of perfectly pressed uniforms on hangers.

Something occurred to him as he hoofed down the stairs, and he went back to the study. No laptop, no desktop. No printer or other peripherals. *Why did the number two guy in the US Cyber Command have no home computer?*

He left the house the same way he entered and locked the door behind him. A moment later he jogged down the street, satisfied he found a way to take the general peacefully. Only a few details to figure out.

I'm coming for you, General Brown.

THIRTY-EIGHT

Fort Meade, Maryland

Preparations to take down General Brown took most of the day. Despite a midnight black bag job at a local veterinary hospital, Max enjoyed a hot breakfast of eggs, pancakes, bacon, and black coffee. Wearing a hat and sunglasses, with a scarf around his neck to ward off the cold, he paid cash for a bare white panel van, and drove to a parking garage where he swiped a set of Maryland plates from a Honda Accord. To be safe, he took a set of plates from a Toyota and put those on the Honda.

Next, he stopped at a mortuary, where he paid the son of the funeral director five hundred bucks for a cheap wooden coffin, saying he needed it as a prop for a haunted house. The kid gladly helped Max load it into the van.

Last on the list was a big box hardware store where he easily avoided the scarce employees as he loaded his cart with zip ties, duct tape, a razor blade knife, a hammer, standard wood nails, a sheet of neoprene plastic, a cordless drill, four opaque plastic bins, and various other tools. He paid cash and loaded his items into the van next to the coffin before making the drive back to Fort Meade.

By the time he reached the outskirts of Odenton, the streets were full of workers on their way home. He pulled into a Red Roof Inn parking lot a mile from General Brown's house and backed the van into a spot in the rear next to a dumpster. He found a generic chain restaurant and ate a tough steak and an iceberg lettuce salad while watching a basketball game on the bar's television. The Wizards were up on the Pelicans in the third quarter, and the lackluster athletic performance made him long for a soccer match.

As darkness descended, he once again donned his jogging outfit, placed the Glock in a pocket, tugged on the stocking cap, and jumped in the car. He left the rental four blocks from the general's house and took off for a jog. When he reached the brick house with the red shutters, he stopped to tie his shoe and look around. Seeing no one, he jumped the hedge. A few minutes later he was back in the darkened house.

This would take two minutes, three tops. From a jacket pocket, he withdrew a small vial of clear liquid and opened the cap while entering the study. He stepped to the credenza and lifted the crystal decanter's heavy top. Three inches of the brown liquid remained in the carafe. He dumped the vial's contents into the Scotch, swirled the decanter, and took a sniff. No sign of the drug. After thinking for a second, he emptied half of a second vial into the decanter before replacing the top. He stuffed the vials into his pocket, turned to leave the office, and froze.

Standing in the doorway was General Brown holding a silver-plated pistol pointed at Max's stomach.

THIRTY-NINE

Fort Meade, Maryland

"Tell me you didn't just ruin a perfectly good decanter of Macallan."

Max held his hands waist high, while General Brown was partially hidden by the doorjamb. "Hello, Bluefish."

The general's baritone voice boomed in the small room. "Yes, your friend the Hawk is exceedingly capable. She managed to dodge my attacks. Got help from that idiot the Monk, and disappeared before I found her. Very resourceful, that one."

Working to keep his movements hidden as he talked, Max held the general's gaze. "Jig's up, Bluefish. Or should I call you General Brown."

The general's face remained blank. "What jig exactly are you referring to?"

Max inched his hands lower. "MI6. They're down the street."

With a shake of his head, the general chuckled. "No,

they're not. Your man Baxter is safe inside the British Embassy, royally steamed at how you gave him the slip. The only people down the street are my men parked behind your rental."

Max gave a loud sarcastic laugh. "Come on, general. You don't have any people. You're a loner. A lonely man with no family and no friends who uses his vast computing networks to fuck with people's lives." His hand slid closer to the Glock in his tracksuit pocket.

Hiding more of his body behind the doorjamb, the general waved his pistol. "Toss the gun. Get down on the ground."

Max slid his hand into his jacket pocket as he talked. "Bluefish. Where did you get that name, anyway? Don't see any Dr. Seuss books around here." He slipped his finger through the trigger guard and fired through the material of his jogging jacket. The room was filled with a popping sound as the general returned fire with the silver-plated pistol.

When he started shooting, Max was ten meters from the general's position but only a meter from the desk. With adrenaline coursing and heart rates elevated, handguns are notoriously inaccurate, even in the hands of experts such as General Brown and himself. Max counted on this and the loud surprise of his gunshots to buy him a split second.

Max hurled himself at the enormous desk while firing and banged down hard on his shoulder, knocking the breath from his lungs. Gasping for air, he scrambled to kneel behind the desk while holding the pistol in a two-handed grip. A searing burn radiated from his left forearm where blood seeped through his track suit. A yank on his sleeve revealed a thin furrow in his radialis. Grazed by one of General Brown's bullets.

Cold air hit Max's back. The sliding glass door had shattered in the gun fight, leaving a gaping hole to the deck and darkness beyond. He grabbed his Blackphone from his pocket, turned on the camera, and put it against the floor so the lens showed the room. The general was no longer in the doorway.

Staying low, Max crouch-walked and stopped behind a leather chair, gun pointed at the hallway. When the general didn't show, Max darted across the room and put his back to the wall next to the door. A glance into the hallway revealed it to be empty, but a dark streak of red blood stood out against the hallway's white walls.

Avoiding the glass shards, Max ran through the broken sliding door to the screened deck. He moved through the outside door to the stoop at the rear of the house. The door was unlocked, and he slipped into the kitchen. Empty.

———

God damn it. All these years in the field and I never got shot. Now I'm lying in my own house with a bullet... Shit. Where am I hit?

He scanned his body. Everything hurt. His nerves were on fire. *Legs, won't move. Torso, check. Arms, check. Shoulder, white hot heat. There. This is what a heart attack must feel like. Is there blood?*

His cheek rested on something soft and silky. *My Kashmirian rug. That ornate silk thing I brought back from Islamabad.*

Where's my gun? I better get that and be ready. That damn Russian is around here somewhere. Can't go down without a fight. I might die, but I'm taking that damn Russian with me. They're the ones that fucked up

Afghanistan. It wasn't us. Was it? Maybe it was us. The damn CIA and their stinger missiles. I've got an idea. Let's kit out all the mujahideen with weapons they can later use against us. But there was Yugoslavia. Didn't the Russians kill a bunch of women and children there?

With a force of will, he moved his arm and cast about the floor. A finger brushed cold metal, and he lunged. *The gun.* He grasped it and collapsed on the carpet. Now the rug felt squishy.

Is that blood? Damn, my shoulder aches. Chilly in here. Better call someone. He fished in his pocket. Brought out his phone. It felt slick, slimy. He punched at it. Emergency call.

A *thunk* sounded near his head, and he realized he dropped the phone. *Damn it.* He tried to move his arm, but it was frozen. *Where is that damn thing?*

"Nine-one-one. What is your emergency?" The voice was female, cold, and efficient.

His body was wracked with shivers. "Bullet... Shot... Help..."

"Sir, can you tell me your location?"

In halting words, he recited his address.

The mechanical voice continued. "I'm sending help now, sir. Can you tell me your name?"

A shadow came over his face, and he sensed the gun plucked from his hand. He wanted to fight, but he was frozen in place. Instead, he screamed as something pressed into his shoulder—like a red-hot iron rod sliding into his pectoral muscle. He couldn't stop shivering. A voice spoke, but he couldn't understand it.

That's a Russian accent. He's here.

Damn you, Russian. Damn you.

More words. What's he saying? Blood loss? I'm going to be okay?

Four words were spoken loudly in his ear. Four words that cut through the pain and fog.

"I'm Belarusian, you fuck."

———

Everyone has a plan until they're punched in the face.

This time, it wasn't one of his father's many pithy sayings, but a quote from Mike Tyson, the boxer, someone Max read about during his American indoctrination training at the KGB.

The one person who knew where Kate was now lay on the floor bleeding out from a gunshot wound and was passing in and out of consciousness. The local police were on their way, and even if he got the general out of the house, the mess left behind would cause a huge manhunt. All he had done so far was staunch the man's wound with a cloth napkin.

The house reeked of gunpowder. A large pool of blood sat under the general's inert body. *I need some luck to get out of this mess.*

Speed was his friend. He shoved his gun into the pocket of his track suit and the general's gun into his waistband and used the silk carpet to make a burrito with the wounded man in the center. He dragged the carpet through the kitchen, into the mud room, and down the three steps of the outdoor stoop until the carpet hit the concrete patio.

Hearing sirens in the distance, he sprinted to his car, jumped in and drove without lights to the general's house. Tires squealed on concrete as he jammed on the brakes in the driveway.

Jumping from the car, he squatted next to the burrito and wiggled both hands under the carpet. Using his leg muscles, he lifted the general and the carpet into the trunk. Hoping he hadn't dropped anything in the general's house, he jumped behind the wheel and hit the gas.

Speeding southeast, he stuck to the speed limit, and made a series of right and left turns to take him back to the Red Roof Inn. There he backed into the spot next to the white van. A mother pulling a cartful of suitcases with a youngster in tow was making her way to the hotel's back door. He waited until she entered the building before getting out and opening the sedan's trunk and the van's rear doors. With a heave, he moved the general, still rolled in the carpet, from the trunk to the rear of the van. Another heave got him in the coffin. Blood was everywhere—in the trunk of the car, on the sides of the wooden coffin, and on his hands, forearms, and shirt. He ignored the mess, unrolled the carpet, and felt the general's neck. *Don't die on me, damn it.*

Nothing.

Fumbling along Brown's neck, he found it. A pulse. Faint, but it was there.

He used duct tape to hold the blood-soaked napkin to the general's shoulder and put the lid on the coffin. No time to clean any of the blood. After a cursory wipe of the sedan's interior to remove any fingerprints, he shut the trunk, banged the van's doors closed, and jumped into the driver's seat.

As he wove through city streets to the entrance to the Baltimore-Washington Parkway, a string of vehicles with flashing blue and red lights passed by in the opposite direction. While he dug out his Blackphone, he controlled his breathing.

Baxter is not going to be happy.

FORTY

Fort Meade, Maryland

"You've certainly got yourself into a bloody shitpouch." Baxter's voice was a low growl.

"Bloody is the operative word. These things happen. Are you going to help me or not?"

The silence on the line was so long that Max checked the screen on his phone to make sure the call was still connected. When Baxter spoke, his voice was frosty. "These things don't happen in MI6."

"That explains a few things. Decide. If you're not—"

"One condition."

Oh, boy. Time to pay the piper. By now he was in East Riverdale on his way to downtown Washington, DC. All he passed were signs for liquor stores and strip bars.

"Anything. Tell me," Max said.

"I want to be part of the interrogation."

"Of course."

"And another thing."

Uh-oh. "What?"

"I want you to apologize for burning down my office."

You've got to be kidding. "Baxter, I've got a situation here. This hardly calls for—"

"Okay. Good luck." The transmission ended.

Fuck. Max gaped at his phone.

Outside the van window, the neighborhood was worse. Groups of men in oversized down jackets gathered around fires burning in fifty-five gallon drums. A homeless man pushed a shopping cart laden with duffle bags. A lowrider slid by, the men inside watching his van. *The general will die without medical help, and whatever knowledge he has will die with him.* He redialed Baxter's number.

It was answered after several long rings. "I'm listening," Baxter said.

Max swallowed hard. "I'm sorry for burning down your office."

No response from Baxter.

"Are you there?"

"That didn't sound very sincere."

"For Chrissake, Callum. I'm sorry, okay? I'm sorry I burned down your office. At least I paid for a new one."

Several seconds ticked by until Baxter cleared his throat. "What do you need?"

———

Staying under the speed limit, he made his way through the dark and wet city streets past homeless drunks and by hookers in fur jackets open to reveal too much. More than once he held his breath as a DC police cruiser roared by, its red and blue lights blazing.

Max approached his destination from Connecticut Ave

NW, turned into an alleyway, and backed the van close to the rear door of the Russia House restaurant. Stepping from the van, he scanned the alley to make sure no one was around and glanced at the CCTV camera to confirm one of Rodion's men had spray-painted the lens black. *Done.*

From half a block away came the sounds of a boisterous crowd at McClellan's Retreat, a bar named after a civil war general. Max rapped on the rear metal door of the Russia House before opening the van. A dim yellow light spilled into the dark alley as one of Rodion's men stepped out.

Headlights appeared from around the corner, and the MI6 SUV pulled up next to the van. Max put his hand on the butt of his pistol but relaxed when Baxter stepped out and was followed by another man Max didn't recognize.

He addressed Rodion's henchman, an old Russian named Pavel, who had a craggy face and the haircut of a man who spent most of his life in the military. "Quick, help me get this coffin inside and downstairs."

The two men slid the wooden box from the van and carried it through the door and wrestled it down the narrow stairs into the dank cellar where they set it on the dirt floor. Max flicked on an overhead light and swept cooking utensils, pots, and food stuffs from a long prep table. With a heave, Max and Pavel lifted the general from the coffin onto the metal surface. Max was fixing Brown's ankles and wrists to the metal table legs with plastic zip ties when Baxter and the second man entered the basement.

"Oh, bloody hell," Baxter exclaimed when he saw the unconscious general with his shirt saturated with blood. The second man, pudgy with tiny round glasses and a balding head, snapped on latex gloves, extracted a pair of safety shears from a brown leather bag, and cut away the general's shirt.

Mildew, rotting vegetables, and raw onions pervaded the room. Cockroaches scurried underfoot, and rats scattered to the dark corners. Max stooped to keep from hitting his head on the ceiling's cross beams. Boxes of vegetables were stacked in a pile, and a cobweb-covered wine rack took up the opposite wall.

After removing the general's shirt, the doctor poked and prodded around the wound while muttering to himself in a British accent. "Lost a lot of blood. Bullet hole in the upper pectoralis major just below the clavicle and two millimeters from the deltoid. Missed the bone. Help me roll him."

Max helped the doctor roll the general on his side to examine his back. "This man can't die, doctor. It's important."

"No exit wound." The doctor held out his hand. "Forceps."

Baxter fished in the bag for the surgical tool as the doctor poured antiseptic into the bullet hole and felt around inside the wound. "Bullet lodged in the subscapularis."

Baxter slapped the tool in the doctor's waiting hand. The doc held the wound open with one hand while reaching into the man's shoulder muscle with the forceps.

Heavy footsteps sounded on the wooden stairs and Rodion appeared, his girth taking up the rest of the available space in the tiny basement. "What the hell, Mikhail? Who are all these people?" He leaned over to see what the doctor was doing and let out a string of curses in Russian. "This wasn't the deal, Mikhail."

"These things happen." Max shrugged as the doctor extracted the slug from the general's shoulder.

"His favorite phrase," Baxter mumbled.

The doctor dropped the tiny hunk of metal in Max's

hand, and he rinsed it off in the sink before examining it and slipping it into his pants pocket.

Rodion pounded his fist on a wooden pillar. "Who are these people, Mikhail?"

Max reached into his pocket and rolled the slug between his fingers. "Don't worry. They're MI6."

Raw Russian expletives flew from Rodion's mouth before he switched to English. "Just what I needed. A dead body and British intelligence in my basement."

Max smiled at his friend. "He's not dead. Yet, anyway. Got any of that famous borscht of yours?"

The doctor waved a finger in the air. "Bottled water, too. Quickly."

With an angry grunt, Rodion signaled to Pavel, who squeezed around his boss and went up the stairs.

FORTY-ONE

Washington, DC

They did everything they could for the general, and now it was a waiting game. A check of the dog tags around his neck determined his blood type as AB-positive, a very rare type, and Baxter coordinated with his team at the British Embassy to obtain as many units as possible. Meanwhile, the doctor set up an IV with fluids, and without anything else to do, he went home.

While they waited, Max filled Baxter in on the operation.

When the narrative was done, Baxter shook his head. "Foolish. How did he know you were there?"

Max shrugged. "I must have missed some kind of motion sensor or surveillance cameras. I was moving too fast. He knows where Kate is. I didn't have the luxury of time."

A grunt from Baxter. "Next time you're rushing around, you might not be so lucky. Maybe this is a lesson?"

Max turned his back on Baxter, went up the steps, found a pan of cold borscht in the cooler, and returned to the basement.

As the minutes ticked by, Max devoured the beet root and beef stew while Baxter tugged on his goatee. When Harris arrived with two units of blood, Max set up the IV. After the first bag slowly emptied, Max switched bags and pulled out a pack of cigarettes.

Baxter put his hand on Max's wrist. "Don't. The man is fighting for his life, for God's sake."

Max put the pack away. "Where's Cindy?"

"Embassy. Sleeping on a cot."

As the second bag slowly drained, Max flicked the lid of his lighter open and shut, each time with a soft *ping*. "I say we wake him and get on with it. You sure you want to be here for this?"

Baxter moved into the shadows and out of the general's line of sight. "Don't let him turn around."

"Okay. You're going to see some things you're not going to like. Stay there and keep your mouth shut. And hold this." He handed Baxter his Blackphone, which he set to record an audio file of the interrogation. Rummaging in a sack, he removed a roll of duct tape and a packet of smelling salts. After slapping a piece of the tape over his captive's eyes, he snapped the tube of ammonia and waved it under the general's nose.

The man came to and started coughing.

Leaning over the table, Max blocked out the light. "Hello, sir."

Brown struggled, his veins popping out of his neck, until he realized he was secured to the cold table. "Where am I?"

"You're in Russia, general."

Max used the shears to snip along both of the general's

pant legs. "You've been shot, and you've lost a lot of blood. You're not out of the woods, so take it easy." With a jerk, he yanked the general's pants from his legs and cut through his boxer shorts. A minute later, the general was naked. His pink and hairy chest heaved, and his skin was puckered from the cold.

Through gritted teeth, the general growled. "You're making a huge mistake. Do you know who I am?"

Chuckling, Max said, "I know exactly who you are. And you know who I am, so let's get down to business."

General Brown's teeth chattered while Max filled a pot with water from the industrial sink in the corner and poured it on the man's chest, letting it drip onto the metal table. "Chilly down here, isn't it?"

General Brown sputtered. "What...the..."

Max put his face over his captive's. "Here's the situation. You have information I want. In exchange for that information, I'm willing to let you live. If you insist on delaying or holding out or deceiving me, I'll kill you and bury your body where no one will find it. Do we understand each other?"

The general's lips quivered. "What...information?"

Max drizzled more of the cold water along the man's torso. "You know where a friend of mine is. A friend I want to find very badly."

Brown grimaced. "What makes...you think—"

A wall of water hit the general when Max tossed a full pot of ice water at his face. "No time for games. You're slowly dying from shock. You need a hospital. The longer this goes on, the longer it takes us to get you there."

After spitting and shaking the water from his head, Brown set his jaw. "You're going to kill me anyway."

"That's where you're wrong. I can always use a contact

in the United States Cyber Command, sir. We can work out a deal where you walk out of here." Max filled the pot again.

As the general's body shook uncontrollably, Max dribbled some water on the general's chest. "You've lost a lot of blood. Shock can kill, you know."

"I'm not telling you anything."

Max splashed water on the man's genitals and went back to the sink for more water before setting the pot on the table next to his captive's elbow. "By now your pulse is weak and rapid, and you're thirsty. You're feeling confused. Soon you will black out."

The general's lips were blue as he quaked uncontrollably on the table.

Max dumped the water on his face and chest and refilled the pot.

The general coughed. "You might...as well...kill me."

"Why do you want me dead so badly?" Max asked.

Brown whipped his head back and forth.

Leaving the general shivering on the cold metal table, Max returned with a blanket. He ripped the tape from Brown's eyes and waved the covering at the general. "All you need to do is tell me where she is and you'll get the blanket instead of the water."

The general tightened his jaw and stared at the ceiling.

Max stepped into a back room and returned with a bag of ice. He ripped it open and poured some of the cubes on the general's skin. Max waved the blanket as the table creaked underneath the Brown's trembling body.

It took another thirty minutes of alternating water and ice treatments before the general opened up and gave them Kate Shaw's exact location. No amount of threats or continued torture revealed the identity of Kate Shaw's captors.

He must not know.

Max fired the audio file off to Goshawk and did a quick Google Map search on his phone to see the location. In the dark shadows in the back of the room, Baxter typed furiously on his phone.

Shoving the Blackphone into his pocket, Max placed the pot on the shelf. "You work for us now, General Brown. Next time I call, you answer or we'll leak this audio file to the FBI. Got it?"

After injecting the general with a powerful sedative, Max dried him off, wrapped him in the blanket, and headed up the stairs to find Pavel.

———

When he reached the top of the stairs, the door to the kitchen was open a crack. He stepped into the kitchen to find Pavel's body lying on the tile floor, a crimson pool of blood spread under him. Max checked for a pulse. Nothing.

Drawing his pistol, he ran to the door leading into the alley and toed it open while holding the gun in both hands. The alley was empty except for the white van.

The muted roar of a V-twin engine reverberated in the darkness. Max ran toward the sound and emerged from the alley onto a street next to a sign that read *Embassy of Costa Rica*. A single red taillight raced away from him. A second later the motorcycle turned and disappeared. The roar faded into the distance.

FORTY-TWO

Unknown Location

I'm suffocating. Are these hot towels around me? This is one of those herbal wraps like at the spa, isn't it?

My arms won't move. Am I tied up?

It doesn't smell like a herbal wrap. All floral and medicinal. Instead she detected odors of sweat and something that reminded her of hibiscus.

Another effort resulted in the shift of a leg. Her calf felt something soft. *Is this a new outfit? It's soft, like I used to wear to yoga.*

Gradually she opened her eyes. At first, everything was fuzzy. *Nothing new there.* After a moment things cleared. A pale whitewashed adobe ceiling was overhead. The blades of a ceiling fan turned lazily. *Can someone turn that up? I'm suffocating here.*

A shift of her ankle moved the sheet and exposed her to the thick air before she rolled onto her side. A washbasin sat in the corner next to a white porcelain toilet.

This is a new room. The furniture is strange, but looks nice. Mediterranean, maybe? Worn stone flooring. A plush daybed in muted earth tones. Some ambient lighting. Is that music coming from hidden speakers or is it in my head? Must be a dream. Or I'm finally dead. Please let that be it.

A struggle to prop herself up on two elbows. A swing of her legs. *Wait. I'm going to throw up.* The feeling passed.

Her feet touched a plush white rug where a pair of sandals awaited. She slipped into them. *Aah. Soft and fuzzy.*

Where's the switch to make the fan turn faster? The stucco walls were blank except for a pair of watercolors showing scenes of ocean and sand. *Remind me to ask management about that.*

The thought made her giggle, but no sound came out. With an effort, she used the headboard to help her stand before letting go to test her balance.

If I fall, please let me fall on the bed.

The room turned around her, but she remained standing. Eventually the furniture stopped moving. When she was confident of her footing, she took a step. And another. Five more steps were taken before she settled on the commode, the cotton pants around her ankles. *So this is what it feels like to use a toilet. Aah soft tissue.* She stood and flushed.

Let's take an inventory. Was there a bottle of wine from the previous night? Or three? My tongue feels like it's covered in fur. She filled a small plastic cup with water and drank it down. *Better, but not great.* She rubbed her temples with her fingertips. *This cotton in my head won't go away.* She flexed her bicep. *Great, just great. No muscle left, all sponge.*

A splash of water on her face sent a chill through her, so

she splashed again. And again. *Mm-hmm... This towel smells like spring flowers.*

Thank you to whoever decided against putting a mirror over the washbasin. One step at a time. I don't need to see the damage.

An arched wooden door was inset into the far wall. She padded over and tried the latch. *Locked. No surprise there.*

A series of window vents were spaced out near the ceiling and the fan stirred a breeze through the room. *Wait a minute. That's a seagull. There's an ocean out there.*

Another scan of the room. *Nothing I can use as a weapon. Well, that's random. Where did that come from? What about this glass pitcher? I'll just keep it here in easy reach.*

A bookcase of ratty paperbacks was in a corner. She selected the classic from Harper Lee. *I always enjoyed this book.* She settled in to read on the couch with her feet curled under her.

———

A gentle knock sounded at the door and her calm evaporated when a series of hazy visions rushed back at her. The betrayal by Bill, her father's oldest and closest friend. The snatch in the park by the CIA men in the blue suits. The incarceration in the military prison where she was mistreated by her handlers. The long interrogations where they pulled everything out of her mind. The abduction by the commandos dressed in black. More interrogations and torture until she spiraled into darkness and stopped eating and talking. *But I don't care anymore. There's nothing left. So why do they keep at it? Just kill me. Death has to be better than this.*

When the door opened, the book dropped from her hand. Retrieving it, she knocked over the empty water pitcher, which shattered on the stone floor. *Damn it.*

A Caucasian man wearing a pressed white Oxford shirt stepped through the door wearing a pair of neat rimless spectacles and clutching a worn leather portfolio. His face was upturned so he looked through the bottoms of his glasses. Two granite-faced guards positioned themselves on either side of the door.

Who is this guy? What happened to that fat man who stank like rancid meat? The one who won't leave my dreams alone.

The newcomer sat, opened his leather portfolio, and crossed a tassel-loafered foot over one knee while studying her through the bottoms of his glasses. "Hello, Kate. How are you feeling today, hmm?"

She retrieved the book from the floor and set it next to her.

A slow nod from the man. "I see."

Something about this guy's voice. Nasal, but in charge. The boss. Is that a hint of German? Or Austrian? I've talked to this man before. But where?

The man consulted his notepad. "Let's go back a few years to when you were CIA station chief in Moscow. Do you remember the time?"

Visions of her younger self floated through her subconsciousness. She was energetic, her career was on the rise, and her side was winning the cold war. Gorbachev's reforms were taking hold while Yeltsin was drinking and losing his grip. The Soviet Union was crumbling, and the wall was about to fall. *Yes, I remember.*

She glanced at the book on the couch next to her. *What page was I on? Damn it.*

The interrogator smiled. "Recall a man you worked with. A Russian—no, a Belarusian, hmm? A senior man in the Belarusian KGB. Big bear of a fellow. You recruited him as an asset. He provided you with years of intel on the Russians."

The craggy face of Andrei Asimov materialized in her mind. Hair wild and unkempt, lips full and red, skin weathered gray. Hard eyes that saw everything, and hands that could rip a phone book in half. Disillusioned with the promise of communism. *I got a lot of information out of him, didn't I? I was on top of my game.*

The interrogator nodded and beamed. "Good, good. I see recognition in your face. We know he provided you a lot of intel over the years. Information that helped dissolve the Soviet Union. But he also entrusted you with some of his personal secrets. Something classified that was important to him. Information about his personal war with a group known as the Russian petroleum council. Ring a bell, hmm?"

I'd like to help. But this means nothing. Nothing. I'm empty. She shook her head.

The man scribbled something on his pad before removing a watch from his pocket. It was the old-fashioned kind with a chain like men used to carry in a vest pocket. Light glinted from its etched gold surface. Leaning his elbows on his knees, the man dangled the watch in front of her. "We're going to get into the depths of your mind, Kate, just like before, hmm? All you have to do is follow the watch and listen to my voice."

The door opened, and a man dressed in a suit made for the tropics walked in holding a panama hat. He leaned against the wall. Her eyes left the moving watch and inspected the man's face.

Hey, I know you. Hello... Wait, what's your name? And what are you doing here?

The man with the watch snapped his fingers and directed her to look at the swinging timepiece, which she did.

No, I don't want to look at that. Can't help it. Damn it.

FORTY-THREE

Salzburg, Austria

Whenever, Nikita Ivanov went out in public, he was forced to drag along a phalanx of security. Long ago, he made a life choice that prevented him from enjoying restaurants, cafes, cinema, theater, and other activities like the general public. Or more accurately, the decision was made for him. It was his heritage, his lineage, that forced him into this life. A life of controlled celibacy from all life's enjoyments. And so he maintained a monk-like discipline over his natural urges. There was too much at stake for it to be any other way.

So it was with mild trepidation that he watched the streets of his beloved Salzburg speed by through the thick tinted windows of his limousine. Ahead of his car and behind it came his Land Rovers bristling with bodyguards. They sped down the 155 until the Salzach River came into view, crossed over the wide body of water, and exited into the Altstadt—Old City—where they ground to a halt in heavy traffic. Soon, he'd have to leave the vehicle and proceed by foot through several pedestrian streets to his meeting.

To distract himself, he reviewed what he knew about his killer for hire. Disturbingly, little was known. Born in China and orphaned at birth, she floundered through several institutions until disappearing from the system at age eight. She reappeared three years ago after the deaths of four highly placed Japanese Yakuza bosses. The Japanese media caught wind of the killing spree, linked all four deaths, and dubbed the murderer The Sushi Killer because all four slayings took place in sushi restaurants local to the boss's neighborhoods. Of course, the Japanese authorities never identified the killer.

Ivanov's team established contact. Since then, she had performed several jobs for him, all successful, and all for vast sums of money. She was a pain in the ass—impetuous, rash, and prone to violence—but deadly effective and worth every penny.

After her fight with Magnus, Kira refused to meet him in private. Instead, she picked a small church in a tourist section of Salzburg. Surrounded by three of his men, Ivanov made his way down a pedestrian mall and into the empty church.

"You're late. And leave those Neanderthals outside." Her husky voice came from the shadows near a rack of prayer votives.

Ivanov signaled his men to wait by the door. "Discourage anyone from coming inside."

The church was small and empty. Five prayer candles were lit causing shadows to flicker around the nave, but otherwise the lights were off.

"Take a seat on the front pew."

Ivanov bristled but did as he was instructed. "Why all the theatrics?"

"Why do you think?"

"Still angry about the Magnus thing, I see."

"Angry is the wrong word."

She was a tiny silhouette in the shadows, one hand playing with her shoulder-length hair.

Crossing one leg over the other, Ivanov put his arm along the back of the pew. "You should thank me for letting you get it out of your system."

"Could have gone either way."

"It didn't, so let it go. What do you have for me?"

"Asimov found Kate Shaw."

The news jolted him to his feet. He took a step with his arms outstretched. "And?"

"Don't come any closer."

"You wouldn't kill your golden goose, Kira."

"Try me."

"Damn it. Enough with the games." He took another step.

"I'm serious. There's a pistol pointed at your stomach. Stay the fuck over there."

He froze. "Fine. Where is she?"

She told him.

By the time Ivanov strode from the church with a bounce in his step, they had agreed to the bones of a plan.

FORTY-FOUR

Somewhere in Bavaria

Kidnapping a Russian oligarch is not easy. Logistics for the operation took weeks and required Ivanov's small team to utilize one of their pre-canned plans called Case White, named after the Nazi's fourth enemy offensive against Yugoslavia during World War II. The target's name was Andrey Pavlova, and he was one of the Russian president's closest cronies, number three on Ivanov's council, and the CEO of Russia's largest oil and gas conglomerate. The snatch had to look like it was carried out by a lone individual, and later, when the body washed ashore, the killing had to look like the work of a highly effective assassin.

Ivanov's team took advantage of Pavlova's trip to Munich where the CEO attended a summit on the proposed expansion of a natural gas pipeline from Russia, through the Baltic sea, to the shores of Germany. On the second night of the conference, several of Pavlova's bodyguards were mysteriously stricken with incapacitating bowel cramps and diarrhea. In the ensuing chaos, a gunman entered the hotel and killed the three remaining security personnel and a prostitute using a silenced .22 caliber pistol. Pavlova was drugged, bound, gagged, and snuck down the service elevator in a laundry cart to a loading dock, after which he disappeared into the Munich night. Later, German authorities found a keycard belonging to a housekeeping supervisor in the dumpster and discovered that all the hotel's security footage from that night was missing.

"Hello, Andrey."

Ivanov strode across the blue mat, now cleaned of Magnus's blood, and regarded his captive. The billionaire sat naked, his pink skin quaking, strapped to a device called the Iron Chair. A gag made from duct tape prevented him from speaking. Felix stood to the left and behind Pavlova. Otherwise the room was empty.

"Welcome to my training room. I trust my colleague here has explained why you're here."

Pavlova's eyes were wide, and blood trickled down the backs of his legs and made little pools at the chair's feet.

"Are you aware of how these contraptions work? You can nod or shake your head. I have no stomach for screaming, so we'll leave the gag on."

The billionaire shook his head sending drops of sweat flying onto the blue mat.

"Right. Not many people do. It's called an Iron Chair, or in some circles, a Chinese Torture Chair. As you can feel, the five hundred little spikes you're sitting on are designed to only slightly puncture the skin. Even a man of your... ahem...girth. Those metal bars across your thighs and chest can be tightened, which will push your body into the spikes." When Ivanov walked around his captive, the astringent odor of urine assaulted him. "The diabolical thing about this device, Andrey, is that the spikes will keep the wounds cauterized until you're released from the chair. At which time, you'll bleed to death."

Pavlova screamed through the gag, making a sound like a horse stuck in a barbed wire fence. Felix slapped him and the man went silent.

"Now, now, Andrey. There's no need to scream. If you just tell me the truth, I can spare you the pain. Are you with me?"

Emphatic nodding.

"Great. My team uncovered digital voice transmissions between you and Ruslan Stepanov that paint you in a negative light. Do you know what I'm referring to?"

The billionaire nodded his head and tried to talk through the gag.

Ivanov signaled to Felix, and the utility man ripped the tape from Pavlova's mouth.

"Yes, yes," Pavlova panted. "Anything. I'll tell you anything. Just don't—"

Another signal and Felix replaced the tape and turned a series of cranks on the back of the chair. Pavlova screamed through the cloth in his mouth.

Ivanov grimaced as Felix turned the crank a second time, tightening the bars across the captive's thighs. Blood ran in rivulets down his legs. When the screaming subsided, Ivanov continued. "You're probably wondering why we did that. It's important for you to have a good understanding of how the Iron Chair works. It will ensure we're as efficient as we can be, no?"

The captive nodded his head hard enough to send his hair, soaked with sweat, flying.

"Good. Now that we're done with the demonstration, we can get down to business."

Felix removed the gag as Pavlova sobbed and his chest heaved.

"Ruslan wants you dead," Pavlova sputtered. "He wants the chancellorship. He won't stop until he's in charge."

"I know that, Andrey." Ivanov's arms were crossed and his feet planted. "What I don't know is how he intends to accomplish it. What can you tell me about that?"

"I...I...I don't know."

Ivanov signaled to Felix, who walked behind the chair.

"Wait! Wait...Don't...I'll tell you what I know."

With a motion of his hand, Felix stopped.

Catching his breath, Andrey Pavlova hung his head. "He's going to have Fedorov arrest you, and they're going to jail you in Russia on tax evasion. While you're in jail, they're going to have you killed."

Right out of the Russian president's playbook. Ivanov paced. "And how are they going to get me?"

"On your way to next month's Komissariat."

The location of the Komissariat for the Preservation of State's monthly meetings was a closely guarded secret, as was Ivanov's route to the meeting venue. Even as a minister of the Komissariat, Ivanov was forced to take draconian measures to preserve secrecy. If Ruslan planned to take him down en route to the meeting, it meant Ruslan had inside help from the Komissar himself. Which meant the Komissar wanted Ivanov off the Komissariat for the Preservation of State. No changes were made to the governing structure of the Komissariate or the various sub-councils without the

Komissar's approval. Ivanov stroked his chin and forced himself to remain calm while he paced.

"Felix, get the details." Ivanov stopped with his hand on the doorjamb. "Then toss his body somewhere it will be easily found."

FORTY-FIVE

Over the North Atlantic

"Not good, Max. Not good."

Baxter paced the aisle between the caramel-colored leather seats of the Lear while Max sat cross-legged with a cup of tea. Cindy, as usual, was hunched over her laptop. The MI6 man repeated himself over and over as he strode back and forth and madly yanked his goatee.

Max chuckled. "Is this getting too deep for you?"

Coming to an abrupt halt, Baxter glared at Max. "Let me summarize. We're in a race to find an ex-CIA officer who is held captive against her will alongside the abducted CIA director and another former ex-CIA operative. Your sworn enemies, along with a half dozen intelligence agencies—that we know of—are in race to find these people. We've learned via a video from a dead man that this ex-CIA agent has information hidden in her head that everyone wants. Hidden in her head, for bollock's sake. How is that even possible?"

A shrug from Max. "That dead man is my father. Pretty good source as far as I'm concerned. Isn't this what you wanted?"

Resuming his pacing, Baxter muttered under his breath so Max almost couldn't hear. "And now we're flying to Cyprus, a country the Turks and the Greeks have been fighting over since the seventies."

Max grinned. "Lots of rich Russians there."

Cindy cleared her throat. "I wondered about the hypnotism, so I did some research and called around. According to a guy I talked to at Harvard, it's possible to hide information in someone's brain using simple hypnosis techniques. Retrieving it usually requires a specific trigger phrase."

Baxter harrumphed. "We don't know what this information is, nor do we know how to obtain it. We don't know who is holding them, and we don't know whether they've already obtained the information and have disposed of her. Turns out, none of this knowledge is known by the assistant director of America's cyber warfare military department, who by the way, we just broke about a hundred laws by abducting and torturing. All we know is her location, which, of course, we obtained from a man under extreme duress who might say anything to end the pain."

Max blew on a cup of hot tea before reaching into his pocket to retrieve two round white pills. He tossed them into his mouth and chased it with a gulp. "I know who has her."

The MI6 man stopped pacing and whirled. "You what?"

After another sip, Max looked up. "You heard me."

Slapping the leather seat, the MI6 man took a deep breath. "And?"

Max said nothing.

"Out with it, damn it."

Max shook his head. "I ran a little side operation. It's only a guess."

Baxter sputtered and cursed. "And how long will you keep us in the dark? We have a team we can put on it."

Max shook his head again. "No. Intelligence agencies leak like, how do you say? Sieves? The less people who know the better."

Baxter threw up his hands, stormed down the aisle, and disappeared into the lavatory.

Max's Blackphone buzzed in his pocket. Cindy had helped him connect the device to the Lear's Wi-Fi which ran off a satellite data connection. A message had come in from Goshawk. There was a brief line of text followed by a link.

Cyprus dossier is available.

Max tapped on the link, which opened up a secure browser and prompted him for a password. After supplying the required credentials, a set of files appeared, including a country report on Cyprus. The other files contained a briefing prepared by the CIA on Russian influence over the tiny country and blueprints for the compound where Kate was being held. He began reading through the information.

He glanced up to see Cindy staring at him. As he caught her eye, her blue irises flickered to the right before returning to Max's. He followed her gaze. Baxter had finished in the bathroom and fallen into a chair. His chest moved slowly as he snored gently. When Max looked back at Cindy, her forefinger was up against her lips.

He returned to his reading. A minute later, a floral scent caused him to look up. Cindy was crouched next to him. He tried to hide his Blackphone, but she had already glimpsed the screen. He narrowed his eyes at her.

She jerked her thumb in Baxter's direction and whispered, "Sorry, but something has happened that I think you should know."

Max raised his eyebrows and caught another whiff of her hair as she put her lips next to his ear. Her warm breath on his neck caused a pleasant distraction.

"Callum had me prepare a report of what we learned from Bluefish. He asked me to blur over the details of how we learned the information."

"Okay. Not surprising."

Cindy's lips brushed his ear. "He intends to send the report to C before we land in London."

"But we're not going to—"

Baxter stirred, and as Cindy pulled away, her eyes caught Max's.

They aren't heading to Cyprus. Baxter told the pilot to land in London. A slow burn started at the base of his neck and traveled to his forehead. *Damn it, Baxter.*

The MI6 officer shifted again, and his breathing settled into a soft purr.

After a moment, Cindy touched Max's arm. "He's planning to get Vauxhall Cross to lead up the search for Kate with us in support. He thinks MI6 beating everyone to the punch would be good for Great Britain."

"Why are you telling me this?"

She shrugged. "Not sure, but you can't let on that you know. Otherwise he'll know I told you." She winked at him before sitting back down to hunch over her laptop.

MI6 will screw it up. There will be a leak. Too much red tape. There isn't time. Kate will be dead or compromised by the time they get there. A vision of the disappearing motorcycle taillight crossed his mind, and he rubbed his face with this palm.

He didn't have time to stop in London.

Minutes ticked by as Max considered his options, Baxter's purring the only sound in the cabin. *Only one thing to do.*

Max crouched next to Cindy's chair after checking that Baxter was still asleep.

She looked up. "What are you thinking?"

The glint in her ice-blue eyes twinkled as he explained his plan. "I'm sorry," Max said.

Taking him by surprise, she nodded with a smirk. "I figured as much."

I just got played. But why?

He glared at her before walking down the aisle to where Baxter sat snoring. He jostled the MI6 man's shoulder while simultaneously plucking Baxter's pistol from its shoulder holster and shoving it into his waistband.

Baxter started. "What the—"

Max grabbed him by the front of his Oxford shirt. "Two choices. You can either order this plane to take us to Cyprus, or I can tie you up, stuff you in the lavatory, and hijack the airplane."

Baxter scowled in Cindy's direction.

"Don't look at her." Max yanked on his shirt. "She's got nothing to do with this. What's your choice?"

The MI6 agent shook himself awake. "Don't do this. I'm telling you that we're better off if we prep C and get the full force of MI6 behind us instead of marching into Cyprus with guns blazing."

Tightening his grip on the lapels, Max put his face close to Baxter's. "What's your decision? I'm going to count to three, at which point it will be too late. One..."

"This is the—"

"Two." Max yanked Baxter up and forced him to march

to the back of the plane. "Three." He opened the lavatory door and shoved Baxter in so he stumbled against the toilet. Max frisked him and removed his Blackberry before slamming the door. Using the lavatory's reverse lock, known only to fight attendants and air marshals, he secured the door from the outside. Marching up the aisle, he knocked on the cockpit's door. The copilot stuck his head out.

Max kept his voice low. "Change of plans, boys. Head for LCA." LCA was the airport code for Larnaca International Airport on the island of Cyprus.

With a frown, the copilot tried to look around Max. "Where's Callum?"

"On the phone. Asked me to relay the message."

When the copilot hesitated, Max shifted so Cindy was visible. "LCA, right? Isn't that what Baxter said?"

Cindy looked up from her laptop and grinned at the pilot. "Yup. Cyprus. Thanks, James."

"No problem, ma'am. We'll let you know when we're thirty minutes out."

Max shut the door, sat down next to Cindy, and put his hand on her arm. "Thank you."

"Hope I'm not fired." She laughed before turning her computer, allowing him to see the screen. "We have some planning to do."

"We'll tell him Goshawk figured it out by tracing our flight pattern and messaged me. You'll be fine."

FORTY-SIX

Kokkina, Cyprus

Moving from tree to tree at a fast pace, he disturbed nothing in the thick undergrowth. Dressed in green camouflage, his boots were scuffed and his face was covered with green and black paint. An encrypted comm device was in his ear. Fitted to his tactical cap was a set of night-vision goggles. A leg holster contained a Berretta APX 9mm, and he carried a Heckler & Koch assault rifle. A backpack thumped against his shoulders as he ran.

Gunfire sounded from the other side of the ridge. He picked out three different calibers. Easiest to discern were the high pitch of the AK-47s. The more alarming sound was the sporadic large caliber fire that sounded like a heavy-duty ratchet. He guessed they were 30mm GIAT revolving cannons from attack helicopters. There was also a different caliber signature that sounded like an air defense system. The compound was already under attack. *Am I too late?*

Max vaulted over a downed log and weaved between

saplings and branches as he ran up the hill. Goshawk spoke in his ear, although he dared not reply. She was illicitly patched into the MI6 and CIA communications channels.

Goshawk's voice crackled in his ear. "The US picked up the fighting and are monitoring. They're as baffled as we are about who the attackers are. You should be coming up to a ridge where you can see the battle."

As he crested the outcropping, he saw movement and froze. Pulling a knife from its sheath, he crouched. Just ahead were two sentries, their attention focused on the battle below.

Step by step, Max edged closer until their body odor made his nostrils twitch. Like an apparition, he emerged from his hiding spot and raised the black-bladed knife. He grabbed one guard by the chin from behind, swiped the blade across his neck, and allowed the dying man to sink into the scrub. Pivoting, Max plunged the knife into the second guard's chest in a thrust aimed to miss the sternum. The soldier let out a gurgle as Max eased him to the ground.

A quick frisk of both sentries revealed Turkish cigarettes, two-way radios, and little else. Max helped himself to one of the radios and stuffed the smokes in his pocket before concealing both men in the foliage. After edging east along the ridge, he found a hiding place where he could observe the compound below.

As he surveyed the wide-open area below the ridge, he was surprised at the scale of the attack. The compound took up a crescent-shaped area of land surrounded on three sides by towering mountains and to the north by the Mediterranean Sea. According to Goshawk's intel, the tiny swatch of land was known as Kokkina by the Cypriot Greeks and Erenköy by the Turkish Cypriots. At one time, Kokkina was a military outpost for the Turkish Cypriots but eventually descended into disuse due to the difficulty of getting to the area over land. Someone had recently rejuvenated the enclave into a militarized compound. And now the compound was under attack by parties unknown.

The buildings contained within the walls were rebuilt into a military base. He counted at least three antiaircraft bunkers and three more beachhead fortifications. No roads led in or out of the compound—everything came in by sea—so the facility relied on the jutting cliffs that surrounded it on three sides for rear and flank defenses.

Four Eurocopter Tiger attack helicopters were in the air, their 30mm cannons blazing at targets on the ground. The soldiers in the compound returned fire with the antiaircraft guns and small arms fire. No markings were visible on the attack birds. No evidence of beach landing ships or ground forces.

One of the birds let loose a volley of four missiles, white in color, short in length, that found an antiaircraft installation and exploded making Max's feet shake.

Another bird was hit by antiaircraft fire and spun out of control before the fiery mess hit the water.

A third helicopter launched a set of missiles that found a target on the far side of the compound. As that helicopter banked hard to its right, a flurry of antiaircraft fire caught one of its rear blades and flames erupted on the tail. The injured Tiger peeled off to the west and disappeared behind a mountain ridge. *There must be at least one ship out of sight supporting this attack.*

A Tiger was hit by small arms fire and disappeared into the blackness of the sky over the ocean. The remaining attack bird retreated a moment later, and cheers from the soldiers rang out through the compound below.

His earpiece crackled before Goshawk said, "The CIA

is reporting the attack was repelled. Kind of a big deal. Four helicopters attacking a sovereign country. Who does that?"

Max clicked his comm mic once before picking his way down the slope. If the maps were correct, he would soon reach a sheer cliff. There were three ways off this ridge. One was to go around to the west and follow a well-patrolled trail down to the far side of the compound. A similar trail ran to the east and curved north before switch-backs led down to the water's edge.

After pulling a length of narrow-gauge black nylon rope from his bag and securing one end to a stout tree, he grabbed a rappelling device, called a GriGri, and threaded the line through. Before tossing the free end of the rope over the cliff, he peered out over the chasm. *Nothing there but darkness.* He let go of the line, gave the fixed end a yank, and stepped out over the void holding on to the rappel device handle. He plummeted as fast as he dared while bouncing with his feet off the rock face. The bramble at the bottom of the cliff scratched his bare arms as he landed. After stowing the GriGri and shouldering his assault rifle, he picked his way down the remaining slope to the rear of the compound, where he clicked his mic three times to signal his safe descent.

Goshawk's voice came over his earpiece. "Max, we have a problem."

FORTY-SEVEN

Kokkina, Cyprus

The plan was simple, but not easy. Goshawk's research led her to the Cyprus civil development office archives, where she unearthed old blueprints to the compound. The plans showed a tunnel leading out of the subterranean levels of the main building. The tunnel ran southwest and culminated at the bottom of the cliff, in what was likely an old escape route. The Cyprus civil development office archives hadn't been updated in decades, so there was a chance the old tunnel was sealed off at the entrance or at the exit.

Using a tiny handheld GPS unit, he picked his way through overgrown vegetation that towered over his head and made his way around chunks of concrete with sharp rusty rebar that stuck up at all angles. The walls of the compound were half a klick to the north, and the bitter tang of gunpowder and concrete dust from the battle permeated the air.

Goshawk's warning rang in his ears as he reached the supposed geolocation of the tunnel entrance.

"Max, we have a problem."

He clicked once on the mic.

"My access to the CIA's comm link with MI6 has been cut off. I'm hitting roadblock after roadblock. I'm guessing your friends at MI6 are the reason."

He clicked once and continued his search for the tunnel entrance. Stepping around a chunk of concrete, a shadow moved in his periphery.

He froze.

Someone is out there.

While keeping his right hand on his rifle, he eased his knife out with his left hand.

Come on. Show yourself.

Another minute passed, and nothing moved in the surrounding brush.

The breeze died, leaving the salty scent of the Mediterranean intermingled with the smells of the battle. Another five minutes went by before he eased from his hiding place to circle around the old concrete foundation and broken walls. Nothing indicated a human was recently in the area. No footprints in the sandy ground. No vegetation was disturbed.

As he made concentric circles in the area where the tunnel was indicated by the GPS coordinates, he stepped on something firm and unyielding. Crouching, he used his knife to poke in the sand, hitting something hard just below the surface. Something like metal. With a gloved hand, he brushed aside dirt to reveal a large round metal manhole cover. A broken-down foundation partially hidden by overgrown vegetation surrounded the manhole cover, indicating the portal was once concealed in a building.

Using the knife, he dug around the edge of the round metal cover until he was able to pry it up. Heaving with both hands, he slid it to the side. A dark hole gaped back at him. Flashing his light revealed a sandy floor six feet below. Without hesitation, he dangled his feet into the opening and jumped down before dragging the heavy metal cover over his head, sealing himself inside. Crouching to keep his head from hitting the top of the tunnel and using his night-vision goggles, a grainy green hole extended in the direction of the compound. No marks or fresh footprints were in the sandy floor of the tunnel. He clicked his comm device four times to indicate that he was in the tunnel.

Goshawk's voice sounded worried. "I'm still in the dark, but working on it. Good luck, Max."

As he crouch-walked down the tunnel, he clicked, wondering if the comm's transmissions would end as he traveled farther underground.

No response.

The concrete roof and cinder block walled passageway was narrow, with enough room for only one person. A five-minute crouch-walk took him to the end of the tunnel, where he found a rusted metal door with a marine hatch. The latch was rusted and corroded, and the wheel wouldn't budge. Using an aerosol canister from his pack, he applied a liberal amount of the chemical to the rusted seal and rested a minute. A single click on the mic resulted in silence.

He tried the hatch handle and was able to wiggle it but not spin it open, so he sprayed more of the lubricant on the rusty handle and waited. It took three applications of the penetrating oil before the lock spun freely. Shouldering the rifle, he teased the door open and peered through the crack.

FORTY-EIGHT

Kokkina, Cyprus

Quiet darkness greeted him on the other side of the portal. His green-lit night-vision goggles illuminated a cramped room filled with boxes and rickety shelving holding a jumble of spare mechanical parts. A pulsing hum sounded beyond the walls and the floor vibrated under his feet. Moving fast, he stepped through the storeroom, rifle held up, and touched the door open a half inch.

A hallway stretched in both directions. He crept through a series of empty corridors and vestibules before reaching a set of concrete stairs. He paused while standing in a ragged cutout in the cinderblock wall. Heavy footsteps came from behind him, and he brought the rifle up in time to see two men appear.

They wore black tactical uniforms, sidearms in holsters, and carried a large box between them. They talked in halting English with some kind of European accent, and the load caused the men to stagger. Max stepped from the cutout, fired twice, shifted, and fired twice again, his suppressed rifle dulling the loud pops. The two men crumpled to the ground, and the box hit the concrete floor with a crash.

He sprang up two flights of stairs and pushed his way through a door into a corridor with rows of doors along each side. Here the floor was free of debris. His memory of the floorplans indicated this was a barracks. He pressed himself into an inset doorway to watch and listen. Somewhere above was raucous shouting and pounding feet. Yelling, the bark of an order, and more feet. He peeled from his spot to the stairwell, where he bounded up to the next level.

Where is that damn cell block?

Dim lights shone from bulbs on a cord spaced along the wall and held up with nails. Max balanced the night-vision goggles on his cap and blinked his eyes against the brightness. His shoes were quiet as he crept down the hallway.

Voices came from somewhere ahead, and Max froze before he backed into a corridor that branched to his left. He took a knee and kept watching the oncoming passage.

Two men appeared, both in torn and dirty black tactical uniforms. Each wore a black cap with an insignia he didn't recognize. One gestured wildly while they marched. Max fired four times, and both men fell. He rushed to the bodies and patted them down. The men had swarthy skin, black facial stubble, and black eyes. Nothing was on them other than radios, pistols, and cigarettes.

A sound like a kicked pebble came from behind him. He whirled, rifle ready, but the hallway was empty. Creeping toward the noise, he kept his finger tight on the trigger.

Nothing again. Must have been a rat.

After hustling down the hall, he came to a stout metal

door. The handle hung free, like someone with great strength wrenched it from its fastenings but left it hanging by a single screw. The deadbolt, however, looked shiny and new. A narrow window at eye level was reinforced with wires crisscrossing the center. Max put his ear to the door for a moment. *Nothing.* He peeked through the window.

A long room stretched away from the door, illuminated by a string of bulbs. On the room's far side was a single cell with thick bars and a locked door.

The cell was empty.

From his angle of view, only a sliver of the room was visible. The door didn't budge when he pushed.

Drizzling water from his canteen on a handkerchief, he tied the cloth around his face to cover his nose and mouth. From his backpack, he removed a small metal box with a magnet on one side and affixed the box to the metal door next to the new deadbolt. With a flick, he activated a switch on the box, stood back, and covered his ears.

Knock, knock, here I come.

A crackle was followed by a loud pop, and a cloud of smoke wafted from the door. He pulled the trigger on a smoke bomb canister and rolled it through the open doorway. Rifle up, he sprinted for the opening and stepped to his left when he entered the room. Smoke billowed from the smoke bomb filling the space with a gray cloud. He scanned the room with the rifle held to his cheek, his finger tense on the trigger.

Through the smoke came the flash of a black shadow. He fired twice. Shots careened past his shoulder followed by the loud pop of a 9mm pistol before a thud and a clatter sounded through the smoke. Three steps, and he almost stumbled over a black-uniformed soldier laying on the concrete, a trickle of blood on his chin.

From the swirling smoke came a familiar voice. Weak, but distinctive. "There's one more."

Max swung the rifle to his left and caught the silhouette of a dark figure moving through the swirling smoke. He squeezed the trigger twice, and the form went down. Stepping to the wall, he spun slowly. Nothing moved in the swirling smoke.

As the cloud dissipated, the room became clear. Along one wall was a table and two wooden chairs with a deck of cards and a full ashtray. There were six cells, each set into the wall, and each fronted by a set of round bars.

The voice came again, feeble and dry. "Over here."

Rifle up, Max walked through the smoke in the direction of the voice. A tall, thin figure materialized behind a set of bars. Wearing ragged green cargo pants, a pair of scuffed cowboy boots, and a dirty white T-shirt covered in blood, was Spencer White.

The former CIA black-ops man gripped the bars. "Took you long enough."

Max chuckled. "Stand back."

Spencer crouched in the cell's corner while Max attached another charge to the cell's locking mechanism. A second later, a crack sounded and the door swung free. Max handed his old friend the silenced Beretta. "You okay?"

"I'll survive. Lucky for me, they had other fish to fry."

"Where's Kate?"

Spencer's brow narrowed. "Haven't seen her." Gesturing with the gun, Spencer said, "The CIA director is over there."

"Okay. Watch the door."

The smoke swirled as Max walked across the room to the opposite cell. Sitting on a soiled and limp mattress was a thin woman, her blond curls matted with blood, and her face crusted with dirt. Her clothing was ripped and soiled, but her blue eyes were bright.

As Max approached, she stood, wavered, and held on to the bars for support. "Well, well. If it isn't the world-famous Max Austin. Or should I call you Mikhail Asimov?"

Max spit on the ground.

The director put her face close to the bars. "If by some miracle you have a way out of this godforsaken prison, I assume you know the kind of honors that would come your way."

He put his finger on the rifle's trigger. "Where's Kate Shaw?"

Montgomery chortled. "Honey, I have no idea. I haven't seen that woman in weeks."

Max glanced at the door where Spencer stood with the pistol gripped in two hands. "There's not a lot of time. We get discovered down here, we're toast. I need answers, and quick."

Montgomery shrugged. "Ask away."

"Why did you submarine Kate's career?"

Looking surprised, Montgomery backed away from the bars. "Why—"

"Answer the question."

"She was too old-fashioned in her approach. The CIA needed new blood, new thinking. Drones are more effective than on-the-ground—"

"Bullshit. What's the real reason?"

The director hesitated.

Max turned his back to her. "Let's go, Spence."

"Wait. Don't leave me here." The director's voice cracked as she gripped the bars with tiny fists.

Halfway to the door, he turned. "So?"

She sighed, and her eyes searched the ground. "I'm dead if I stay here. I'm dead if I talk too much."

Again, Max turned. "Let's go."

"Wait. She was too close to you."

Max spun. "How do you mean?"

"We didn't want to be seen working with you, hiding you, giving you a home. The CIA. I had a deal with Ivanov—"

"Nikita Ivanov? The head of the consortium?"

The director nodded.

Max took a step. "What kind of deal?"

Silence overcame the room as she looked away. Something crashed to the floor over their heads.

"What kind of deal, damn it?"

Another big sigh. "My career is over anyway," she mumbled. "We had to force you out of protective custody so the consortium could get to you. And in return..."

The truth hit Max hard in the chest. *Was Kate's pain and suffering his fault?* "In return for what?"

Another big breath. "The consortium was supposed to pass us intel on the Russian's spying on US soil. Ivanov was to provide intelligence about how the Russian president influenced elections, spread false information over social channels, and details about their cyber warfare capabilities..."

Her voice faded as he stopped listening. *Kate's life is at stake because of me. She was snatched because she took me in and gave me protection. This is all my fault.*

Montgomery gripped the bars tighter. "Even after we cut you and Kate loose, we got no valuable intel from the consortium. Ivanov is a fucker. I don't trust him any farther than I can throw him."

Another crash from above startled Max. "But we were cut loose. You didn't have to take her into custody."

The director of the CIA nodded. "We nabbed her once we uncovered the fact that she knew information about the consortium. If we got to that information first, it would give us leverage over Ivanov and the consortium. Leverage we need to make him pay up on his debt to us." She leaned her forehead on the bars.

"So what did you learn? You interrogated her for weeks."

Montgomery slowly lifted her head, her eyes placid.

An overwhelming urge to grab her by the throat and wring her neck consumed him. He moved so he was close enough to grab her through the bars. "Tell me, damn it. Tell me, or I swear I'll kill you myself."

She stumbled back, out of his reach. "Nothing."

"What? What do you mean?"

"Zilch! Nada." She curled her hands into fists and shook them. "We got nothing out of her. It's bullshit. No one could withstand what we put her through. She knows nothing."

I don't believe it. Something isn't right. There has to be more. "So who snatched Kate from your custody?"

She released her fists and shrugged. "No clue. Could be any of a number of interested parties. It's not Ivanov, though, I'll tell you that. He's steaming mad and scared as hell that she'll end up in the wrong hands."

"Who are the wrong hands? What's he scared of?"

She rolled her eyes. "You don't know much, do you?"

Spencer cleared his throat. "We need to go."

Max raised an index finger at him. "So why is everyone looking for Kate?"

The director's eyebrows shot up. "You don't know?"

Max looked at his watch while he turned away from the cell. "Let's go."

The bars rattled behind him as Montgomery shook them with both hands. "Wait. Fine. I'll tell you. She's—"

Pounding feet came from behind him, followed by Spencer's shout. "Look out!"

A split second later a muffled boom and bright flash filled the room.

By instinct, he dove to his left, waiting for the slugs to pound into his torso. He landed hard, forced himself to a knee, and brought the rifle around. Muffled sounds came and went like he was underwater. "Spencer?" *Can barely hear.*

A muted voice came from the corner of the room. "Here."

"You hit?"

"Negative."

What just happened? Max stood on shaky legs, his rifle aimed at the doorway, taking in the cellblock, searching for a target. As he turned, he did a double take.

Piper Montgomery was sprawled on the cell floor, her dirty white shirt covered in blood.

FORTY-NINE

Kokkina, Cyprus

Spencer reacted first by pinning his back to the wall next to the door, pistol held in an outstretched hand. Using hand signals, he indicated Max should cover him as he peeked out the door.

Max sprinted to the door and took a knee, rifle to his shoulder, with a field of view into the hallway and to the right of the doorway. He saw no one. *Is that someone running or are my ears playing tricks on me?*

Spencer counted down from three with his fingers and peeled into the hallway to take a position at a doorway to cover Max. Max followed and ran ten meters and took a knee. They moved down the hall, covering each other, without seeing any sign of the intruder.

Why are we alive? Who wanted her dead, and why? To conceal information. But what information? She was about to reveal why everyone was looking for Kate. That must be it.

Was the killer hovering outside the room, waiting and listening?

They came to a branch in the corridor with a set of stairs. A hallway to the left led to more doorways, and wooden pallets along the wall held familiar-looking crates.

Rockets exploded, and small arms fire came from above. Someone cried out in pain. A man yelled. A massive explosion shook the building. The assault on the compound had resumed.

The two men fell back to the cellblock and talked in hushed voices. Max told Spencer about the escape tunnel. "Stay or go?"

The lanky operative crouched with his back against a wall. "If you got in that way, is it possible someone else came in that way too?

Shifting to scan the hallway, Max nodded. "Possible. Maybe they escaped that way."

Spencer ducked involuntarily as a rocket exploded somewhere overhead, causing concrete and mortar to rain down on their heads. "Your information is that Kate is here?"

"Yup."

"We stay. I'm not leaving without her."

Max crouched, his back to the wall nearest the door. "The battle gives us cover. Chaos hides our movements."

Another bomb exploded. Plaster fell from the ceiling and filled the room with dust. Cries of men mingled with small arms and antiaircraft fire. Spencer waved the dust away from his face. "Unless we get killed by a rocket."

Max studied his old friend. Deep bags hung under his eyes, blood crusted over scratches on his face, and he had lost weight. His hand shook as he held the pistol. Max took an MRE from his pack and threw it to the former CIA commando. "Eat it. That's an order."

Running footsteps and yelling men came from down the hall. Another series of explosions rocked the building. *Is that the same attack force, but with reinforcements, or another group?*

Spencer ate the food with a quivering hand.

"You go out." Max motioned with his rifle. "I'll stay. Once you exit—"

Spencer finished the ration and brushed crumbs from his stubble. "The fuck I am."

Max grinned. "Thought so. Let's go."

Leading Spencer to the door, they took up covering positions. Max was about to move to the hallway when he heard the thunderous pounding of dozens of booted footsteps, followed by a voice.

"Mikhail Asimov! I know you're in there. Drop your weapons and come out with your hands on your heads. Don't make us come in there. I don't want it to get bloody."

I recognize that voice. I hate it when I'm right.

It was the voice of Victor Dedov, his father's former boss at the Belarusian KGB and his sister's current lover.

FIFTY

Kokkina, Cyprus

Weaponless, arms secured behind them with plastic cuffs, and surrounded by men in black uniforms, Max and Spencer marched through the compound's lower halls. They were pushed up three flights of stairs until they emerged into a wide-open courtyard surrounded by high walls and battlements. The fresh air tasted good after the smoke and dust in the lower levels of the compound. The fighting had entered a lull.

They were forced to their knees in the center of the courtyard under a cloudless sky while a hot morning sun beat down. The compound's defenses resembled those of a castle. A set of steel reinforced double doors were inset into the high wall in front of them, which Max knew led to the beach. The high wall ringed the massive courtyard and was interspersed by a half dozen battlements and fortifications, all bristling with armament. Except now the fortifications were in varying states of destruction from multiple rocket attacks. Only three still supported soldiers, and only two had operational antiaircraft guns.

As a haze of smoke hung over the compound's sandy field, and the pungent odors of gunpowder, blood, and salt dominated the air. Dozens of men in black uniforms lay mangled and bloody among concrete and wood debris. The remaining soldiers wore grim looks as they raced to shore up defenses during a lull in the fighting.

Victor Dedov, his face haggard, stood in front of the two captives while six of his men stood guard. A holster hung on Dedov's belt. The former KGB director toyed with the undone flap. His uniform was dusty and ripped in several places. His men were equally war-torn.

"You're losing, Victor," Max said. "You're not going to hold the compound much longer."

Dedov sneered. "You're a fool, Asimov. Just like your old man. He never knew when to walk away. Well, now it's over. This whole mess will come to an end."

Despite the pain in his knees from kneeling and the ache in his shoulders from having his hands secured behind him, Max's mind was clear. *I get it now.* A slow burning anger tightened at the bottom of his neck and crept across his chest until his throat constricted. His voice came out choked. "It was you. You killed my father."

Dedov chuckled and shook his head. "You still don't get it, do you?"

With a glance at Spencer, who looked at him curiously, Max lowered his voice. "You were the one that planned and executed my father's murder. It was you who held back the security detail so the truck with the bomb could get close to the house. It was you who covered up everything, using your power at the KGB. You've pulled the strings all along. Now you're just using my sister to stay close to me." He flexed his arms in an attempt to break the plastic straps, but only succeeded in forcing the zip ties to cut into his skin.

Pushing his face close, Dedov sneered. "Don't try to think, you dumbfuck. You'll never figure it out. You see things in black and white, just like Andrei."

Wait a minute. The leader of the consortium was named Nikita Ivanov. No record of the man had yet been uncovered, and the name was common in Russia. It has to be a fake. "You're Nikita Ivanov! You're the leader of the consortium. You're using an assumed name to hide your identity."

After laughing and turning away, Victor gave a command, and three men scurried to obey. Turning back, he refocused on Max with a resigned look on his face. "This whole affair pains me, Mikhail. Your father and I went way back to the early days of the KGB. I trusted him as my lieutenant for years. We had many successful operations together. He was a strategic and tactical genius, but he went outside the boundaries. If he had played along, he could have become a very wealthy man. Instead he picked the wrong side, and so here we are."

What role does Dedov play in all this? The list of the consortium members flipped through Max's head. *Number one—Nikita Ivanov, true identity unknown. Number two is Ruslan Stepanov, head of Russia's military intelligence. Number three is Andrey Pavlova, the CEO of Russia's largest oil and gas conglomerate. Number four—Lik Wang, Chairman of China's largest oil company. Spartak Polzin, former Russian army major and arms trader, is number five and now deceased. Number six is Leonid Petrov, another Russian oil executive. Seven is Sergei Fedorov, a Russian army general and the director of the FSB, Russia's post-Soviet replacement for the KGB. Eight is the head of Ukraine's largest oil and gas company. Victor Volkov, head of Russia's largest crime syndicate, was number nine, also deceased. Ten is another Chinese name, a man who Max understood to be the Chinese Republic's head of State Security. Eleven is Aleksei Grishin, a Russian four-star general. Twelve is Erich Stasko, the Latvian Banker who I forced to help uncover the name of the Brompton Street bomber.*

The courtyard grew quiet. Dedov looked around, distracted, like he expected something to happen.

Damn it, I should have figured it out sooner. "You're not Ivanov. You're number eleven. Aleksei Grishin. I thought it was the Russian general, but it's an alias. Aleksei Grishin was also the name of the Belarusian freestyle skier who took the first winter Olympic gold in 1992. It's your alias!"

Dedov smiled with a glint in his eyes. "Very good, Mikhail. Too bad you'll never see your sister again to warn her. All this time, she's been living safely under my roof where I can watch her, available to me when I need her."

Max's brow furrowed. "But why keep her alive? And me—I've been to your castle now twice. Why haven't you already killed us?"

Dedov shrugged. "If you don't know, all the better. Let's just say that keeping you alive served my purposes. Until now. It's all coming together, and soon you'll all be expendable."

A commotion came from the far end of the courtyard, and Dedov whirled with a look of anticipation. A team of tall men in the black uniforms of Dedov's security force appeared in the doorway of an outbuilding a hundred meters on the far side of the courtyard.

As the men marched at them, Max couldn't help but

smile. In the lead was a beefy soldier wearing a ball cap similar to those worn by special forces soldiers. Behind him, walking between two soldiers, her curly hair tucked under a floppy hat and wearing a pair of clean cotton pants and a matching top, was Kate Shaw.

FIFTY-ONE

Kokkina, Cyprus

When he saw Kate, Spencer fought against his bonds, flexing his muscles and grunting. One of Dedov's men struck Spencer's neck with the butt of a rifle, sending him tumbling face-first into the ground where he lay motionless.

The little group of Kate Shaw and the team of elite soldiers was on the far side of the courtyard but approaching fast. Kate's face was partially blocked by her guards.

Victor Dedov grinned smugly and gripped the handle of his pistol as he watched the tiny procession. "Well, well, all of us are finally together."

As the group approached, Max caught Kate's gaze. There was no recognition in her eyes. Her gait was smooth, but lacking bounce or life as if she were asleep. Her face was deeply lined and pale, her glasses were missing, and her frail arms were puckered with goosebumps. *She's gotta be sedated.*

The four soldiers marched in tight formation, two of them with a grip on Kate's arms propelling her ahead. Dedov glanced at the sky before listening as a solider whispered something in his ear. The solider ran off in the direction of an antiaircraft embattlement.

Victor turned back to the group with a scowl and gestured urgently to the soldiers escorting Kate. "Hurry up, now." He waved his hand at Max. "Get her on her knees here, next to this one."

It didn't take Max long to figure out what Dedov was up to. His soldiers manned their stations with grim faces. Their uniforms were ragged, the compound was strewn with dead men in black uniforms, the injured left to writhe in the burgeoning heat. They wouldn't last the next onslaught, so Dedov was gathering his chips.

"It's not going to work, Victor. You can't bargain from a position of weakness."

Kate was pushed to her knees next to Max. On Victor's order, one of the soldiers drew his pistol and put it against Kate's head. Victor took out his own gun and pointed it at Max. "Who said anything about bargaining?"

In the distance came the distinctive *whomp whomp whomp* of a Russian Mi-26 Halo, one of the largest helicopters ever made. As the sound grew louder, Dedov's pistol hand twitched.

A high-powered rifle cracked nearby.

Instinctively, Max threw himself to the ground. When he looked up, antiaircraft guns chattered and small arms fire sounded sporadically. The telltale pounding of attack helicopters was followed by *whoosh* after *whoosh* of dozens of AT-9 Spiral-2 anti-tank missiles that exploded into the battlements sending concrete, dirt, and body parts flying. The attack birds hovered out of sight and sent wave after

wave of radio-guided missiles at the walls, antiaircraft fortifications, and compound buildings.

Max and his team were exposed in the middle of the
battle. Men in black uniforms darted for cover as Max kept
a low profile and scanned the grounds for a safe hiding
place.

One of Dedov's soldiers lay in the grass next to him,
unmoving. His head was separated from his shoulders. Or
rather, his head had disappeared and left a ragged bloody
stump. It was the soldier who had held the gun on Kate.

Sniper.

Max struggled to his knees but didn't see the former
KGB director.

*Where is Dedov? The air attack came from out over the
ocean, but where had the sniper bullet fired from?*

Four members of Dedov's elite guard force, the men
who guarded Max, Kate, and Spencer, were each on one
knee with their weapons trained on them, their heads
swiveling to search the compound.

They're looking for the sniper.

The enormous main building rose up four stories
behind them and contained dozens of windows. The wall
surrounding the grounds held a walkway, battlements, and
towers.

The shooter could be anywhere.

A black-uniformed guard's head exploded, showering
Max with blood and gray brain matter. The head explosion
was accompanied by the *crack* of a sniper rifle. A glint of
light came from the fourth floor of the main compound
building behind him. The guards scattered leaving the three
captives alone.

Cursing his secured hands, Max jumped to his feet and
nudged Spencer. "Come on!" He took off running at a right

angle to the compound to reduce the shooter's field of fire. From the corner of his eye came movement.

Victor Dedov was also running. The KGB man sprinted away from the main building, his legs pumping hard, in the direction of the wall's large double doors leading to the sea where a small armored vehicle sat.

Another crack sounded and Dedov stumbled, tumbling to the ground, his pistol flying from his hand. As he rolled onto his back and his screams echoed across the courtyard, his hands grabbed his leg where his foot had once been.

Max's back hit the cinder block wall of the main compound building, his chest heaving, and he searched the crumbing concrete for a jagged edge to sever the plastic zip tie. Grabbing a sharp piece of rusty rebar, he went to work on the plastic while he looked around wildly for Spencer and Kate.

Three guards had run after Dedov, while another scrambled toward the compound's main doors. The rifle cracked again, and one of the running soldier's heads disappeared into a fine mist, his headless body tumbling to the ground like a rag doll. The second runner made it another three meters before a bullet took a chunk out of his neck and he collapsed.

With his arms bound behind him, Spencer tried to shield Kate from the shooter. Kate, who's hands were free, stood and yanked Spencer to his feet. They took off running.

Watching them run, Max expected the sniper to fire at any moment, striking down either one as they stumbled over debris. Time slowed as they scrambled, Kate with her hand gripping Spencer's arm urging him ahead. The din of the battle faded as Max waited for the rifle with a hollow pit in his stomach. When it came, his heart dropped from his chest.

Crack

His two friends kept running, Kate helping Spencer pick through the rubble. Near the double doors, close to Dedov's inert form, another black-clad soldier tumbled headless to the ground and didn't move.

Kate and Spencer fell against the wall next to him, unharmed, gasping for breath. As they reached him, Max's restraints sprang loose. He went to work on Spencer's bindings with the rebar.

Assembling in a defensive position, Dedov's men directed small arms fire at a window on the top level of the compound. Chunks of plaster fell to the yard as bullets chewed up the building. Under cover of machine gun fire, two of Dedov's men pulled their commander to safety behind the ATV.

The antiaircraft fortifications took rocket attack after rocket attack until only smoldering piles of rubble and concrete remained. The concrete wall, a foot thick and reinforced with steel, had crumbled in dozens of places. The grounds were strewn with bodies, some dead, some squirming in pain. As the attack helicopters retreated and the small arms fire slowed, only the occasional moan or scream for help from the injured carried across the blood-soaked lawn. An eerie calm descended on the courtyard.

We need to move.

When Spencer's plastic ties sprang loose, Max signaled to Kate and Spencer to run along the building's wall to a corner where they could take cover and plan their retreat. Spencer urged Kate ahead while Max followed.

He heard the helicopters return before he saw them. Five birds flying in attack formation appeared over the

compound. Four were Russian Mi-24 Hind attack helicopters and a fifth was the larger Mi-26 Halo transport.

I should keep running, but...

Max stopped to watch. Two Hinds let loose a volley of
air-to-surface missiles that smashed into the compound's
walls and exploded, sending enormous chunks of concrete
high into the air.

Spencer grabbed his arm and yanked, and Max started
running again as a second volley of missiles hit the main
compound building. Debris showered them coating Kate's
hair with dust. Razor-like shards of metal raked his back,
and when he touched his neck, his hand came away bloody.
With their legs pumping, they left the building behind,
sprinted across an open section of the courtyard, and disappeared around a small outbuilding next to the wall. From
their hiding spot, they had a good view of the compound.

Two Hinds hovered ten meters off the deck while a task
force of commandos rappelled down and dispersed to the
perimeter. Twelve more streamed from the other two Hinds
to help secure the compound while a brigade of soldiers
emerged from the rear of the massive Halo.

The wall near the sniper's window was shredded,
exposing the room behind to the air. Nothing moved.

That sniper is either dead or gone.

The ragtag survivors of Dedov's forces were rounded
up, disarmed, and forced to lie face down on the ground. A
task force disappeared into the compound and emerged to
indicate the building was secured. The massive Mi-26 Halo
lumbered through the air and settled on the ground, its
humongous rotors, 32 meters in diameter, stirring up dirt
and scree as it settled.

Spencer tugged at Max's shirt. "Let's get the fuck out of
here before we're discovered."

I'm about to get a clue to this whole mess. He held up his index finger.

The first soldiers off the Halo took up defensive positions around the bird, rifles up, as the leader of the ground squad approached the helicopter. A quiet descended upon the compound as the Halo's rotors slowed.

Nothing moved until the side door of the Halo opened and an enormous man stepped into the sunlight wearing khaki cargo pants tucked into gleaming combat boots, a T-shirt, and a large white cowboy hat. A pistol in a polished leather holster was strapped to his waist, and aviator-style sun glasses were perched on his face. But it wasn't the man's attire that struck Max, it was his size. The man stood at least seven feet tall. His hat hid a large forehead, his jaw was square and pronounced, and the lines of his face were hard-edged. He looked like a sculptor's rendition of a giant from Greek mythology. Clean-shaven and ruggedly handsome, the man looked to be in his mid-fifties. Max was certain he had never laid eyes on him before.

Who is this guy?

Max grabbed Spencer's arm. "Have you seen him before?" As Max removed his Blackphone to snap photos, Spencer shook his head.

The newcomer in the cowboy hat surveyed the battle zone, listened to a brief report from his lieutenant, and gestured at the compound. The lieutenant shook his head before the giant walked across the yard to the main building.

There was another tug on his shirt, and Spencer hissed at him. "We need to go."

With a dozen photos secure in his phone, Max relented. All three turned at the same time and disappeared into the thicket near the cliff.

Emerging into a small clearing, they stopped in their tracks.

A small raven-haired woman stood ten meters away holding a Kel-Tec machine gun pointed at them. Her eyes were green like emeralds, and she was dressed in tight-fitting black combat gear. A 9mm compact was strapped to one leg, and a knife was attached to her belt within easy reach. A small pack was slung over her shoulders along with an oblong case that made Max think sniper rifle. Her olive skin was covered with dirt, blood, and dust, and her small mouth was curled into a snarl.

"Hands where I can see them. All slow like."

FIFTY-TWO

Undisclosed Location

The raven-haired woman marched them to the courtyard, where they were cuffed, searched, hooded, and relieved of their possessions by a team of the newly arrived soldiers. His senses dulled by the hood, Max stood in the heat and tried to discern the activities going on around him. After what felt like an hour, they were herded onto the Mi-26 Hind where they were made to sit in spartan jump seats. No one talked to them, no one assaulted them. Cigarette smoke wafted past his nose. Another hour passed before more footsteps clanged on the helicopter's metal floor, the massive rotors started turning, and they lifted into the air.

The Mi-26 Hind had a range of about 430 nautical miles, but could do twice that with auxiliary fuel tanks, which meant any number of North African or Southeastern European countries might be their destination. With nothing else to do, he focused on resting his weary body.

When the helicopter touched down, they were guided

down a ramp into a breeze saturated with the bite of jet fuel. Sounds were muffled by the turbo whine of the Hind's engines and thumping rotors. His legs were stiff and he tried to stop and stretch, but he was prodded along by the guards.

After a short march that included trudging down eight flights of narrow metal steps, Max was pushed and he tripped over a transom and fell hard onto a grated floor. The plastic cuffs were removed, a door clanged shut, and a bolt fell into place with a *chunk*. When he pulled off the hood, he found himself in a metal room he recognized as a ship's solitary confinement brig. The only clue to the identity of his captors were the Russian Cyrillic characters stenciled on the walls. After a thorough examination revealed no means of escape, he stretched out on the thin mattress and fell asleep to the gentle movement of the ship.

Time was marked by meals: two breakfasts, two lunches, and two dinners. The tasteless food was vaguely Russian and the coffee was tepid and weak. He had no interactions with humans, and so he slept, performed long hours of body weight exercises, and kept his mind sharp by reasoning through the events of the past several weeks.

Victor Dedov's position on the consortium was a shock. Now I know who executed the operation to take down my father, kill my mother, and destroy my childhood home. But why did Dedov leave Arina and Alex alive?

And who is the huge man in the cowboy hat? The giant had obviously won the race to find Kate. But what information did she possess that was so dear to the consortium and the various intelligence agencies that were chasing her? What had his father hidden in her head? And if the CIA had had the opportunity to interrogate her for weeks, why were they not able to pry the information from her head?

Assuming Dedov had run the operation to pluck Kate from the clutches of the CIA, why was he not able to extract the information? No human could withstand modern day interrogation techniques, so what super power did Kate have? Or did she even have this information? Was it a wild goose chase started by his father? A gigantic fuck you to the people who killed him?

When he slept, a raven-haired woman with emerald-green eyes filled his dreams, populated the shadows, and chased behind him. A wraith with no face. *Who is she? Who's side is she on? What is her name?*

————

They retrieved him after the third breakfast. Rested and nourished, he was hooded and cuffed and led off the boat. The air smelled of fish and salt and something mechanical. Like docks or a shipyard. Gulls cried somewhere in the distance.

After a long ride in the back of a van over bumpy roads, he was taken into a building and stowed in another cell, this one made of stone and tile that smelled faintly of perfume and bleach. Another incarceration followed, marked by eight meals. The food here was better. Hummus, dolmas, tabbouleh, and even salad with olives and red onions, all served with a pitcher of ice water. A warm salty air clung to his skin. The bed was thin but had cotton sheets. A flush toilet sat next to a sink with running water.

They got him after the third dinner. Four men with sidearms and tasers forced the hood on him, marched him down three corridors paved with stone and up six flights of wooden stairs. He was pushed into an oak chair, and his wrists bound to the wooden arms with thick plastic zip ties.

A large wide-open, airy room with tall ceilings held up with whitewashed columns greeted him after they removed the hood. Wide openings in the walls offered expansive views of an azure-blue ocean. Mosaics in blues and greens depicting ocean scenes covered the walls, and the floor was tiled in a bright white. In the distance came the sounds of water crashing on rock. *Except for the plastic cords binding him to the chair's wooden arms, this would be a nice place to spend a vacation.*

A voice boomed out in English from behind him. "Welcome to Greece, Mikhail!"

He couldn't place the accent. Max stayed silent as the giant man with the square face came around to stand in front of him. He had changed out of his military garb and now wore light linen pants and a linen jacket over an open shirt that billowed in the warm breeze revealing a tan chest. The white cowboy hat was still perched on his head, and he held a large glass with ice and a clear liquid mixed with floating green leaves. A set of amber-colored worry beads were wrapped around his wrist in a makeshift bracelet.

The giant took a sip through a straw. "I'd offer you a mojito, but I'm currently lacking an assistant to help you drink it."

Max shrugged. "Never cared for them myself. The mint gets stuck in my teeth."

The giant roared, his guffaws echoing through the wide-open space. "Touché, my friend. Touché. Hence the straw."

"Very wise."

Meandering to an opening in the wall, the giant looked out over the sea and inhaled deeply "This is a special place, Mikhail. I don't get back here often, but when I do, I try to breath in as much air as I can. Something about the Aegean

Sea always gets me right here." He pounded his broad chest before turning back to Max.

A door squeaked behind him, and wheels rolled on the tile floor. Max craned his neck. Two men wearing sidearms, Bermuda shorts, and flowered shirts appeared, one pushing a wheelchair. They stopped with the chair near one of the open spaces in the wall that looked out over the sea, several meters from where Max sat in the center of the room. Sitting in the chair was a pale and gaunt Victor Dedov, his wrists secured. A clean white bandage was wrapped around the stump of his left leg. The giant thanked and dismissed both guards, and the three men were left alone in the vast chamber.

Max smirked. "Hello, Victor. Nice of you to join us. Nikita here was just offering mojitos."

Again the giant roared with laughter. "I do appreciate your humor under such austere circumstances, Mikhail. And yes, you are correct. I am Nikita Ivanov." Turning to Dedov, his face darkened. "Alas, Victor. There is no mojito in your future."

Max bowed his head. "Thank you for agreeing to meet with me, Nikita."

Ivanov's laughter was muted. "We have much to talk about, Mikhail. But first, we have other business to attend. I understand you two men know each other?"

"Vaguely," Max said.

The former KGB director's face was white, and his hands shook while gripping the arms of the wheelchair. He opened his mouth, but no words came out.

The giant faced Dedov while he spoke to Max. "The problem with organizations of men, Mikhail, is that over time they start to take on a life of their own. Powerful men such as Victor here make up the—what did your father call it? The consortium? Men such as these tend to form agendas of their own. Much like a mafia family might be comprised of those who wish to rise up the ranks, so too is our group made up of ambitious men who aspire to greatness."

Ivanov sipped his drink while he undid the button on his jacket to reveal a sidearm in a worn leather shoulder holster. "As the leader of such a group, I find myself spending more and more time defending my position than I do advancing the cause of our council. It's almost enough to make a man want to—how do the American's say it—toss in the towel."

Another pull on the straw and the mojito glass was empty. Ivanov set it on a table and paced behind the two bound men. "Does it surprise you to know, Mikhail, that this entire caper—the gun purchase in Turkey, the bitcoin locker, the hunt for Kate Shaw—was all orchestrated by me in order to expose a faction of my group that conspires against me?"

I guess that makes sense. "You could have just called me instead of going to all that trouble."

The giant snorted. "Great lengths are required to achieve one's goals, do you not agree Mikhail? You, for one, have employed extreme measures to find and kill the members of my group. I call that a pretty elaborate scheme."

Max shrugged. "Lives are at stake."

"You make my case for me." Ivanov pointed at Max. "Lives are indeed at stake, and great lengths are required. I didn't know the full extent to which the treachery runs through my organization. I couldn't tell who was with me and who was against me." He came to a halt in front of Dedov. "But now I know, don't I, Victor?"

Dedov stared at the floor.

The giant suddenly reared back and launched a dumb-bell-sized fist directly at Victor's face. It connected with a crunch and blood spattered into the air. The wheelchair rolled back a few inches, and when it came to rest, Victor's head lolled sideways. Nikita slapped him twice. "Don't pass out on me yet, you pig."

He strode over to a broad window and gazed out while wiping his knuckles on a handkerchief. He spun and addressed Max. "Spartak and Dedov were against me, that much is clear. Spartak was the dull instrument, and I applaud you for dispatching him, Mikhail. You did me a favor. I didn't know who else was in on it, but now I know that Victor was the ringleader. The so-called brains of the operation." Nikita's laugh came out as a dull roar. "Thanks to our discussions over the past few days, Victor has seen fit to illuminate the rest of the conspiracy for me, haven't you, Victor?"

Victor Dedov, a man known for his tenacity and forti-tude, a man who built his KGB career on guile, cunning, and aggression, was now a shell of his former self. He was too weak to even beg for forgiveness. He said nothing, and instead slouched in his chair and cast his eyes to the ground.

The giant made a dismissive sound and turned to the window muttering under his breath. "Useless." His hand snaked into his jacket before he spun with the pistol out and fired. A deafening pop filled the room, and Victor Dedov's head rocked as the bullet from the .45 cartridge pierced his face at the bridge of his nose. A distorted chunk of metal exited the rear of his skull, spraying gray-red brain matter on the white tile.

Max sat wide-eyed. *Guess this is it.*

FIFTY-THREE

Somewhere in Greece

The echo of the gunshot was replaced by the giant's chuckles. "Never liked that little fucker."

He holstered the .45 as four security guards rushed in, guns drawn. Ivanov issued several commands in Greek, which Max didn't understand. As the door closed, he added a final command in English. "And tell Delphinia to make me another mojito."

The giant turned to Max. "Now we're even, no?"

Max's eyebrows went up. "Not even close, but how do you figure?"

Nikita shrugged. "You helped me by killing Spartak. I helped you by killing Victor. The account is now even."

Max's mouth gaped open for a second before it closed. "I think you have your math wrong. You killed my parents. The price is the twelve lives of the consortium members, including yours."

A knock interrupted them. A man in Bermuda shorts entered carrying a tray holding a glass of ice, rum, and mint leaves. The giant made a show of tasting the drink, announced his approval, and dismissed the servant. "Where were we? Ah, yes, you were suggesting the accounts weren't settled. Let's discuss this idea of yours, shall we?"

Max smiled. "By all means. It's simple. You killed my parents. Now I kill all of you."

The giant made a sound in his throat. "What if I told you I had nothing to do with your parents' death?"

A shrug. "I'd say you're lying."

The giant stroked his chin. "But just for conversation's sake, what if Dedov did it on his own without my sanction? How might that change our position?"

"So Arina, Alex, and I are free to go? Our lives aren't in danger?"

The giant shook his head. "It's not that simple."

"Well then we're right back to where we started," Max said. "Unless you're offering some kind of deal, I don't follow your line of thinking."

Ivanov made a conciliatory gesture with the hand holding the drink. "The consortium, as you call it, is not a static group. Even now with Volkov, Spartak, and Dedov dead, we're grooming new members to take their place. You can't eliminate the group by killing everyone."

"So people keep telling me."

A chuckle. "It's like a parliament or a senate. The body exists independent of its individual members. The institution is greater than its individual parts." He stopped to sip. "Besides, where does it stop? Do you spend the rest of your life killing every member of the council? Eventually we'll wear you down, or it will consume you. If it hasn't already."

Max raised his eyebrows. "Someone once told me the same thing right before I killed him."

"Yes, you're referring to Wilbur Lynch. He was useful, but only to a point."

"Is this where you call me a blunt instrument?"

A deep chuckle erupted from the giant, who took a sip of the mojito. "An animal is bred for survival. The shark hunts because it has to. A chameleon blends into its surroundings to stay alive because it has to. You were taught one thing, and quite well, I might add. You learned from the best, and I was disappointed to see the decision your father made." He gestured at Max with the mojito glass. "You rely on one skill. You're like a shark. You only know one mode of attack."

"Do you have another suggestion?"

Ivanov nodded. "Now we're getting somewhere. You call it the consortium, so I will as well. Do you know why the consortium exists?"

Max shrugged. "My educated guess is to either protect or corner the world market for oil. It's a partnership with China, and you collude to keep oil prices high, control drilling and distribution, and ensure Russia and China's access to the scarce resource for generations to come."

The giant slapped his thigh. "They told me you were smart, but I didn't believe them. Of course, you're partially correct. That is our outward aim." Ivanov paced. "What if I were to provide you information that proved without a shadow of a doubt that Victor, and Victor alone, was behind the killing of your parents? That he acted independently, without authorization from me."

"I'd say you're fabricating the information in order to get me off your back. And with Victor dead..."

The giant snorted. "This is an interesting conversation,

no? Here you sit, shackled to a chair. I might blow your brains out at any moment. I offer you an olive branch, which you toss away like garbage. What's wrong here?"

He wants me alive. But why? "I'm not dead yet. Until I am, your life is in danger."

Ivanov scrunched up his eyes, took a mobile phone from his pocket, dialed a number, and issued a command in Greek.

Footsteps sounded at the door and a phalanx of guards entered the room. A chair was set on the tiled floor, and an obese man was guided to the chair. His white Oxford shirt was soiled and wet, and his eyes shifted around the room with nervous energy, lingering for a moment on the dead form of Victor Dedov. The guards were waved away, and the three men were left alone.

Ivanov smiled broadly. "Hello, Dr. Diego"

The fat man nodded his enormous head. "Holá."

"My people tell me that you, Doctor, are one of the preeminent experts on interrogation and extracting information from the dark depths of the human mind, no?"

Dr. Diego smiled revealing yellow teeth. "That is correct.

Ivanov caressed his chin. "And you agree there is none better at this kind of work?"

The fat man shrugged. "It's hard to say. I'm by no means the only expert in this field."

"I'm told you're in the top five."

"I guess you could say that is correct."

"Fair enough. I'm told by the late Victor Dedov over there that you spent several weeks interrogating and questioning Kate Shaw. You've applied many methods, including sleep deprivation, various forms of pain including shock therapy, water boarding, and many drugs designed to persuade her to talk, is that not correct?"

The fat man shifted in his seat. "It is."

"And what have you learned from our good friend Ms. Shaw?"

"Not much, I'm afraid. Any information she possessed would have come out. I'm afraid you're barking up the wrong tree."

Ivanov nodded as if perplexed by this conundrum. "The wrong tree, as you say." His cotton trousers billowed in a light breeze. "My people assure me the information is in her head, as does an independent source I trust. If true, how is it that a man of your expansive skills cannot make Ms. Shaw reveal it to us?"

Another shrug. "I cannot say."

Ivanov spread his arms. "Is there anything we have not yet tried? Interrogation techniques? Chemicals? Perhaps more distasteful methods?"

The doctor shook his head and his voice quivered. "As I've written about many times, pain is not a favorable method for knowledge extraction, it simply incents a subject to lie. We tried shock treatment, as well as many psychological methods such as sensory deprivation, water, extreme noise, sleep deprivation, and other techniques to break her down and build her back up. We used various drugs and even hypnosis. My assessment at this point is that there is no information she possesses in her mind that has not come out. I can only surmise that your sources are incorrect or deliberately misleading you."

Max held his breath.

Nikita Ivanov reached under his jacket, removed the pistol, and fired. The room was filled with the odor of gunpowder as the large body of Doctor Diego fell dead from his chair.

Holstering the weapon one more time, Ivanov faced Max. "It's not that I mind being told something I don't like. I suspect he's partially correct and they did try everything. I killed Dr. Diego not because he failed, but because he simply knew too much and had outgrown his usefulness. Let me ask you something. Do you trust your father?"

Max nodded.

"Of course you do. This may surprise you, but before he...um...went off the reservation so to speak, I also trusted him. Despite our differences, I knew your father to be a man of deep honor. He spoke the truth, and unfortunately it got him killed in the end. I have good intelligence that he told you, in a video made only for your consumption, that Kate has the information in her head. I doubt he would lie to you, and therefore I suspect the information has been coded into her brain in such a way that only you can extract it from her."

This is why I'm not yet dead.

The giant's arms hit his sides. "What do we do now?"

Max tested his restraints. "I don't know. Not sure I know what—"

Nikita held up a hand. "Before you say you don't know, think about this. If you truly can't extract what's in Kate's head, I have no use for you either. Do we understand each other?"

Rolling his shoulders, Max stretched his muscles. "If that's true, I'm in a predicament. I stay alive while there is the potential to uncover the information. But the second you learn it, my life is over. And so is Kate's. Wouldn't I be better off dead so the information remains forever buried?"

The giant's massive head bobbed up and down. "Very

good, Mikhail. I've thought of that too. Lucky for both of us, there is one last chip on the table."

Ivanov retrieved a tablet from a small table by the door. "If I have the information I'm looking for, there is no reason to prevent your sister and nephew from carrying on with their lives. They have no knowledge that puts the consortium at risk." He held the tablet in front of Max. On it, a video showed the inside of the Swiss compound where Arina and Alex lived. "You see, Victor imparted much information before he left us."

Max's chest tightened as he watched Alex playing with a radio-controlled race car in the keep's ward. The wooden chair creaked as he yanked at his bonds. "How do I know you will keep your word?"

A shrug from the giant. "You don't, but do you have a choice? Besides, I honestly don't care about those two. I'm not going to expend the energy and money to kill them if I don't need to. It's not good business."

Max kept his face blank. *Where are Spencer and Kate? Baxter and Cindy can't, or won't, help. Not after I hijacked the MI6 Lear. There's the detail of the plastic cords holding me to this chair, and the contingent of guards securing the property.*

Max eyed the dead form of Dedov slumped in the wheelchair. "So, where is she?"

"Now we're getting somewhere." Ivanov put the tablet on a small table near a wide open window.

A beep emitted from Dedov's wheelchair. Both men whipped their heads around.

Max hurled all his weight to the side in an attempt to overturn his chair. It teetered for a second before falling. As his world tipped sideways, Max glimpsed Nikita Ivanov standing by the opening to the cliff below and watching him with a frown on his face. When the wooden arm of his chair hit the white tiled floor and splintered, a horrific boom sounded, followed by a concussion blast of hot gasses. Max was blown sideways along the smooth tile until he hit the plaster wall. Deafened, he was barely able to hear the far away sounds of debris raining down on the porcelain tile.

And everything went black.

FIFTY-FOUR

Somewhere in Greece

Something pulled on his arm. Everything radiated pain. His head was in a vice, and he couldn't feel his arms.

Except for the yanking.

Each pull shot pain through his spine and up into his neck.

Stop. Please stop.

Nothing came out of his mouth. From somewhere far, far away, someone called his name.

"Mikhail! Mikhail!

Sounds like my foster mother.

Another yank, and he almost screamed. *Did I scream?*

Let go! He attempted to dislodge his arm until another shot of pain fired through his spine.

Maybe it's better to stand. He allowed himself to be pulled up by a blurry form.

Bad idea. Whatever was in his stomach came up and out

his mouth. He staggered, but a strong hand kept him upright while he spit out bile.

"Let's go, let's go!"

The words were close and loud. One foot in front of the other, and he dry heaved. Something cold and hard was pressed into his hand and he gripped it instinctively while he staggered.

One of his feet came down on a chunk of concrete, and he wavered. Something strong and solid held him steady. As he walked, the world became more clear. A gaping black crater stood where the white tile floor used to be. Little remained of the vibrant colored walls and pillars. A chunk of the ceiling near where Dedov's chair had been was gone, revealing a cobalt-blue sky. The odor of motor oil tinged with plaster and pulverized tile permeated the room.

Smells like C-4.

Shredded paper and swirls of dust flurried in a salty breeze. A sea gull screeched. Something propelled him along, step after step.

The source of his propulsion came into hazy view. A short young woman with raven-black hair and tight-fitting commando gear supported his arm around her shoulders. When she looked up, he looked into two pools of green, verdant and lush, like emeralds. They swam in his vision before coming into focus.

"We need to move, Mikhail."

Confusion caused him to resist. "What are you doing?" His voice was distant.

She urged him in the direction of the door. "Go now. Talk later."

Something didn't make sense. "Where's Ivanov?"

"Dead. Blown down the cliff. Go!"

Her strength drove him three more meters until he

stopped. From far away the roaring cadence of waves crashing on rocks filled his ears. He pulled away from her grip and lurched around the crater to look out the ragged hole. Although his vision was hazy from the concussion, black and wet jagged rocks glistened far below.

An arm wrapped around his waist and pulled. "God damn it, what are you doing?"

"I need to know." A gray gull made lazy turns as he peered at the rocks, willing his eyes to focus. *The body. Show me the body.*

"Shit. There's no time. We need to go. Men are on the way."

She pulled a weapon from behind her back and leveled it, aiming the suppressed assault rifle at the doorway.

There was something in his hand. A pistol.

He racked the slide and a bullet fell to the floor. Reaching for the bullet, he staggered, caught himself, but kicked the projectile into the bomb crater. *Damn it.* He slipped the magazine into the pistol and rammed it home with his palm.

Far below, the surf bashed against jagged rocks, sending white sea foam skyward. Three gulls floated in the air, looking for morsels. The cliff plummeted down at a steep angle and was covered by rocks and scraggly brush. The sapphire-blue ocean, dotted with whitecaps, was empty of sea craft.

With a hand firm on the craggy plaster wall, he scanned the rubble below. Something silver flashed in the sun, and he caught his breath, but it took to the air and spread its wings. No human body. No evidence of Ivanov.

He scanned the cliff until the shouts of men and the *spit, spit, spit* of a silenced rifle jolted him. Pivoting, pistol up, he fired twice and a flower-shirted guard stumbled. Three bodies sprawled among the explosion debris.

Adrenaline focused his vision. Gun up, he followed the mysterious woman around the crater and through the destroyed double doors.

———

"This way. Move faster."

The whitewashed walls moved in and out of focus as they hastened down a corridor littered with the bodies of Bermuda-short wearing security personnel. They moved fast without using cover tactics. A wide sweeping set of stairs led down to a domed entryway where they turned right into another corridor. Rifle up, she pointed with a gloved hand and started running.

When they paused at a doorway that was blown apart by explosives, she slapped him hard on the cheek.

"Ow. What the—"

She spoke in a whisper. "Pay attention. We're going four flights down. We might run into resistance. Slower now. Hand signals, and cover each other. Got it?" She reared her hand back to hit him again.

He held up a palm. "I'm awake. Shit."

With a glare, she raised her rifle and stepped through the doorway.

They dispatched two sets of armed guards on the way down the four flights of wooden stairs. Emerging into a spartan hallway of tile and concrete lit by long fluorescent bulbs they were greeted by a volley of fire from the hall to their right, forcing the woman to fall back into the stairwell. From her backpack she removed three canisters, pulled the pins on two, and hurled them down the hallway. They bounced several times on the tile before two muted explosions sounded, at which point, she pulled the pin on the third and tossed it.

"Go. Go. Go."

She darted into the hallway with Max on her heels. When he saw the fog of smoke from the third grenade, he sucked in his breath and held it. No rifle fire sounded, and ten meters down the hallway, he stepped over two bodies torn apart by the grenades.

To his right came the *spit, spit, spit* of the woman's silenced rifle. Her hand gripped his arm and yanked him through a doorway, where two guards lay dead on the ground, and two more human forms lay on cots.

Waving away the lingering smoke revealed the long inert body of Spencer White. Next to him, on a second cot, was an emaciated and gaunt Kate Shaw, her eyes closed. *How are they sleeping through all this?*

The raven-haired woman slung her rifle over her back. "They're sedated. Grab him. I'll get her. Move. Move."

"Where are we"

She flung Kate over her shoulder like she was a sack of leaves. "Go. Go. Follow me, damn it."

He stuck the pistol in his waistband and grabbed Spencer, lifted, staggered, and caught himself. Another heave got Spencer balanced with one hand in a fireman's carry, and he pulled the gun with the other while following the woman into the swirling smoke.

————

The SeaHunter 45 Tournament roared south east at 65 MPH on quad 400 HP Mercuries as warm water sprayed its occupants. At the helm was a shirtless olive-skinned

Adonis of a man with long dark hair, his shoulder muscles rippling as he gripped the wheel with both hands. Huddled in the tiny cabin just fore of the helm were Spencer and Kate, both covered with a wool blanket, watching the horizon.

With one hand on the canopy's post and his pistol in a firm grip, Max surveyed the surrounding water for signs of pursuit. The raven-haired woman stood at the bow, feet braced against the gunwales, assault rifle at the ready, also watching.

The boat's pilot adjusted a pair of mirrored sunglasses and yelled at Max over the engines. "Good to see you again, *mon ami!*"

"Likewise, Carlu. Likewise."

The Corsican's hearty chuckle rose over the engine's growl, and his hair streamed out behind him as he yelled into the wind. "Couldn't get a cigarette boat over here, but she'll outrun most in this chop."

According to the navigational charts, Ivanov's house was situated just east of Mt. Athos on a peninsula of land sticking out into the Aegean Sea. The mountain towered behind them as they raced east. No pursuit in sight.

He nudged Carlu and nodded at the front of the boat. "Who's your friend?"

The Corsican scratched his chin. "Never seen her. Thought she was part of your gang."

Max braced himself against a wave. "How'd you know to be here?"

"Goshawk gave me a stack of cash and the GPS coordinates. She neglected to mention the guns." His brow furrowed. "But when she calls, I come." He laughed into the wind.

And how did Goshawk know we were here?

Letting his legs brace him against the pounding of the boat's hull, Max made his way forward. His head throbbed, and his joints ached. A constant ringing hissed in his ears. As he walked, his hand trailed on the gunnel. While he focused his attention on the small dark woman at the bow, a large fishing trawler appeared on the horizon.

Rising and falling in the surging ocean, the massive ship plowed in their direction, making good time.

Max glanced back at Carlu, who gripped the wheel with two hands, his jaw set. *Surely he sees it.* The SeaHunter was headed right at the fishing boat.

"Mikhail!"

The yell from the raven-haired woman startled him, and he moved closer. "I have to thank you for rescuing us!" Max yelled.

She shook her head.

The trawler materialized like a hulking rusty building over her shoulder.

"Why did you help us?"

"Doesn't matter."

Fist clenched on the gunwale, he staggered as a wave hit the boat. "It does to me."

She thrust out a palm. "Don't come any closer."

Carlu had the throttle wide open and the engines surged against the waves.

"How were you tracking me?" Max asked.

A shrug and her lip curled into a smirk.

"At least tell me your name," he yelled over the roar.

Carlu put the engines in neutral, and it got quiet except for the purr of the Mercuries and the water lapping against the hull. The other vessel was a few meters away.

The mysterious woman in the SeaHunter's prow eyed the fishing boat as a long rope ladder was thrown from the deck above. She swung her rifle onto her back while Carlu reversed throttle and, with precision that came from many years at sea, brought the SeaHunter's port gunwale alongside the tall metal hull of the fishing boat with a small bump.

A crew of orange-suited fisherman peered from the trawler's rail. Covered with a thick beard and wool cap, the captain's head was visible through the helm's window.

Before Max could react, the young woman vaulted over the SeaHunter's gunwale and scampered up the ladder to the trawler's deck. Carlu reversed engines and swung the bow away from the other boat.

A Chinese woman appeared near the fishing boat's aft deck railing, her hands shoved into the pockets of a dark wool pea coat. Her skin was pallid, and her jowls fleshy. Gray hair waved in the wind. A cigarette was clenched in her teeth. She gazed at the SeaHunter through dark wayfarer-style sunglasses.

As the Carlu pulled their boat away, the raven-haired woman appeared next to the old woman in the pea coat. Ebony hair fluttering in the breeze, her eyes locked on Max's and she cupped her hands to her mouth and yelled, "Call me Kira."

He held her gaze, locking her face into his memory, before he yelled back. "Thank you, Kira!"

Max's last image was of the two women standing together, the older woman's arm around Kira's shoulder. He kept his eyes on them until the trawler disappeared over the horizon.

FIFTY-FIVE

Lisbon, Portugal

"Where is she, damn it?"

The bellow came from Callum Baxter as he pounded across the courtyard of the Jerónimos Monastery. An icy wind singed Max's skin, and his leather jacket did little to keep him warm. Baxter's face was an angry rose color, and his wiry hair stuck out from a gray flannel watch cap. Several paces behind him, Cindy followed in a fashionable wool overcoat, her face unreadable.

Max held out a gloved hand. "Stop right there, Callum."

The spymaster stopped, but he waved a fist. "I demand to see her!"

The wide expanse of the Monastery's lawn contained only three hardy tourists willing to brave the crisp temperatures. The fountains were turned off for the winter, and the grass had wilted to yellow. Cindy stood a few steps behind her boss wearing white ear muffs, her eyes sparkling.

Max lowered his voice. "Do you need your pipe or maybe a cup of tea to calm you down?"

His feet planted, Baxter shoved his hands deep into his overcoat pockets. "You screwed me."

A shrug. "I never agreed to let you interrogate her."

The older man's eyes blazed. "We're MI6, for bollock's sake. We don't torture people. All I want is a debrief. Where is she?"

Max chuckled. "I'm sorry if this didn't go your way, Callum—"

"We put hundreds of thousands of quid into this deal. We taxied you around the globe. We spent a fortune treating her. All you had to do—"

Max clenched his fists in his pockets. "Your bureaucracy gets in the way. She's safe now. No one will find her. If you're nice, I'll share what I learn. But you're not starting off well."

After the rescue in Greece, Carlu had dropped them at Catania, a port city on the island of Sicily, where Goshawk arranged for a series of flights and overland transit that ultimately brought them to London. There Max and Spencer allowed MI6 to perform a lengthy medical examination of Kate by the Royal Army Medical Corp. She remained unresponsive throughout the evaluations, and the medical staff pronounced her malnourished and dehydrated, but otherwise physically healthy. Before Baxter had an opportunity to debrief her, Max and Spencer hustled Kate from the hospital under the cover of darkness and disappeared.

"I'll get to her one way or—"

A dark panel van careened into the quadrangle followed by a short black limousine with tinted windows. Behind the limousine sped a second van. A phalanx of men in dark overcoats poured from the vans and spread around the edges of courtyard. The tourists disappeared, leaving Max alone with Baxter, Cindy, and a dozen security men.

What was Baxter trying to pull? "You can torture me all you want." Max crossed his arms over his chest. "I don't know where she is. Simple precaution in case you tried something like this."

The MI6 agent's face drained of its color, and his shoulders slumped as he regarded the motorcade. "When are you going to get it through your thick skull? We're not the KGB. We don't torture people for information."

The rear door of the limousine opened, and a man stepped out. He wore a dark overcoat similar to his bodyguards, but his head was bare except for a neatly trimmed rim of white hair. A long and pinched face held spectacles perched on a hawk-like nose. An electric-blue silk tie peeked from under the overcoat. The man pointed to the interior of the sedan with a bony finger.

Baxter pivoted and marched in the direction of the limo while he yelled over his shoulder. "Bad idea to keep C waiting."

After a moment, Max followed and surrendered his pistol to a pink-faced bodyguard, and followed his MI6 partner into the limousine. Cindy remained outside, stomping her feet to stay warm, while Max and Callum sat opposite the head of Great Britain's secret intelligence service.

C offered Max a bony hand with a grip of iron. "Been meaning to meet you for a long time, Mr. Asimov. Our country owes you a great debt for your help in locating the West Brompton bomber."

Max nodded once. "More than happy to help, sir."

Baxter brushed lint from his lapel.

"Callum and Cindy have kept me appraised of your

recent progress," C said. "Let me offer you the warmest condolences on the suffering of your friend Kate Shaw. What she endured, first at the hands of the Americans and then in the custody of Mr. Dedov, is reprehensible. I hope and pray she can make a suitable recovery and regain some semblance of normal life."

Max bowed his head. "Thank you, sir. I appreciate that. It will be a long road, but she's tough."

"So I've heard." C formed a steeple with both hands. "Callum here speaks highly of your abilities. Don't you, Callum?"

Baxter typed furiously on his Blackberry and didn't speak.

A glint of mirth appeared in C's eyes. "Success heals many wounds. Despite your...eh...unconventional methods, Callum has assured me that our relationship is mutually beneficial. Tit for tat, as the Americans say. Do you agree, Mr. Asimov?"

"I'd like to think so, sir."

The head of Britain's intelligence agency rearranged his long limbs on the leather seat. "Splendid. In which case I'm sure you'd appreciate some background on our friend Nikita Ivanov and your consortium?"

Max leaned forward so his elbows rested on his knees. "Have they recovered his body?"

C shook his narrow head. "He was either incinerated by the blast or carried away by the tides." He thought a minute. "Your report was silent on the explosion. Do we have any intelligence on where the bomb came from? Who placed it there?"

Max sat back. *How much do I reveal?* "We think someone planted it who worked for Ivanov and had access to Dedov's wheelchair while in captivity. Maybe someone trying to take out all three of us. There is a divide in the consortium after all. It's speculation at this point. We may never know."

"Indeed." C adjusted the crisp pleat on his wool trousers while his gaze lingered on Max. "Before you arrived on the scene, we knew some of Mr. Ivanov's activities but never connected him to the odd and mysterious machinations of what you call the consortium. The man himself is also quite the mystery. This may surprise you, but the West actually knows very little about what went on behind the iron curtain. What we do know we've pieced together from dubious accounts from defectors, a few successful spy operations, and by applying computer algorithms to vast quantities of intercepted data in the hopes we may find patterns. Callum has explained what we believe about the consortium?"

A nod from Max. "Some of it."

"What Callum didn't tell you—" A moment between the MI6 men elicited a brief shrug from Baxter before the director continued. "Right. While we don't know much about Ivanov himself, we have made some educated guesses about the nature of the consortium. Cindy gave you the background on the chekists?"

Max played back Cindy's briefing in the Lear when Baxter cut off her update. Max nodded.

"There has long been the belief among some corners of the intelligence world," C said, "bolstered by lesser known academics, that the Russian president is simply a figurehead acting out the directives of a shadow government. While perceived as an authoritarian ruler by the rest of the world, some very intelligent and learned people believe that he can't hold this kind of power without the support of what were once the chekists."

"Cindy alluded to that," Max said.

"What she didn't tell you is our hypothesis about Russia's shadow government."

Max glanced out the window. Cindy was talking animatedly to one of the guards, a young man with red hair.

The director raised a bony hand. "Shadow governments are hard to pin down. They exist more because of an ingrained set of cultural beliefs than an overt set of charters or dictates. They are hundreds, maybe thousands of people, all with similar aims, working to subvert goals counter to their own, sometimes by tacit agreement, sometimes in alignment with one another, sometimes opposed to each other. There are, however, some common threads. They are often ultra-nationalist in nature, anti-democratic, anti-worker, and secularist."

Max shrugged. "Sounds familiar."

C nodded. "Other characteristics include a heavy military influence with deep state leaders coming from various positions at the heads of the nations' armed forces. There is sometimes a mafia-like influence, autocratic cliques, and high levels of corruption. There is often a pervasive threat of government overthrow by the right-wing military, what's called a Putsch threat after the failed coup in Germany after World War I. Most of these deep states exist to serve an ideological agenda, and as such, there isn't a tangible form to put your finger on."

Max sat back. "No one to shoot."

"So to speak." C spread his hands. "Our hypothesis is that the deep state in Russia is different. Where most of these other regimes are really just different ideologies working to undermine the established government—natural in any ecosystem made up of conflicting beliefs—we think there is a formal organizational system that administers the inner-workings of this Russian deep state, and that maintains a facade of false democracy."

Max felt in his pockets for his cigarettes, glanced around the pristine interior of the car, and put them back. "Doesn't that seem far-fetched?"

A shrug from C. "Not at all. It's happened before. Russia has a long history of maintaining puppet regimes in countries like Poland and Hungary, and the United States did it in Panama."

Baxter chimed in from behind his Blackberry. "Britain's never done it."

C pushed his glasses up on his nose. "As Cindy mentioned, our capable friends in the GCHQ are whizzes with the data. I ran spies in Russia when computers still used punch cards, so sometimes I have to suspend disbelief and listen to what my analysts tell me."

Max crossed his arms. "Let me guess. They've reached a conclusion about the consortium?"

C shook his head. "Merely a hypothesis."

The only sound in the car was the faint clicking of Baxter's fingers on his Blackberry.

Max spread his arms. "And?"

The director glanced at Baxter. "I'm assured there is a decent likelihood their analysis is correct. In fact, I saw a report on my way here where the head of the GCHQ is increasing the odds of their assertions being correct by ten percent."

Baxter snorted. "We went from one percent to eleven percent."

C kept his gaze fixed on Max. "Callum has many qualities. Tact is not one of them."

Max made a show of looking at his watch.

The director peered at his own watch. "Indeed. Before I

share the theory with you, consider one question. How is it possible the current Russian president, a man who held a mid-level position in the KGB before mysteriously being appointed president by Boris Yeltsin not long after the fall of the Soviet Union, has systematically consolidated and held power this long?"

Max shrugged. "The will of the Russian people?"

A guffaw from Baxter.

"Here's the working hypothesis," C said. "The consortium, as you call it, is merely one division of a more elaborate infrastructure buried deep within the Russian military and government. This infrastructure, or set of councils, governs Russia from the shadows with the president as a figurehead."

Max's eyebrows lowered. "You mean there might be more of these consortiums?"

"Consider. Your consortium exists to help control oil and gas production, prices, and distribution. This fits because such a large portion of the Russian economy—and the hardliner's wealth—is based on oil and gas. If oil prices plummet, the Russian economy tanks, the populace gets restless. The fake government keeps improving the citizen's quality of life, which keeps the people placid."

"What happened in 1991?" Max asked. "If they had an iron grip, how did the Soviet Union fall apart?"

A slow nod from C. "They lost control, due in part to subversive action in Ukraine by the US. The chekists learned their lesson. The Soviet Union was the old shadow government, with each country's president and the Chairman of the Supreme Soviet all practically puppet heads except for Khrushchev, who was more liberal, and got away with it because Stalin went too far." He spread his hands. "Now you see how important the consortium is to the stability of the hard-liners."

This is too bizarre to be true.

C cleared his throat. "Our intel suggests there are at least three more of these councils. One for foreign policy, and one for control—media, spin, and in the extreme case, assassinations—and one for administration. But there might be more."

Wait. "Sounds like the list of old KGB directorates."

"Precisely."

"What about the military?"

"Some evidence points to the military being largely in control of these councils. Members of the military are on each board, but they don't have their own directorate."

If what C was saying was true, the task ahead was even more daunting than he thought. *How do I force an entire shadow government to stop hunting us?*

C coughed gently. "We don't know why this system of secret committees has marked your family for assassination, Mr. Asimov. But I can assure you, if you choose to continue our relationship, Her Majesty's intelligence services will do everything in its power to protect and aid you in your quest."

"I appreciate that." *The best way to find out what MI6 is hiding is to stay close to them. To stay close, they have to believe I'll share what Kate knows.*

C gave a brief nod. "Before we part ways, Mr. Asimov, I have two questions for you."

Max shifted to ease the pressure from the large bruise on his back. Since the explosion at Ivanov's, he'd had difficulty sitting for long periods of time. Not even the white pills helped. "I don't know where Kate is."

The director bent his head. "I understand. Callum

disagrees, but I believe our best bet to learn what she knows is by ensuring she gets the love and attention she needs from those closest to her. We'd be happy, of course, to offer protective custody."

Max shook his head. "It's not necessary, but thank you. What do you want to know?"

"Several key facts are missing from Callum's reports." C peered at Baxter before continuing. "Victor Dedov's role on the consortium must have been quite a shock, given his relationship with your father. How did you put the pieces together on his involvement?"

"Two things pointed to his involvement." Max held up two fingers. "One obvious, one not. He didn't need the weapons to defend his keep in Switzerland. I've been there twice and knew he had an ample supply of weaponry. Therefore, Dedov needed the guns to defend something else. The second was something he said when I talked with him in Italy. He said he needed to protect something extremely valuable. If not the keep, then what? So I hid a tracking device in the weapons shipment. When I saw the rifles were headed for Cyprus—the same place Bluefish told us Kate was located—I put it all together."

C pursed his lips. "Dedov and Spartak were working together against Ivanov in a plot to take over control of the consortium. That much we put together with help from our friends in GCHQ."

"Right," Max said. "They were in cahoots."

C inclined his head. "Studying up on American lingo, I see."

"Trying, Sir," Max removed a white pill from his pocket and slipped it in his mouth. *My back is killing me.* "While both Kate and I were held captive, he assumed he had the power. When Ivanov rolled into the Cyprus compound,

Dedov figured he had the leverage to take Ivanov down. What else do you want to know?"

The director removed a small tablet computer from his jacket pocket and tapped a few times and read before regarding Max again. "There was a gap in time between when Kate appeared in the courtyard and Dedov took the bullet that shot off his foot. The details are foggy. Can you fill in the holes?"

"Did you serve, sir?" Max asked.

"Pardon?"

"The military. Did you see any action?"

"Yes, of course. I don't see—"

"The fog of war." Max frowned. "When the helicopters started shooting, we were intent on escape. It wasn't until Dedov appeared at Ivanov's house that I realized he must have taken gunfire that severed his leg."

C appeared to accept his explanation. "What happened to this fellow calling himself Bluefish?"

"That's three, sir."

C's eyes widened. "Pardon?"

Max waved his hand. "Never mind. We dropped him a block from a hospital and made an anonymous call."

The director picked at a fingernail. "Can you explain why you didn't turn him over to the American authorities?"

"He's a current and high-ranking member of the US military. I was intent on finding Kate and didn't have time to sort it out. We know who he is and where to find him. Besides, we have enough evidence to expose him if he tries anything. He works for us now."

C recrossed his legs while looking at Baxter. "Given the evidence against him—"

Baxter cut in. "We were on US soil and already in hot

water. I didn't want to create an international incident. It was my decision."

Another nod by C as he returned the tablet to his pocket.

This is dragging. I need to get back to the hotel before Kate wakes. "Where does this leave us?"

C gestured at the door. "I know you want to go, but I'll leave you with this thought. What many intelligence agencies tend to forget is that intelligence agencies are just that, they are in charge of intelligence. Our mandate is to develop sources of information into actionable intelligence that our government leaders can act on. So go. Despite Callum's insistence to the contrary, we will not follow or interrupt Kate's recovery. We trust you'll take good care of her. Seek the knowledge that you seek. When you learn what you learn, come to London. We will work together to compile and analyze our intelligence and determine what the Russian's are up to. In the end, that knowledge will set you and your family free." C leaned against the door to open it for Max.

With one foot on the pavement, Max stopped. "I need a favor."

"Name it."

When Max told him, C inclined his head. "It will be done."

Max stepped into the brisk morning, accepted his pistol from the bodyguard, gave Cindy a nod, and strode off in the direction of Portugal's National Archeological Museum. As he saw the sign next to the hulking neo-Manueline style building, he chuckled at the irony. To know the present, he needed to uncover the past.

FIFTY-SIX

Outside Aspen, Colorado

A beam of sunlight cut through the jack pines while a crisp breeze stung his skin, foretelling of the winter ahead. Snow fell overnight, and a crispy frost covered the loamy ground so their feet made crinkling sounds as they hiked. Despite the chilly temperatures, the morning sun warmed their shoulders. Kate walked in front with Max following. Their destination was a ridge that offered a shelf of rocks ideal for sharing a thermos of hot coffee and admiring the jagged snowcapped mountains in the distance.

After his surprise meeting with C, Max, Kate, and Spencer spent three days on various transatlantic flights using the air travel for surveillance detection. While traveling, Kate spoke little and never strayed far from the two men. When she dozed, Kate held Max's hand and often cried out in her sleep while clamping down on his fingers.

They arrived at the cabin from Europe a week ago. Arina and Alex's trip was courtesy of MI6 and was the

favor Max asked of C. Once settled in the cabin outside
Aspen, Kate ate sparingly and refused offers of wine or cigarettes. Most of her days were spent curled under a wool
blanket in a chair on the porch looking out over the pond or
in front of a roaring fire. Whatever secrets the former CIA
station chief and black-ops commander held in her head
were locked there forever. Still, each morning, Max forced
the group to take a hike in the hopes that the clear mountain
air and brisk exercise might help Kate's recovery.

Some days Spencer joined them, other times he accompanied Alex on a four-wheeler jaunt through the woods or
coached Arina in the finer points of pistol shooting in the
barn's makeshift gun range.

When they reached the rocky outcropping, they sat
with their thighs touching and sipped steaming coffee
while surveying the valley. Velvety tops of pine trees
stretched for miles in all directions, and to the west, a
buildup of clouds foretold of more snow. Max related
stories of his childhood and how his father taught him ball-
room dancing and cooking, not because he needed to know
them as a gentleman, but because they would come in
handy as a spy. When he exhausted his memories of
growing up, he moved to tales from his days at the KGB
academy, like how an upstart young cadet named Svetlana
challenged him to a pistol shooting contest. The loser had
to guzzle a bottle of vodka. She got most of the liquor
down before throwing up. Later, they pumped her
stomach.

When the coffee was gone and a snowflake hit him on
the nose, they began the long hike back. As they descended
the steep trail and approached the cabin, cloud cover dulled
the sunlight and the snow came down heavier. The growl of
an engine grew louder as a large Jeep with oversized tires

pulled up the drive. First to exit from the vehicle was a bundle of energy with blond hair.

"Uncle Max!" Alex rushed over and offered Max a fist bump. Spike, now a medium-sized dog with puppy-sized energy, jumped from the back and ran in circles sniffing the air.

"Hiya, sport. Need help with the groceries?"

Spencer climbed from the truck, his worn cowboy boots crunching on the gravel, and Arina got out of the front passenger seat.

The five of them retired to the cabin, where Kate settled on the couch under a sheepskin rug and Arina busied herself in the kitchen. Spike and Charlie, Spencer's gray-faced golden retriever, bounded up onto the couch and settled in next to Kate, who absently stroked Charlie's back. Max built a fire in the hearth while Alex and Spencer helped Arina in the kitchen.

A large spread of meats and cheeses and vegetables was set on the table, and Max broke out a bottle of aged bourbon and poured generous helpings for Spencer, Arina, and himself. Kate shook her head when Max offered her a tumbler of the light brown liquid.

After the food was eaten and the dishes cleared and Alex was settled into bed, the two men retired to the porch in down jackets to smoke and sip bourbon. Two inches of the liquor was gone before Spencer stirred. "I know the docs in London gave her a thorough evaluation, but do you think we should get her some medical attention? Some kind of head doc?"

Max swirled his drink. "I'm sure MI6 would be happy to provide someone."

With a snort, Spencer drained his drink. "Do you trust them?"

Max scratched his neck. "I don't trust any intelligence agency. But if we have to work with one, they're probably the best of the lot."

Spencer poured them another measure. "Maybe."

Max sipped. "The MI6 doctors said she'll eventually start talking again."

"At least she's safe," Spencer said.

The two men lapsed into silence as the bourbon steadily disappeared. By the time they went inside, Kate and Arina had gone to bed, and the fire was reduced to glowing embers.

———

The next day, the five members of the makeshift family went on the usual hike to the top of the ridge. Arina was as quiet as Kate. The man she loved, the man who rescued her from the dangers of the consortium, the man who took her son under his protective wing and provided them both a safe place to live, had turned out to be a traitor. He had also murdered her husband and her parents. Max left her alone with her thoughts.

Spencer led them along the steep switchbacks, followed by Kate, Alex, Arina, and the two dogs, while Max took up the rear. Both men wore sidearms, and a rifle was strapped to Spencer's back while Max carried a shotgun. Arina was armed with a 9mm on her hip. Alex trotted along, happy to be back in the woods of Colorado. He liked to dart off the trail and return with a stick or leaf or some other treasure. Kate was her normal stoic self. *Is that a renewed brightness in her eyes?* Maybe it was his imagination.

Since uncovering his father's video, Max had played it over and over again, watching it frame by frame. When

Arina and Alex arrived from Switzerland, Max played the video for his sister dozens of times, both of them watching intently for clues. By now, he had memorized the dialog, and he let it scroll through his mind while they walked.

As they crested a ridge with mountain views on either side, Arina halted in the middle of the trail. "I've got it!" she yelled.

Max almost knocked her to the ground before catching her and bracing them both to keep from tumbling to the rocky trail. "Jesus, sis. What is it?"

The rest of the group stopped to listen as she bounced up and down. "The video. I've got it!" Her face beamed.

Max's mouth hung open as Arina recited a quote from memory. "Man cannot possess anything as long as he fears death. But to him who does not fear it, everything belongs. If there was no suffering, man would not know his limits, would not know himself."

Everyone gaped at Arina. Spencer, Kate, and Alex stood a few meters down the trail while Charlie sat on his haunches and Spike sniffed at the ground.

Max touched Arina's arm. "Are you okay?"

She bounced up and down on the balls of her feet. "It's a quote from Tolstoy's War and Peace. Papa made me memorize it, but would never tell me why."

A melodic voice came from behind Arina. "Nikita Ivanov is actually Anton Pushkin."

Everyone turned to stare at Kate. Her eyes glinted with electricity as she recited from memory. "Anton Pushkin, born in 1952 in St. Petersburg, is a direct descendent of Felix Dzerzhinsky, also known as Iron Felix, who was the first Director of the Bolshevik secret police. Pushkin grew up in St. Petersburg, son of that city's Governor. At age seventeen, he disappeared into the KGB's training programs, eventually becoming Head of Second Chief Directorate in charge of counterintelligence. Five years after assuming that post, Pushkin's death was faked and he disappeared."

The whole group was stunned into silence, and even the dogs sat quietly. Max stepped closer to Kate. *This is the information his father hid in Kate's mind. What everyone was looking for. The quote was the key.*

"A decade later Pushkin reemerged as Nikita Ivanov after undergoing significant plastic surgery. Now he leads a top secret and tightly controlled group of men descended from the first secret police organization instituted by Vladimir Lenin in 1917."

Spencer cleared his throat. "Except he was killed by a bomb hidden in Dedov's wheelchair."

Kate shrugged. "Ivanov/Pushkin is also one of three ministers who form the Komissariat for the Preservation of State."

"The what?" Max shifted his feet in the snow. A komissariat was an old term that meant government department in the old Soviet Union, but the word hadn't been in use since the 1940s.

"The Komissariat for the Preservation of State governs four groups. The first, the council of internal security, is twelve men charged with disinformation and propaganda along with suppression of uprisings. The second group, called the council of external security, oversees the military. The third group, called the council of petroleum and natural resources, manages a monopoly on oil and gas production, and the fourth group, called the council of monetary policy, handles banking and finances. These groups all operate outside the rule of the law and serve as a shadow government. The Russian president is a puppet, who serves at the pleasure of the Komissariat for the Preservation of State."

So MI6 is right. Except they left out the part about this Komissariat thing. "Who are the three ministers of the Komissariat?"

Kate smiled. "The Komissariat for the Preservation of State is comprised of three men, all of whom are direct descendants from families who formed the Cheka. This lineage is strictly maintained through bylaws and secret ceremony. We've discovered that Ivanov/Pushkin is one such minister. The identities of the other two ministers remain secret." She paused and smiled. "More accurately, their identities were not revealed to me by Andrei."

Max turned to Spencer. "This is good information, but hardly worthy of pursuit by so many intelligence agencies."

The ex-CIA man gazed at the sky. "To be fair, they didn't know what information they were looking for."

Kate gripped Max's arm. "There's more."

Everyone stared at Kate.

"I know when and where the Komissariat for the Preservation of State holds its monthly meetings. It's a closely held secret, known only to the Komissar himself and the other two ministers. The next meeting is in mid-January." Her hand tightened on his forearm. "Max, your father wants you to be there."

———

The pitch darkness of the moonless morning forced the sky to blend with the murk of the trees. Max stepped outside, careful to tread lightly on the wooden porch. Pea gravel crunched under his boots as he made his way to the edge of the pond. A cloud of no-see-ums encased his head before he batted them away. A chorus of cicadas kept a constant background buzz.

Stopping along the water's edge, his boots sinking into the soft earth, he removed a crumpled pack of Marlboro Reds and his Zippo, the one he received from his grandfather just before his death.

How had Kira tracked him so easily?

He had replaced his clothes, including his boots and beloved leather jacket, so he knew there was no tracking device hidden on his person. Goshawk performed a scan on his Blackphone, ensuring it too was clean. He bought a new backpack and wallet. Baxter scanned him and his gear with a bug tracker, which revealed nothing. He was clean, yet she had easily followed him between Europe, the US, and Cyprus.

A flick of the lighter and he held a flame to the end of a cigarette. The tobacco flared, and an ember formed. He inhaled the acrid smoke into his lungs. As he exhaled, he stowed the remaining cigarettes and ran his thumb over the old Belarusian flag burnished on the side of the Zippo lighter as he had so many times before. The image reminded him of home, of growing up in Minsk, of the good times with his father. Of his homeland. He flipped the lighter around his fingers and caught it in his palm like his grandfather had.

The reminder of his homeland made him yearn to set down roots. To create a place where Alex and Arina would be safe. A place where Alex could get an education and start a normal life. Another flip of the lighter.

A pink hue appeared over the jack pines and cast a purple glow over the frosted mountains to the west. The locals call it alpenglow. He gave the lighter a flip but fumbled it, and it fell and bounced on a rock.

Cursing, he stooped to pick it up. The lid was dented, and the inside case had slid partly from the bottom case.

It couldn't be, could it?

He removed the lighter's inside case. The felt pad was dry.

Wait. I tossed Baxter the lighter so he could light his pipe. I forgot it at his office. Baxter flipped it to me when I boarded the Lear before flying to Moldova. Was it possible Baxter was working with Kira?

He hurried into the house and flicked on the light in the kitchen, where he disassembled the lighter, piece by piece. When he was done, dozens of tiny parts rested on a white towel. He rummaged in a drawer and emerged with a bug sensing device similar to the one Baxter used. He flicked it on and waved it over the bits and pieces. The device remained silent. The lighter was clean.

So much for that theory.

With care, he reassembled the lighter, soaked the felt with lighter fluid, and took it with him back outside. By now, the sky was bright enough to reveal a cold clear morning. As he stood by the pond and lit another cigarette he glanced up to see a large bird soaring high above the trees, her brown back contrasting with a snowy white breast. She flew lower revealing a bright white crest and hooked beak. An M-shaped kink in her wings gave her away as an osprey.

She circled high over the pond, wings beating hard, before soaring on an air current and diving feet first into the water with a splash. When she rose with a mighty flap of her wings, she carried a flopping fish in her talons. As the osprey glided over a ridge and disappeared, Max saluted her and remembered one of his father's many quotes.

Son, the number one rule when duck hunting is to go where the ducks are.

The aroma of bacon, pancakes, and coffee welcomed him into the kitchen. Arina smiled with bright eyes as she set the table for breakfast. They hugged before she pushed him away and held him by the shoulders. "You're leaving again, aren't you?"

Max bowed his head as he set out the butter and syrup. "Soon. But not today."

EPILOGUE

Corsica

She felt safe in the ancient wooden chair under the over-hang but pulled the light shawl around her bare shoulders for warmth. A patter of rain hit the roof and drops tapped the exposed wooden deck. The wind picked up, tossing the palm fronds and creating whitecaps in the sea. A purple and blue evening sky bore angry dark clouds, and flickering lightning lit the surf. Thunder rumbled before another spark of lightning cracked over the sea. For now, Goshawk relished the cool break from the Corsican heat.

A half-drunk bottle of French rosé sat at her feet. She didn't bother with a glass and instead drank straight from the bottle.

I miss Paris. With Bluefish's exposure, my compound there will be safe again. Besides, this cottage is too small for two.

A set of warm desires mixed with trepidation floated through her body, centered on her heart and loins. These disturbances in the fabric of her ordered universe confused and alarmed her, and even now, her stomach roiled with anticipation and dread and wonder. It was weeks since she called Carlu to her cabin—she didn't want him around. Instead, she was haunted by a fantasy where a different man was by her side. The idea sent flashes of heat through her belly and prickles of cold on her skin, feelings she didn't want yet was powerless to stop.

A ding came from the netbook laptop on the table next to her. She took a slug of the wine before touching the keyboard to wake the machine. A message appeared in a secure chat window.

Kira: Are you pleased with my work?

She drummed her fingernails, fresh with new polish, on the chair's arm before responding.

oDD17Y: Lucky your bomb didn't also take out Max.

Kira: I had eyes on the whole time.

oDD17Y: And Ivanov?

An inch of the wine disappeared before Kira replied.

Kira: I believe he's dead. Are we done?

oDD17Y: For now.

Kira: It won't be so easy next time. He's aware I exist.

Goshawk took another swig. oDD17Y: Let's see what next time brings.

Kira: You'll complete the payment?

Goshawk brought up a command line, tapped a few keys, and returned to the chat window. oDD17Y: It is sent.

There was a ten-minute pause before the chat window dinged again. Kira: Xiè xiè

oDD17Y: You're welcome. Pleasure doing business with you. I turned off the tracking on his phone.

Kira: I noticed. Until next time.

oDD17Y: Until next time.

Goshawk closed the chat window and opened another command line window. *Can't hurt to be sure.* It took only a few keystrokes to launch the preconfigured algorithm that sent a secure command to Max's Blackphone. Without giving any indication to its user, the code shut down the secret GPS tracking algorithm Goshawk had programmed into the phone.

The wind grew stronger and blew a spray of rain that dowsed her, the chair, and her computer. Thunder rumbled and lightning flashed over her head. The whitecaps turned into frothy waves. As the skies opened and water came down in sheets, she shut the laptop, grabbed the bottle, and went inside where she found the dog and her new room- mate huddled next to a fire.

She poured some rosé into her new roommate's glass and found a spot next to her dog, who quivered at the thun- der. "It's for his own good, right?"

Julia Meier raised her glass. "What he doesn't know won't hurt him."

IF YOU LIKED THIS BOOK ...

I would appreciate it if you would leave a review. An honest review means a lot. The constructive reviews help me write better stories, and the positive reviews help others find the books, which ultimately means I can write more stories.

It only takes a few minutes, but it means everything. Thank you in advance.

-Jack

AUTHOR'S NOTE

So, yeah. This installment took a while. A look back through my writing logs shows that I started this book—the working title was Max #4—on January 21, 2017. Recall that The Attack—Max #3— was published in November 2017. So there I was in late 2017 and early 2018, merrily pounding out prose about Max, Mueller, and Julia up against a sect of white supremacists, when I started to get a lot of emails.

"Where is Kate?"

"What happened to Kate?"

"You can't leave us hanging about Kate!"

"Kate has to be rescued!"

Sheesh.

I had no idea that Kate Shaw was such a beloved character. So into the scrap heap goes the manuscript, and I went back to the drawing board. I'm confident when I say that none of the original Max #4 story made it into the final draft of The Hunt. And maybe, just maybe, dear reader, we find out what happened to Kate.

The Hunt is the fourth installment in a six-novel saga that tells the story of Max Austin's fight against the evil forces of the consortium, a group steeped in Russian history, that will stop at nothing to erase Max's family from the face of the earth. The Abyss, Max #5, is underway and should make it to the presses in late 2019. Endgame, Max #6, will be available sometime in 2020. After that, maybe Max will ease into retirement and another character will take center stage.

As always, drop me a line if you have feedback or if you want to say hi.

Jack Arbor
April 2019
Aspen, Colorado

ACKNOWLEDGMENTS

"If you want to go fast, go alone. If you want to go far, go together." That's a quote that the internet says is either an African proverb or is made up by Al Gore. Either way, it sure applies to novel writing. As you know, I have no intention of going fast, but I will keep writing until I keel over facedown on my keyboard for the last time. For me, writing is a team exercise. If it's a good story, all these people get the credit. If it's crap, I get the blame.

In no particular order, I want to lavishly thank these good looking, super generous, and amazingly fastidious readers on my Advanced Reader Team: Bob Kaster, Hugo Ernst, Wahak Kontian, Dr. Edward White, Keith Kay, Mark Fussell, Jenni Adamstein, Patrick Lockhart, Robin Smith, Tim Dickenson, Robin Eide Steffensen, Ken Sanford, John Rozum, Ken Monk, John Bilancione, Kerry Kehoe, Rashna Panthaki, Nick Brown, Jen Close, Linda Bryant, Murielle Arn, Judith DeRycke, Mel Laughton, Susan Boyle, Josiah Cook, Mike Johnston, Pete Adkins, Phil Taylor, Jan Haggerty, Vince Gassi, Mary Enge, Gregg Backemeyer, Catherine Baldwin, Ruth Hall, Harvey Ascher,

Cheryl Lewis, John Sims, Terry McEachern, Lois Dean, James Farmer, Laura Kevghas, Don Bershtein, Patrick Welch, Kathy Mischka, and Alex Neubert. You all rock the free world.

Mark Twain said, "A successful book is not made of what is in it, but of what is left out of it." The first manuscript I sent to my editor was over one hundred thousand words. The final draft is just under eighty thousand. You and I have Martha Hayes to thank for trimming the fat. Martha, we're lucky to have you.

Last but not least, Max Austin would not be the man he is today without my wife Jill's everlasting support for the long weekends and late nights, patience with the living room floor covered by red ink-stained manuscript pages, and tolerance of my long daydreams to work out story problems. I love you, sweetie.

JOIN MY MAILING LIST

If you'd like to get updates on new releases as well as notifications of deals and discounts, please join my email list.

I only email when I have something meaningful to say and I never send spam. You can unsubscribe at any time.

Join my mailing list at www.jackarbor.com.

ABOUT THE AUTHOR

Jack Arbor is the author of five thrillers featuring the wayward KGB assassin Max Austin. The stories follow Max as he comes to terms with his past and tries to extricate himself from a destiny he desperately wants to avoid.

Jack works as a technology executive during the day and writes at night and on weekends with much love and support from his lovely wife, Jill.

Jill and Jack live outside Aspen, Colorado, where they enjoy trail running and hiking through the natural beauty of the Roaring Fork Valley. Jack also likes to taste new bourbons and listen to jazz, usually at the same time. They both miss the coffee on the East Coast.

You can get free books as well as prerelease specials and sign up for Jack's mailing list at www.jackarbor.com.

Connect with Jack online:
    (e) jack@jackarbor.com
    (t) twitter.com/JackArbor
    (i) instagram.com/jackarbor/
    (f) facebook.com/JackArborAuthor
    (w) www.jackarbor.com
    (n) newsletter signup

ALSO BY JACK ARBOR

The Russian Assassin, The Russian Assassin Series, Book One

You can't go home again...

Max, a former KGB assassin, is content with the life he's created for himself in Paris. When he's called home to Minsk for a family emergency, Max finds himself suddenly running for his life, desperate to uncover secrets about his father's past to save his family.

Max's sister Arina and nephew Alex become pawns in a game that started a generation ago. As Max races from the alleyways of Minsk to the posh neighborhoods of Zurich, and ultimately to the gritty streets of Prague, he must confront his past and come to terms with his future to preserve his family name.

The Russian Assassin is a tight, fast-paced adventure, staring Jack Arbor's stoic hero, the ex-KGB assassin-for-hire, Max Austin. Book one of the series forces Max to choose between himself and his family, a choice that will have consequences for generations to come.

The Pursuit, The Russian Assassin Series, Book Two

The best way to destroy an enemy is to make him a friend...

Former KGB assassin Max Austin is on the run, fighting to keep his family alive while pursuing his parents' killers. As he battles foes both visible and hidden, he uncovers a conspiracy with roots in the darkest cellars of Soviet history. Determined to survive, Max hatches a plan to even the odds by partnering with his mortal enemy. Even as his adversary becomes his confidant, Max is left wondering who he can trust, if anyone...

If you like dynamic, high-voltage, page-turning thrills, you'll love the second installment of The Russian Assassin series starring Jack Arbor's desperate hero, ex-KGB assassin-for-hire, Max Austin.

The Attack, The Russian Assassin Series, Book Three

It's better to be the hunter than the hunted.

A horrific bombing rocks the quaint streets of London's West Brompton neighborhood and Max Austin finds himself the target of an international manhunt the likes of which the world hasn't seen since the hunt for Osama bin Laden. The former KGB assassin must put his fight against the Consortium on hold while he seeks redemption.

As Max chases the bomber from the gritty streets of London through the lush Spanish countryside and into the treacherous mountains of Chechnya, he's plunged into a game of cat and mouse with a wily MI6 agent determined to catch Max at all costs.

Can Max find the terrorist and clear his name before it's too late?

The Attack is the third installment in The Russian

Assassin adventure thriller series that pits Max Austin against his arch-enemy, the shadowy consortium of international criminals that will stop at nothing to kill Max and his family. If you like heart-pounding, page-turning thrills, grab this adventure starring Jack Arbor's grim hero, the ex-KGB assassin-for-hire, Max Austin.

Cat & Mouse, A Max Austin Novella

Max, a former KGB assassin, is living a comfortable life in Paris. When not plying his trade, he passes his time managing a jazz club in the City of Light. To make ends meet, he freelances by offering his services to help rid the earth of the world's worst criminals.

Max is enjoying his ritual post-job vodka when he meets a stunning woman; a haunting visage of his former fiancé. Suddenly, he finds himself the target of an assassination plot in his beloved city of Paris. Fighting for his life, Max must overcome his own demons to stay alive.

Made in the USA
Lexington, KY
10 June 2019